THI
IMMORTALITY
CLOCK

For Stephen — with so many thanks always.

Richard Pierce

Richard Pierce

logo © Marianne Pierce-Saunderson

First published in 2019 by
NoPapyrus Press
Spring Cottage, Church Street, Stradbroke, IP21 5HT

© 2019 by Richard Pierce

ISBN: 978-0-9551279-3-9

Front & back cover illustration
Oleg Gamulinskiy from pixabay

For Elliot and James

ACKNOWLEDGEMENTS

Thanks to Elliot and James for inviting me to the Cheapside Hoard exhibition at the Museum of London in 2013, a visit which inspired this story.

My main work of reference for this novel has been Hazel Forsyth's wonderful *The Cheapside Hoard – London's Lost Jewels*. Although I have never met Hazel, I want to thank her for providing such accurate descriptions of the Hoard, as well as giving me a starting point for this history, as I think I should call it.

Thanks, too, to Sharon Ament, Director of the Museum of London at the time of writing, for her interest and support.

Although I wrote the book in 2014, accompanied entirely by Catfish & The Bottlemen's first album, the time never seemed right to send it out into the wild, but with England now once again embroiled in a civil war of sorts, it struck me that now was that time. I hope reading allows you to escape from the harshness of everyday life for a few moments whilst still pondering on how hard-won our freedoms are, and how much they are worth fighting for.

As always, thanks to Marianne, Oscar, Charlotte, Kara, and Alex for enduring my absences when I'm travelling the countries of my imagination. I owe you everything.

Richard, November 2019

The long unmeasured pulse of time moves everything.
There is nothing hidden that it cannot bring to light,
nothing once known that may not become unknown.

Nothing is impossible.

Sophocles

Prologue

London, June 1912

The sweat pours from his face as he raises his pick-axe again. He's sick of this digging, digging all the time, here there and every bloody where. Why'd they decide to knock down Cheapside in the middle of the summer, anyway, when London's so hot and dusty and vile? He wants a proper drink, a nice pint of something, to wash the dirt out of his mouth. And then a few more. Only a couple of hours till the working day's done.

He brings the pick-axe down. The ground splinters and tears apart, a new void opens beneath the chalk floor he thought was the very bottom of the new foundations at Thirty and Thirty-Two Cheapside. He shakes his head, and smashes more of the floor out of the way. This has never happened to him before, to find a hole under a hole. In his excitement, he breaks away the floor in double quick time. When it's done, he jumps down into the new cave he's made. The debris has fallen into what looks like another cellar. Brick walls, old, and some signs of mould. The river's not far away. Dank is the word. He takes a deep breath, shivers in the sudden cool of the pit. The sun slants shadows into the void.

He starts clearing away the mess, strikes soft, muddy ground. His shovel changes its tune to wooden. He looks down. There's a glittering mess by his feet; gold, silver, pearl. Shining stones of all colours. He kneels down, puts his shovel to one side, puts his hands into the chaos of splinters and glitter. *What?* And there, in the middle of the broken wooden box, a tiny, green diamond, a shimmering prize. He picks it up, wipes the mud from it. He turns it this way and that, holds it out of the shade into the sun. There's a hinge on the stone,

9

and a dial under one side of the gem, smeared with his fingerprints and the brown mud. He gasps at the beauty of it, puts it back down on top of all the other things he's uncovered

'Lads! Lads!' he shouts. 'You've got to come see this.'

They round the corner, see the unexpected hole, jump down into it next to him, see the jewels surrounding him, dive in, hold them up to the light in wonderment.

'Bloody hell, Will, you've struck gold here.'

'We'd better let Stony Jack know.' He gets up, runs his fingers through his sweaty hair, feels slightly faint. 'He'll pay us well for this stuff. Fetch a sack, somebody, and we'll fill it.'

George Lawrence, the pawnbroker and antiquities trader known as Stony Jack, is just about to leave for the pub from his office a few blocks away from Cheapside, when Will and his friends arrive, breathless and sunburned.

'Jack,' Will says. 'You know you told us to look out for stuff worth saving for history and the like? I think we've found a load you'd be interested in.' He drops the heavy sack off his shoulder and empties its contents onto the carpet of Jack's office. 'Is this what you meant?'

'My God, lads,' Jack says. 'This is wonderful.' He drops to his knees, hands quick amongst the mud-caked jewels. There are chains here, and necklaces, enamelled pieces, loose jewels, empty fittings, what looks like ear-rings, flowers and blossoms made from multi-coloured stones, and bound in gold and silver. He shakes his head. 'Where did you find this, Will?'

'Cheapside,' Will says. 'Number Thirty. On the corner of Friday Street.'

'D'you think you got everything there is?'

'It's all we could find right away, Jack,' one of the

other men says.

'Go back and see if you can find any more. I'll wash this stuff in the meantime. I'll pay you good money, you know I will.' He starts putting everything back in the sack. 'And if you find more, bring it straight back here.'

They storm out of the office, and he, pub forgotten, drags the sack into the workshop out back, where he always cleans the things the navvies bring him. Even if they bring him rubbish, he stands them half a pint. It's useful to be friends with them. If not he, who else? And if not he, who knows how much of London's history would have been lost?

He picks one piece out of the sack and washes it gently, under a stream of lukewarm water, and puts it in the drying rack. He repeats the process for every single piece they've brought him. He gets through a hundred of them before they're back, this time with a smaller sack and even muddier hands. He gives them five pounds each. 'There'll be more, boys, once I've worked out what all these things could be worth. I thought you'd like to go get yourselves a well-earned drink first. Come back at the end of the week. And if you find anything tomorrow, or the day after, or in a fortnight, bring it to me.'

The next thing he picks out of the first sack is the watch made from a single emerald. He daren't wash it as simply and crudely as the other pieces, so instead wipes it as clean as he can with a soft cloth. He opens the hinged lid, puts his ear to the watch face, sprinkled with shards of emerald, laughs at himself. 'Why would it still be ticking, you old fool?' He puts it in the rack, and sits down on his chair. This is beyond fantastic, beyond amazing; it's a miracle. He can't believe it. Is it real?

In one of the drawers of his desk, he keeps a bottle of

old single malt whisky. He opens the drawer, gets out the bottle and a chipped crystal tumbler, one of the worthless finds from the past he decided to keep, and pours himself two fingers of the amber liquid. He leans back and takes a small nip, lets out a deep breath of satisfaction. He places a phone call to one of his friends on the board at the London Museum, Lewis Harcourt.

'Lewis, I've had a significant find today,' he says. 'Do you want to come over here and take a look?'

'Of course, dear boy. I'll be there in half an hour.'

When Lewis arrives, Jack is on his second glass of whisky, pours one for his visitor, and takes him through to the workshop. 'I've no idea how many hundreds of pieces they might bring,' he says. 'But even if they bring nothing more than this, it'll be the most significant find of jewellery in London since Lord knows when.'

'Since ever, George, since ever. A Cheapside Hoard.' He picks up the tiny clock, puts it in the palm of his hand. 'And you'll never find anything better than this. I wonder who buried it, and when.'

'I don't think we'll never know.'

The next few weeks are a flurry of activity for Lawrence. Three days after the initial find, he is appointed Inspector of Excavations for the London Museum, and the trustees tell him to make big payments to the men who found the treasure. As the days go by, the navvies bring him more objects they find in the hidden cellar. When the finds stop, he has over four hundred pieces. He washes and catalogues them all. He finds out that some pieces have been taken elsewhere, some sold to the British Museum and some to the Guildhall Museum. It irritates him, but he consoles himself with the thought he must have secured the bulk of the jewels for the London Museum.

Every day, he opens his safe, and takes out one or

other of the pieces, still breathless at their beauty. About one set of ear-rings, he scrawls a line in his notebook – *They are fashioned so tenderly as to intimate touch, not imitate it.* He's never been moved to poetry before, and never will be again.

Chapter 1

Antwerp, January 1642

The final day of her childhood she spends with her father. She watches him, in the study, across the desk, his face creased behind his glasses, his eyes on the book in front of him, in another foreign language he's taught her. Wherever he's travelled, she's travelled, too. They speak rarely when they're reading, and today is no different. They haven't travelled for some time. She thinks he could be feeling his age. Or maybe there's no trade to be done that's to his liking.

As always, he has one hand inside his shirt, cradling the watch he brought back from one of his trips, before she was born. It hangs from his neck by a simple strap. Cut from a single emerald, the cover is attached to the body by a tiny hinge of gold, and the numbers on the face decorated with splinters from the carved emerald. It's an unconscious act, something he doesn't even notice anymore, clinging to the warmth of the precious stone, a present for the wife he lost when his daughter was born.

The room is rich with coffee and the heavy aroma of old books. The girl turns the page of the book in front of her. It's over three hundred years old. *Rubaiyat.* She doesn't see the words. She's tall for her seventeen years, rangy, with the delicate features and fair hair, almost albino, inherited from her mother, the double of the portrait hanging from the wood panels behind her father. Every day she watches him grieve and wonders why he doesn't hate her.

'I should be proud of what I have, not envious of what I wish I had,' he mutters.

She ignores him, turns the page, its crisp sound clean in the stuffy room. She feels the roughness of the parchment between her fingers, keeps her head down.

'It wasn't supposed to be a sound,' he says.

The questions are there, questions she's asked since she could speak, questions he;' never answered. She wishes he would, but, for all his love, she's never found a way through to him.

'You should marry again,' she says, against her wishes.

He doesn't get angry, just lifts his eyes over the edge of his golden glasses. 'That's not possible, Fien,' he says.

She knows she's beaten. She always knows. 'More coffee?' she says, instead.

'I should get it.'

'I've reached the end of the verse.' She jumps from her chair, takes his cup and saucer, gentle porcelain burning in her palm. *And I'm nearly eighteen, for God's sake.*

'Don't be long.' He's always kept her close, never let her run wild like other girls she's seen, from a distance, always near to her, within a shout's length, always there, his eyes on her, his hand within reaching distance.

'The kitchen *is* only out there.' Her words surprise her; the first words of rebellion. As she walks from the study to the kitchen, she notices how yellow the sky has become. It will be night soon. She's distracted by movement outside the front window, a tall man with a tall face. *It's nothing*, she thinks.

There's a clamour as she reaches the kitchen. Her father's up out of his chair, rushing into the kitchen behind her, drags her into the study, pulls to one side the desk and the carpet under it. A brass ring where she never knew a brass ring was. He pulls at it, his face strained. A trapdoor opens, and the scent of damp and dark is threateningly strong. 'Go down, now,' he says, sweat on his face. 'Don't open it to anyone. Ignore any sounds you hear.'

'What … ?'

'Go now.' He kisses her, wraps his arms around her, briefly. 'Go.'

'Why?'

'Now.' He has never shouted at her before. 'I love you.'

'I love you, too.' She trips down the steps, rough and uneven. The door closes over her. She drops to the floor. Mud. Clay. Cold and uncomfortable. She wants her book and the scent of coffee.

'So here you are, Herr Piet Brants.' It's a voice she's never heard before, an English voice, muffled by the floor. 'We'd heard that someone in the Low Countries was doing some interesting business with old things.'

'What do you want?' Her father's voice.

'Everything you've got. The king needs it.'

'Then he should come and get it himself.'

'Oh, he's too busy for that.'

'Watching masques and starting wars?'

'He does what he must.'

The clash of weapons, moans and groans. She shudders under the floor. An oath.

'This is honest work,' her father says. 'A collection.'

'We could all be collectors. But some of us need profit more than purity.'

Another clash of metal against metal. Silence. She wants to push up against the trapdoor. She sees nothing but blackness, even when she lifts her hand up to her eyes. She knows she hasn't gone blind. Do they know where she is? Do they even know she exists?

'It's all the king's.' That voice again, strident, triumphant. It's the tall face talking, she's sure of it. 'Don't make it so difficult.'

Nothing.

And then heavy footsteps, rushing around the study above her, cackles and laughter, and the joy of those

16

safe in numbers and triumphant because of it. She scrabbles away, fingertips finding the way, away from the madness the silence and the noise tell her about. So much for the poems of the Persians. She drops to the ground, the mud heavy between her fingers.

Renewed silence wakes her, she doesn't know how much later, cocooned into a back-aching shape, despite what she knows to be true, although she has no proof. She feels a heat bearing down on her from above, hears a crackling that can only mean fire. She reaches out, searches the ground, blind, with her blind hands, teaching them to be seeing. This can't be real. Everything was as it should be a few short hours ago. Her fingers touch something square; a firebox, she thinks. *Did he plan this? It can't be.* Her finger grasp, curl around the shape she imagines, almost automatically open, and strike. There's light in her dungeon. She sees the smoke first, dropping through the cracks in the wood. And then she sees something else, a solid shape leaning against the crooked wall.

Chapter 2

She reaches for the silhouette, brushes her dirty hands against what turns into wood under her touch. A tall cupboard, drawers from top to bottom, light wood, pine it seems. She stops, listens. Still nothing from above, just the smell of smoke around her. Where should she start? She chooses the drawer at the very centre, pulls it open slowly, soundlessly. They could still be there, above of her, their ears to the floor, listening for her. She holds her breath. The drawer's empty except for a solitary envelope, a letter folded and sealed to the shape of an envelope. She holds the firebox into the drawer. A candle, at the very back. She sets fire to its wick and light floods into this cellar, a finite, flickering, expanding and contracting circle of luminescence.

The seal cracks under her long fingers, the sound as loud as a gunshot to her. She freezes, holds the paper next to the candle, her hands shaking. She takes a deep breath, steadies herself against the ancient furniture, brings the black ink scrawls into focus.

My dearest Fien,

I had hoped this day would never come, but if you are reading this, it has. I have, we have, for years, been collecting, collecting things of value, objects which have not only monetary worth, but historical worth, too, and sometimes more than that. But now, as I feared, someone has come to take them away from us, not to preserve them for the people of the world, but for profit, to sell them to the highest bidder, to gather money for Lord knows what purpose.

Yes, some of my trades in the past, to start this whole venture, may have been tainted, one way or the other, though never with blood, but my aim, even before you were born, even before you were conceived, was to create a repository of history, to keep intact some of the world's greatest treasures, and I received many gifts for our collection. Yet, as you read this, they will have taken all the gold and jewels, and left the books behind, or even burned them, books which have more value than the most sophisticated jewellery, the biggest diamonds.

You will ask me how I let this happen. There is no defence against the real world. You will have been frustrated by how close I have kept you over the years, by how little I have let you experience of the outside. But I have let you read. I have travelled with you. That will have taught you everything you need to know. I have talked with you past the bed-times normal girls must keep, talked through sleepless nights with you, because we had to try to answer one of the many questions life poses.

So here you are. I am dead or captured, and we will never see each other again, in this life. What are you to do? These drawers are full of what you need. Move slowly, carefully. Take your time to gather it all together. I can give you no full inventory, because I filled the drawers year after year without much thought, always thinking, as young men do, and old men shouldn't, that I was immortal. I do know, though, that there is a money belt, coins in different currencies, and a belt full of knives. I know how much you love knives. Use them. Retrieve them.

It would have been wonderful to grow old with you, to become a grandfather, to have watched you mature into the beautiful woman you'll doubtlessly be. It's a shame not to. I will be watching over you. Never doubt my love for you.

Always, your father.

She doesn't fall onto the floor, nor scream nor shout. She folds the letter neatly back into its original creases, and begins to search the drawers. The one to the right contains some men's clothes, and a note telling her to disguise herself as a man, because the world won't recognise her that way. The other drawers are full of the coins her father's letter spoke of, and the money belt, which she straps to herself under her white shirt, and short sharp throwing knives fixed into a leather belt of holsters he must have sewed himself. It's only when she's emptied all the drawers but one that she realises she's rich, that she could buy her way through life without having to work again. Already, she misses the books.

The candle gutters when she opens the last drawer. There are countless leather pouches in here. She opens one. Diamonds, lustrous in the yellowing light. She gasps. There are at least ten of these pouches, each one worth a fortune. Her father has left her an empire of jewels.

What now? she thinks, checking each drawer again and finding them all empty now. How to get out of this cellar, how to find safety? All the wealth in the world isn't enough if the enemy's outside your front door. She's thirsty, her men's garb already soaked through with the sweat of fear and grief. She puts her hands deep into the first drawer she opened, in hope and superstition, and finds a tiny lever, no bigger than the nail on her little finger. She wraps her palm around the tiny fault in the wood and pulls. The cupboard slides to one side, without a noise, on well-oiled rollers. He must have spent so much time down here. And when it finally rocks to a purring halt, cold airs pour down into her face, and she thinks she sees real light at the end of a narrow tunnel.

Chapter 3

The fresh air conflagrates, and the house collapses onto the hidden cellar. Under the tremors, calm beyond her understanding, she binds up her hair with a length of leather she found amongst the fortune her father's left. She bends, onto her elbows and knees, crawls into the cave towards the imagined light, closes her eyes, and prays.

The mud is dry and rough under her fingers. Her hands guide her along the uneven ground. There's nothing but the rush of air past her, and she doesn't open her eyes until it is freezing on her face. She sees fragments of light, through the uneven shelter of tightly-knit bushes. She pushes her way through them, ignoring the scratches on her face, and stands up. It's dawn where she expected darkness, still. The sun is a smudge on the horizon, and silence dances around her. She turns. Where she used to live is a widening column of smoke and the dark orange of dying flames. She hears shouts, far in the distance, tries to work out how far she has come, how long the tunnel must be. It's a long way.

There's nothing she can do now. She walks away from the sounds of destruction, walks away towards the sea, an adult now, and her childhood years past. Her only comfort is the weight of the belt full of knives around her.

Along the streets lined by tall houses, there's no life. It's still early, and her breath freezes into her face. She's drawn to the water, to the docks, where the ships are, where she'll find an escape from the tears that still haven't come, away from the nightmare of the tall man with the tall face.

The day begins, and familiar and unfamiliar faces begin to pour out of the houses. None of them look at her, none take notice, and none greet her. She's changed and disguised, become a stranger in a land that was always the resting place on her travels with her father. His features are beginning to fade already, and his voice starting to dim. She waits in vain for grief. It won't come until she's had her revenge. The muscles in her jaw tighten, the skin drawn hard over her bones. No longer is she Fien, the dutiful daughter, the adoring daughter. She's Fien, the avenger, the schemer, the angered angel.

Her long legs take her down to the docks before she has time to wonder what she'll do if she finds Tall Face there, boarding his ship with his men and her treasure. She'll not look for him now, and he doesn't know to look for her. The shadows of a thousand masts fall across her path, and of their thousands of furled and unfurled sails, swaying to the motion of the water. Seagulls cry and swoop, sailors shout and holler, their hands raw and chapped, ropes are cast away from the side, and old wood creaks and scrapes and hurries off into the ocean on another new journey.

'You look lost, young man.' A voice drags her out of her anger and search for pain. The old man has a beard, white with age and yellow with tobacco. 'Looking for work?' He rubs his hands together again the cold.

'I could be,' she says, her voice unnaturally deep.

'Anywhere you want to go?'

'I haven't thought about it.'

'You're not very good at making up your mind, are you?' he says. 'I've been watching you wander around like a lost soul for an age.'

'I must have had too much to drink last night.'

'Tell me another story I don't know.'

'Any ships going to Persia?' she says, thoughts of the *Rubaiyat* suddenly alive. Somewhere warm.

'That's a long way,' he says, rubs his beard with his

calloused fingers. 'I wonder what you're trying to get away from.'

'It's somewhere new.' Her heart beating fast, the steam from her mouth dense.

'And you've been plenty of places, have you?' He grabs one of her freezing hands before she can stop him. 'Galley boy, eh?' He laughs gruffly. 'Those hands haven't seen much work now, have they?'

She shrugs. 'I just look after them.'

'Then you're the first boy who does.' He jerks his head towards the very end of the docks. 'Up there,' he says. 'Some trader's ship heading for Gombroon. I think they're still looking for someone stupid enough to make such a long trip. They're supposed to be leaving today. Ship's not got a name on it. Tell 'em Dirk sent you.' He spits on the ground, and the ice sizzles. 'And good luck to you.'

'Thanks,' she says. 'Thanks very much.' She starts running, her feet skating on the ice.

'Thank me when you get back,' he calls after her. 'Now's too soon.'

She waves at him without turning, runs even faster towards the ship without a name, hops up onto the gang plank, rushes up it, onto the deck. Hands grab her, throw her to the ground, slipping and sliding.

'Hey, hey.' Another voice, young and strong. 'And what do you think you're doing?'

She wrestles herself free, jumps up, dusts herself down. 'Dirk sent me.' She gasps for air. 'He said you were going to Persia and needed a galley boy or something.'

'Not so quick, not so quick.' The young voice turns into a skinny dark face with a body to match. 'We don't just take anyone, you know.' He puts his hands on his hips. 'You don't look like you've been on a ship before.'

'I've been on lots of ships,' she spits back, stares at his chest.

'Oh, I'm sure. And what did you do on those ships? Watch the clouds pass by while everyone else did the work?'

'Who are you to be asking, anyway?'

He leans against the railings, folds his arms, warm in a leather jacket. 'I'm the one who hires all the boys.'

'Ha. Tell me another joke.'

The nameless youth doesn't move. 'I'll throw you into the water.'

'Just you try.' She's cold, wants to get into somewhere warm.

'What's your name?'

'I don't have one.' She suppresses another shiver.

'Even better. Running away from home, are we?'

'Don't be stupid.' She spits on the deck. 'What's your name?'

'Ben, they call me. And I decide who comes aboard and who doesn't.'

'I want to talk to whoever runs this ship.'

Ben grins at her. 'You want an audience, do you?' He scratches his hairless chin. 'Even if it ends with you in irons?'

'Stop messing me about.'

'Stop invading my ship.'

'I'm not invading …'

'You could've called up to us instead of rushing the plank.'

'I thought you might be leaving any minute.'

He shakes his head, laughs again, out loud. 'Ah, so much experience you have.'

'So, do I stay or not?' She walk across to him, leans towards him, her face almost touching his. She feels warmth.

'How about a test?' he says. 'Follow me.'

'What sort of a test?'

'You'll see.' He starts away without even looking to see if she's following him, across the deck, polished under the ice, and through an open door into a darkened corridor, a warm corridor.

'Wait,' she calls, and chases after him. When she catches up with him, he's in the galley, a hot room, fire glowing in a primitive stove.

'You can make our commandant some coffee and breakfast,' he says. 'You've got ten minutes. And then we'll let the commandant judge if you've passed the test.'

She opens and shuts her mouth without saying anything.

'Not up to it?' he says. 'Then I guess it's the water for you.'

'Ten minutes,' she says. 'It'll be done.'

He bows to her. 'I'll wait outside for you.'

'You're not going to watch?'

'I don't need to,' he says. 'I already know how to make breakfast for someone.' He disappears.

She tears around the tiny room, ripping open cupboards and stove, burning her hands and not caring, because it's better than the cold, reaching up to the very top of the shelves, bending down to see what there is that she can turn into something edible. She throws coffee grounds into the kettle sitting on the stove, finds a pan and throws into it some dried meat she finds. In another niche, she discovers some flour, mixes it with some water into a smooth dough she kneads until it's thin, throws it into the oven on a tray, counts to a hundred while she's busy finding anything resembling a plate and a tray.

One hundred counts reached, she pulls the unleavened bread out of the oven with her finger tips, throws it onto the plate, piles the hot meat up next to it. She finds a cup, pours coffee gingerly into it, makes sure none of the grounds spill from the kettle with the dark liquid. She finds what she thinks are a knife and fork, drops them onto the tray next to the plate and cup. She lifts it all up, and walks out into the corridor.

'Done already?' Ben says. 'It'd better be good.'

They step out onto deck. The ships sways, but she keeps her feet. Land is miles away and moving. She says nothing.

'Follow me,' he says, and finds his way across the shivering deck to another door, dark oak. He opens it without knocking. 'After you.'

She walks in ahead of him, her head high, the tray growing heavier in her hands.

'Welcome. Just put the tray on the chart table.' A woman's voice, and she's the most beautiful woman Fien has ever seen.

Chapter 4

'So you're the wonderful new cook Ben's told me all about,' the woman says. 'The cook with no name.' She stands next to the chart table, even taller than Fien, red hair cropped too short, blue eyes, and sun-burnished freckled skin.

Fien says nothing.

The woman smiles. 'You're not afraid,' she says. 'I can see that. So why won't you speak?'

'I'm surprised,' Fien says. 'That's all.'

'Why surprised?'

'I've never heard of a woman captain before.'

'Commandant,' Ben hisses from behind her.

'Oh, Ben, stop teasing the poor girl.'

Fien blushes. 'How did you know?'

'Oh, my dear, isn't it obvious? It takes one to know one.' She looks past Fien. 'You couldn't tell, could you, Ben?'

He shakes his head, pulls a face. 'Taste the breakfast, Commandant,' he says. 'And if it's no good, I'll throw her over the side.'

'We'll see about that,' the woman says. She picks up a morsel of meat with the fork. 'I'm not sure I remember how to use one of these.'

'Then use your fingers,' Fien says.

'Thank you. Maybe I will.' She pops it into her mouth, chews and smiles. 'Not bad, not bad at all.' She picks up the flat bread between her thumb and index finger. 'Now, this isn't an Antwerp dish.' She takes a bite. 'A well-travelled girl, obviously. You've been to Persia before?'

Fien nods.

'And you've learned from being there, too. Impressive.' She chews her way through two more bites of bread. 'Tell me, can you read?'

'Of course.' Fien bridles.

'Poor old Ben still can't read,' the red-haired woman says. 'Perhaps you can teach him.'

'Haven't you taught him?'

'Oh, I don't have the patience or the time.' She gulps some coffee from the cup. 'And good coffee, too. There's something about you, girl, something that makes me think you could be good for us and bad for us.'

'D'you want me to take her away now?' Ben says from across the room.

'Oh, be a little more patient, boy. I'm sure it wouldn't be much of a challenge for her to swim back the little distance we've covered.' She puts both her elbows on the table, the maps rustling as she moves this way and that. 'Are you going to tell me your name?'

'My name's Fien.' She inclines her head a little. 'And yours?'

'Com ...' Ben's voice is cut off by a sharp nod.

'Lilian,' the woman says. 'You can call me Lilian.'

'Thank you.'

'Ben, go get yourself a cup, and one for Fien here, and bring them back. I think we should all have a little chat.'

Ben nods, and turns on his heels.

'Come, Fien, come sit.'

It's only when they're on the chairs, under the long windows at the stern of the ship, that Fien notices Lilian is wearing trousers as well.

'They're not just for men, you know,' Lilian says. 'Much more comfortable and useful than those bloody dresses they say we should wear. I'd like to see them in one.'

Fien can't help laughing at the thought.

'You do laugh then,' Lilian says.

Fien thinks of her father and stops.

'Before that fool of a boy comes back, tell me what a

fine girl like you's doing jumping onto the first strange ship she finds.'

Fien feels the weight of the knives and the coins and the diamonds around her, and doesn't know if she can trust this woman. She hesitates. 'And then what?'

'I'll listen.'

'And throw me off the ship?'

'Why would I do that? It'll be nice to have some female company for a change.'

'Are you a pirate?'

It's Lilian's turn to laugh. 'I've heard it said.'

'So you are?'

'I just trade for myself. That's all. Just because I don't pass my profit on to any government doesn't make me a pirate.' She leans back into her chair. 'And, anyway, whoever's heard of a woman pirate?' She looks at Fien. 'You don't know if you can trust me, do you?' She puts a finger to her lips, closes her eyes. 'You're carrying any number of knives, you're wearing a money belt, and you're running away from something.'

'And I'm on a ship heading into the middle of the ocean.'

'So all these things are true.'

Fien nods, clutches a hand to her chest.

'Let's drink that coffee and then I'll show you something,' Lilian says. 'Perhaps it'll persuade you to tell me what's driven you to me.'

'Coincidence.'

'There's not such thing, my dear girl, there really isn't.' She looks towards the door. 'Ah, here's Ben now.' She stands. 'What kept you, boy?'

'My clumsiness, Commandant,' he says, and puts down the two steaming cups.

'Sit, Ben, sit, and listen.'

He sits down next to Lilian, narrow against her tall frame, picks up his cup, his little finger as far away

29

from its edge as he can manage.

'Fien here, she doesn't trust us. Is that your fault for taunting her?'

Ben turns red, just a little, and shakes his head. 'Just protecting you, Commandant. We can't have just anyone on board, can we?'

'And yet you chose wisely, boy. She can make coffee and flatbread.'

'I could tell from the start.'

'You're a fool.'

'Your fool, Commandant.'

Lilian smiles. 'Such a little diamond you are. And if you're so clever tell me how we'll get her to trust us.'

'I'm not clever enough for that,' he says. 'Maybe we should just throw her in the water.'

'Oh, stop it. You've had your little joke now. I don't want you to frighten her any more. Tell her you're sorry.'

'I'm sorry, Madam,' he says, and bows to Fien. 'Forgive the japes of an uneducated boy.'

'Will you teach him how to read?' Lilian says.

'If you want me to.'

'I'd like you to.' Lilian drains her cup and gets up. 'Now, drink up. Let me show you what I promised.' Her trousers are white silk, held up by a red sash, a white shirt tucked into it. She pushes through the door, walks through a group of unshaven sailors who bow to her, and across the swaying deck towards the bow of her ship, to the forward hold, and pulls open its cover on the deck. She jumps down the ladder, two rungs in one step. Ben and Fien follow her. It's darker down here, and the smell of sea storms into Fien's nose.

'I told you I trade for my own profit.' She lights a torch. 'And here's the profit from this trip.' She walks across to a line of chests all neatly stacked, secured to the floor with ropes. She opens one of them. It's full of glittering stones.

Fien gasps.

'Ah, I see you understand, child,' Lilian says. 'A lot of diamonds.'

'More than my father gave me, and I thought that was a fortune.'

'So we get nearer the truth. Why did your father give you diamonds?'

'Only a few small bags. He hid them for me.'

'And where is he?'

'He's dead.'

'Oh. I'm sorry.' She hands the torch to Ben and comes across to Fien, puts her arm around the girl. 'No tears?'

'I can't find them.'

'When did he die?'

'Last night. An Englishman killed him.'

'A tall man? With a tall face?'

Fien nods. 'How do you know?'

'He's been crossing me for some time.'

'So why didn't he come for you instead of my father?'

'I don't know,' Lilian says. 'Perhaps he wasn't looking. He can be very blinkered.'

'Who is he?'

'Ah, now there's a question.' Lilian drops the lid back down. 'He works for the king of England. He's supposed to be a harmless old man but he's not. They think he just sits in his big house and influences things. But he's as hard as nails. He doesn't know I know that he goes on supposedly secret missions all the time.'

'Why?'

'Because the king spends too much money and needs more. Because he's milked all the English dry and needs money from other places to stop his palaces from falling down. And to fight a war against his own people. Because he thinks he'll save his kingdom that way.'

'So he lets this Lindsey go into foreign countries and kill people?' Fien's rage rises.

'That's just about it.'

'And no-one does anything about it?'

'What can anyone do?'

'Can't you do something?'

Lilian stands at the foot of the ladder, one slim arm stretched out, her bony hand holding on to one of the rungs. 'Believe me, I've tried. He's a slippery customer. And he's always surrounded by his private army.'

'Didn't you see him this time?'

Lilian shakes her head. 'I've no idea how he got here, nor how he heard of your father.'

'I want to kill him.'

'Your time will come, I'm sure of it. But now's not the time.'

'Why?'

'Because we're sailing to Persia, not to England. Because you're too young, and he'll kill you even more easily than he killed your father.'

'He doesn't know I exist.'

'You need more of an advantage than that.' Lilian starts to climb up the ladder. 'I can teach you.'

'What's in it for you?'

Lilian brushes imaginary dust from her shirt. 'I can always do with an ally, someone I can absolutely trust. And I tell you, never trust a man, not ever, because a man will soon forget about what he's promised when he sees something he thinks is prettier or richer than you are.'

'Is that what happened to you?'

Lilian shrugs. 'It happens to all of us.'

Chapter 5

A hundred miles at least from shore, Lilian takes Fien around the ship, introduces her to the crew, all of them men, all of them bowing to her, and smiling at Fien, all hard men, too, by the look of them. She can't remember all their names.

'Don't they mind serving a woman?' Fien says when they're back in Lilian's cabin.

'Why should they? I treat them better than any man would.'

'Don't you feel threatened?'

'Should I? I'm probably stronger than them, and I wouldn't ask them to do anything I wouldn't do.'

'But on long trips men get … you know.'

'Randy, you mean, or are you too young to know the right words?'

'I know the right words.' Fien blushes.

'You just don't know what to do with them.'

'Answer my question.'

'Oh, you can be a fierce one, can't you?' Lilian picks up a pipe, stuffs tobacco into it, lights it. 'I can get randy, too. And like them, I have to wait until we can find what we want, or what we need. It's as simple as that. That's the one rule there is, if we have any rules.'

'That can't be easy.'

'There's plenty to keep us occupied,' Lilian says. 'Like the storm that's about to hit us.' She takes a deep drag of her pipe. 'Did you see the clouds?'

Fien shakes her head.

'I'll teach you to read the weather if you teach Ben to read by the time we get to Persia.'

'Persian or English or Flemish?'

'I think English will be enough.' Lilian nods, her eyes closed. 'You can read Persian?'

'My father taught me. We travelled a lot.'

'Lucky you.'

'Are you English?'

'Now that would be telling.' Lilian's eyes twinkle. 'I don't belong anywhere, and I belong to no-one.'

'Is that why your ship has no name?'

'She has a name alright. But I choose not to have it painted on her.'

'What is it?'

'*The Odyssey.* That makes sense to you, doesn't it?'

Fien nods. 'Who are you?'

'I'm what you see, my girl.' Lilian points at the long bench under the long window. 'You'll sleep here.' She smiles. 'No-one's ever shared this cabin with me. Be honoured.'

'I am.'

The sky darkens more suddenly than Fien thought it could.

'Stay here.' Lilian throws her a length of rope. 'Tie yourself down. I'll be back.'

As she ties knots around her waist and to the wall, Fien hears Lilian's voice, out on deck, shouting commands to her men, makes out words that call them to the main mast, words that reassure, words made to inspire, that warn of danger and are full of kindness and entreaties and threats all at once. And then the wind roars in from the northeast and darkness is complete.

Fien can't remember a storm like this. Never, on her travels with her father, did she encounter such ferocity. The lightning rips through the black sky, jagged yellow forks of fire, and the thunder so loud, as if some malevolent god were ripping apart the clouds around the tiny ship. Fien isn't afraid. She doesn't close her eyes. She doesn't scream. She doesn't cry. The rain slaps against the stern windows, and the wind howls across the thin glass, invisible fingers grasping for a hold, trying to break into the cabin, reaching for her.

I can't just sit here waiting, she thinks. *I need to help.* She
unties herself from the seat, leaves one end of the rope
coiled around her waist, and forces her way across the
uneven, dancing floor to the door. She can't hear the
crew's shouts anymore, just the voice of the storm, and
the wind battering against the oak in front of her. She
pushes her way out, and the door slams shut behind
her. She reaches forwards and finds a railing, ties
herself to it with one of the sliding knots her father
taught her, pushes into the opposing forces, the rain in
her eyes, running down her neck into her shirt, soaking
her in a couple of seconds. She can see nothing.

Another flash of lightning illuminates the deck. It's
chaos. Raindrops as large as her fist bounce off the
boards. A crash of thunder, and another flash. A
fragment of vision. Men hanging from the rigging,
pulling heavy sails in to the outriggers. Blackness. The
ship bounds, bucks, throws itself from the crest of one
wave down into the endless valley of another, and
struggles to climb the face of the next invisible
mountain of sea. The ocean breaks over the side of the
ship, a whip of water blasting across the buckling deck,
punishing and breaking anything in its way.

Fien edges away from the door, secure on her rope,
trusting her instincts in the black ink darkness. Three
flashes of light in quick succession, and three huge
thunderclaps at the same time. She finds her way to the
steps that lead up to the wheel. She unhooks the rope
from one railing, binds it to the next, just with the
touch of her fingers, quicker than thought. She
stumbles up the stairs. More lightning. She's at the top
now. Another buck, another groan of bursting wood.
She feels it more than hears it, senses the splintering of
something, somewhere, a weight tumbling through the
thrashing air, down, down towards the wheel. Flash.
Lilian, knuckles white, forcing her will onto the ship's

rudder, a shadow, falling.

Without thinking, Fien rips loose her knot and throws herself at Lilian, knocks her to the ground and to one side, with a force she didn't know she had. The impact of the wooden beam rips a gash into the deck an arm's length away from where Fien lands with Lilian. The ship leaps. The thunder louder than ever.

'You could've got killed.' Fien's scream is thin over the noise.

'So could you.' Lilian jumps to her feet, hauls Fien up with her, ties them both to the wheel with the rope. 'But thanks.'

'You should've tied yourself to it in the first place.'

'Then I would have been dead.' Lilian wrestles the ship back to where she wants it, panting, sweating.

Fien, next to her, feels the woman's raw energy, intent now on nothing else than saving her ship, her crew, thanks done, almost death forgotten.

'Head back to port,' Fien shouts.

'We're too far away.' Lilian spits salt water. 'Do you want Lindsey on your back so soon?'

'Hell.'

The storm shows no sign of weakening. The hours pass too slowly, hours of brute force and pain, a few seconds of windlessness when they can both hope the end of the chaos is near, and then the howls start again, with a new force, with nature's hatred for those who try to tame it. The salt water burns in the scratches in Fien's face, and the wind rips at her skin, at the bruises underneath. But she refuses to give in, refuses to let the tiredness drag her down, asks herself how exhausted Lilian is, how she finds the strength and skill to hold the ship, wonders if the crew is safe, where Ben is.

And then it's over. One last tumultuous wave which threatens to overturn the ship, and then a flat sea. The clouds scud away towards where Fien thinks the land should be, the sun carves a last blade of light across the horizon before sinking away to the other side of the world. The main mast still stands, like a tree shorn of most of its branches, and a mess of ropes and cracked wood litters the decks.

Lilian unties the rope, puts her fingers into her mouth and whistles. The crew appear, as if from nowhere, sodden ghosts, water and blood.

'Drop anchor,' Lilian says without raising her voice.

A second later the rattle of the chain echoes through the stillness.

'All present and correct?' Lilian says.

'All present and correct, Commandant,' Ben shouts up, salutes with his thin arms. 'A few knocks, but that's it.'

'No thanks to you, boy,' an old sailor calls, with an enormous white beard and no hair, wraps his arms round Ben's neck from behind, the smile never leaving his face. 'Thank God.'

'Better get this mess cleared up,' Lilian says, a smile on her lips. 'Another close scrape for Lilian's Lads, eh?'

'Aye,' the bald man says. 'There's always the next one to look forward to.'

'That'll do me for a while, Harry,' Lilian says. 'I need us to sail on as soon as possible. Can we?'

'We always can, Lil,' Harry says. 'That's what we do.'

'Thanks. Let's get to it.' She turns to Fien. 'Go brew as much coffee as you can if the galley's still workable. The boys will be needing it.'

Fien wipes the wet from her face. 'You don't want me to help up here?'

'Best coffee I ever tasted, what you gave me before.' Lilian laughs. 'Thanks for that, my girl.'

Lilian skips down the steps, finds her way to the galley. It's cold in here now, pots and pans everywhere, the floor covered in a slime of water and food. She sighs, digs her way to the wall, grabs a broom and starts to clean. Oblivious to the noise of the decks being cleared, she turns the mess into tidiness, the dirt into cleanliness, until, at last, she can throw wood into the stove and light it. A few hours later, the galley is warm again, and innumerable pots of coffee bubble away on the red-hot plates. She sticks her head out into the hubbub. 'Coffee,' she calls. 'Four at a time.'

Soon she's busy handing out mugs of steaming coffee, the intensity of the smell reminding her of her father's study, and the smiling faces of the men making her feel at home and safe. 'There's no reason for tears,' she says to herself, aloud, in a quiet moment. 'This is where I was meant to be.'

'Going mad, are you?' Ben interrupts her meditation.

'Is that what you think?' She realises his arms don't look so thin now.

'I'm sorry. I can't help it. A joke always seems easier than being serious.'

'Even when the joke hurts?'

'I didn't mean …'

'You didn't,' she says. 'Not now.'

'I'm just the ship's fool,' he says. 'There'd be no use for me otherwise.'

'How did you get to be here?' She offers him some coffee.

'She saved me.' He takes a sip, sits down on the floor, wipes his hand across it. 'It's never been this clean.'

'What did she save you from?'

'Bad things, she says. That's all you need to know.'

'What do you know about her?'

'She's Lilian. No-one knows where she came from, or why she does what she does. All that talk about profit is just talk. She gives a lot of it away.'

'Is she English?'

Ben shrugs. 'She talks like an English. It doesn't mean

she is.'

'Have you ever heard her talk anything else?'

'She talks all sorts of words to all sorts of people. I can't tell what it is she says, though.'

'You all love her, don't you?'

'Don't you, now, already?'

'She's amazing.' Fien blushes.

'There's nothing wrong with thinking that,' Ben says. 'There's something about her. And it's not because she's a woman doing what women aren't supposed to do. It's because of the person she is.'

'That's what I think, too. It's odd, though, because I've only just met her.'

'She's hard and soft; that's what it is. She'll kill to protect, and I've seen her do it, and she's vicious. But if there's something wrong with anyone, she's there. It's like she can read minds, like she can feel things none of us can see. I don't really understand it.'

'I suppose there's no point thinking about it. It's just the way she is.' Fien wipes the top of the stove with a cloth. 'Where is she now?'

'Still out there with the boys.'

'Take her some more coffee.'

'Why don't you take it?'

'I want to keep this place clean and warm.'

'We could do with a decent cook and cleaner.'

'It's a good thing I came to you then, isn't it?'

'Did I ever say anything else?'

Fien slaps him with the cloth. 'I'll throw you into the water if you're not careful.'

Ben laughs. 'Now that's more like it. I think we're going to be best friends from now on.'

'Not if you don't take her that coffee now.'

Chapter 6

The sun is almost up again when Fien gets back to the cabin. Lilian is a few footsteps behind her.

'That was fun,' Lilian says, drops into one of the chairs. 'You should never have come out.'

'You'd be dead now if I hadn't.'

'I'd have got out of the way, somehow.' Lilian grabs her pipe. 'But thank you, anyway.'

'You don't have to thank me.'

'Oh yes I do. We all have to be thankful to those around us.' She chuckles. 'I must have the most polite bunch of thieves and murderers around me.' She waves the pipe through the air. 'That's quite an amusing thought.'

'Is Ben a murderer, too, then?'

'You've taken a shine to the boy, have you?'

'No.' She feels the blood rising in her face. 'He just said you saved him from something bad, but he wouldn't say what.'

'Then you'll have to wait until he decides to tell you. I can't tell you what he won't.'

'You're a strange woman.'

'Am I? I'm just honest. … I never asked you about your mother.'

'She died when I was born.'

'That's sad.'

'Yes. I don't think my father ever recovered from it.'

'But he loved you.'

'I think so.'

'I know.'

'How can you know?'

'Because you wouldn't have turned into this adventurous girl sitting next to me if he hadn't. You wouldn't be half as brave and tough as you've proved to be in the last twenty-four hours. That sort of thing doesn't just grow by itself. It has to be nurtured.'

'I'd just started to feel hemmed in by him. I wanted to be free.'

'And now you feel guilty.'

Fien nods.

'Don't. We all feel like that, whatever we do, wherever we are. It's natural.'

'Is that why you became this, whatever it is you are?'

'Maybe. It's so long ago I can't remember.'

'You're not that old.'

'Perhaps not in years.'

'Won't you tell me anything about you?'

'You know as much as the lads do, and that's enough.' Lilian knocks the dead ashes out of her pipe into the ashtray. 'Enough now. You need to sleep. And so do I.'

'Don't you need to steer?'

'Oh, Harry and the others know where we're going. They can point the old girl in the right direction on their own. I was only at the wheel because it was a question of saving the ship and the crew. And I can't let them carry that burden, even though they gladly would.'

'W ...'

'Enough, I said, young lady. Bed down now. The sun will wake you before you know you're asleep.'

Fien lies down in the cot, and pulls a cover over herself, watches Lilian lie down on her bed, without a cover, on her back, her arm over her face. They're both asleep within seconds.

'This is the only day you're allowed to sleep late,' Ben says, as he shakes her shoulder. 'The Commandant told me to let you. And then she made me cook breakfast.'

Fien sits up, rubs her eyes, instantly dislikes the felling of having slept in her clothes. 'I'm sorry.'

'You'll just have to make me breakfast tomorrow to make up for it.'

'What time is it?'

'About noon. That's what the sun says, anyway.'

'She let me sleep this late?'

'She said you'd had a bit of a difficult time.'

'And what now?'

'We'll find a way of making you useful.'

'So what do you do during a long trip like this? It'll take us three months to get to Persia.'

'Not quite that long,' Ben says. 'You must've been on slow ships if it took you that long before.'

'Oh, so this is a mysteriously fast craft then, is it?'

Ben laughs. 'No, there's no mystery about it. She just knows how to get the most out of her ship. And so does Harry.'

'So we're not about to attack other ships and steal all their treasures.'

'Is that really what you think we do? She's an honest trader. And that's why we're going to Persia. To trade.'

'The diamonds for what?'

'You ask too many questions.'

Fien jumps off the bed. 'You didn't even bring me any coffee.'

'You know where it is and how to make it.'

'You brought me some yesterday.'

'Only because she told me to.'

'Oh.'

'Come on. I'm sure some part or other of the deck needs scrubbing.'

'I'm going to the galley to make sure it's clean,' Fien says. 'I don't trust you boys to keep it the way I want it.'

'Then you should've got up sooner,' he says. 'Because I think you'll find there's a lot of cleaning to do now.'

'You bastards.'

'Right in one.'

It takes her an age to get the galley back to the state she left it in after the storm. She swears her way through the cleaning and tidying. And afterwards she feels better, like she's accomplished something real. She leans against the warm stove, takes a breath, and smiles at herself, wonders if her father would be proud of her. It stokes a rage inside her.

'You think it's odd you're not sad, don't you?' Lilian's voice perches into the silence like conscience on her shoulder.

Fien nods, rubs the wet cloth over an imaginary stain.

'I can understand it. I'm still like that when I think of some things.' Lilian wipes a finger across the stove. 'Spotless.'

Fien says nothing.

'Pretend I'm the sister you never had. Talk to me about anything. Whenever. Maybe you never will, maybe you'll never want to.'

'We'll see.'

'Yes, we will. Now, have you thought about how you're going to teach the boy how to read and write?'

'Oh.'

'Never forget bargains you've struck,' Lilian says. 'One day, it could cost you your life. ... Yes ... Your life. ... Check my room for books that might help.'

'Why haven't you ever taught him?' *And he's not really a boy anymore, is he?*

'He won't listen to me. And I haven't really got the patience. Too many other things on my mind.' Lilian looks at her, daring her to ask more. 'Go.'

Back in the cabin, Fien's surprised at all the books she never noticed, books kept in place on their shelves by rails. *That's why they didn't fall out during the storm*, she thinks. She pulls out one of the rails to free the books, pulls out one after another. Many of them are practical books, in the language of all seafarers, English and German. Huge volumes, leather-bound, heavy, almost impossible to lift from their places, hide skinny pamphlets made from flimsy paper, in languages Fien has never seen, never mind learned.

She works her way from the top shelves to the bottom. Some books she places in a pile next to her bed, not because she thinks they'll be any use to Ben, but because she wants to read them herself, although she doubts she'll find the time. She surprises herself with her curiosity, until she remembers, somehow, moments with her father when she was still a very young child, when he used to let her sit on his desk, when he'd be leafing through books he'd just acquired, his glasses on his nose, his hand in his shirt. And sometimes, he'd lean back, and look at her over the top of his glasses, encourage her to turn the pages in the book he'd given her, smile at the way her small, pudgy fingers would struggle with the heavy parchment. He'd point out pictures to her, and the shapes of letters and symbols she didn't know about, when that tell-tale wrinkle across her forehead would deepen and her widening eyes would ask him questions he'd answer without her talking. How had she learned to read and write? She tries to remember, but besides her father's benevolence and joy she can remember nothing. She sighs.

'What is it?'

'Does a red-haired pirate princess really have the time to follow her newest cook everywhere?'

Lilian raises an eyebrow. 'Whoever said I was a princess?'

'Poetic licence.'

'Well, be more of a teacher than a poet, my girl. Please.'

'I don't think any of these books will help.'

'What about that stack by your bed?'

'They're the ones I want to read.'

'You do, do you?'

'Have you any parchment and quills?'

'In the drawers of the chart table. I'm surprised you haven't looked already.'

'I don't like to delve into other people's things.'

Lilian bows.

'You didn't trust me, did you?' Fien says.

'To say I didn't anticipate your politeness would be more accurate.'

'I'm glad I've exceeded your expectations.'

'Only a few of them. I expect a lot more from you.'

'I think I realise.'

'Good. What do you want the parchment and quills for?'

'I think it's best to draw words for him to begin with.'

'I want him to be able to read and write by the time we get to Gombroon.'

'That'll take a couple of months. That's plenty of time.'

'And I don't just mean child-speak,' Lilian says. 'I want him to be able to write properly, to read properly, to understand most of the words in these English books here.'

'That won't be easy.'

'I don't care.'

'Why the hurry?'

'That should be no concern of yours,' Lilian says.

'You're planning to sell him, aren't you?'

'Don't be ridiculous. The one thing I won't trade in is people.'

'Why can't you explain it to me?'

'I've only known you for a week, girl.'

'So?'

'We'll see in a week or two, shall we? I expect you to spend most of your time teaching him, not keeping the galley clean.'

'Those tasks go hand in hand.'

'So be it.'

'What if he doesn't want to learn?'

'He'll want to learn from you, alright. I can tell.'

Fien blushed. 'What do you mean?'

'I think he has a soft spot for you. You've noticed that, haven't you?'

'I … I don't know.'

'That's you knowing the words again, but not being able to use them.'

'That's because I've never lived in the real world.'

'I know. You told me. Well, you'd better start living in it quickly and get used to it.'

'I'll go to find him now.'

'I'll send him to you. Get whatever you need ready. And don't let me down.'

'I don't plan to.'

'Good.'

Chapter 7

Ben won't sit still. His long legs protest against the hot weather they've reached now, protest again sitting down, being still.

'This was her idea, not mine,' Fien says.

'I know.'

'Now try again. Look at the paper and tell me what you see.'

'You draw well.'

'Tell me what I've drawn.'

'An ant.'

'So what do those three letters under the picture say?'

'Pig.'

'Stop it.'

'Alright. ... Cat.'

'You know what'll happen if you don't try harder?'

'You'll make me clean the galley for you? You'll teach me how to make good coffee? You'll leave me in peace?'

'She'll throw me in the water.'

'She'd never do that.' Ben balances his chair on its back legs.

'Yes, she would. She told me.' She pushes him so that he overbalances and crashes onto the floor. 'But I guess you'd like that, wouldn't you?' She makes no effort to help him up.

He scrabbles to his feet, stands the chair back up. 'That was mean.'

'You're being mean.'

He sits down again, pulls the chair back under the table, sighs through sullen lips. He's too tall to be treated like a little boy.

'So, let's try again. Sound out those three letters. You know the shapes and you know the word.'

'A ... n ... t.'

'That wasn't so difficult, was it?'

'Why do I have to sound them out?'

'If you know how to sound them, you can build your own words.'

'N ... t ... a.' He snorts. 'See – that's not a word.'

'I mean you can build words you read from the sounds of the letters even if you don't know the words.'

'Oh.'

'That way you can read all sorts of things.'

'But not all words are made from three letters.'

'True. But we have to start here.'

'Why?'

'Because we all have to start somewhere.'

And so it goes on, for hours, for days, for weeks. By then, Ben, who, against all odds, is proving to be an able pupil, can spell out simple words, can read simple sentences which Fien composes, can read them from pieces of paper, blank except for the letters, with no sketches to prompt him, with no pictures to guide him. Lilian approves, though, in a rare quiet moment alone with Fien, tells her to push him harder.

'We're going as fast as we can,' Fien says into the moonlight shining in through the big window behind them.

'Just try.' Lilian, on her bed without a cover again, fully clothed again, ready to jump up at any moment, sounds tired.

'You should try to get more sleep.'

'That, my girl, is not what we were talking about.'

'Then explain to me why you need him to learn to read and write.'

'He needs to learn to look after himself. And he needs to be able to read to do that.'

'He's got you.'

'I'm not going to live forever.'

'None of us are.'

Lilian says nothing.

'You're not that old. You could really be my older sister.'

'Again, that's not the point.'

'Then what is? I can't understand you if you talk in riddles.'

Lilian sits up, the light silver on her short hair, her face even paler than usual, her eyes a milky blue. She rubs her face. 'There'll be a time, and a time soon, when I'm not here anymore. And then he'll need to read.'

'He's got me.'

Lilian snorts. 'Sorry. That's not supposed to sound like you don't mean anything. He needs to find answers himself, not depend on anyone else.'

'He's your son, isn't he?'

'Leave it.' Lilian's voice shakes.

'Why the secrets? Aren't we in this together now?'

'You don't know what you're talking about.'

'Lindsey killed my father.'

'I know.'

'It could have been you.'

'I know that, too.' Lilian sighs again. 'I'm sorry it was your father.'

'I'm sorry it wasn't you.'

'We know where we stand then.'

'That's not what I meant.'

'It's exactly what you meant. Family.' Lilian jumps up. 'Sleep. I have things to do.'

'In the middle of dead water?'

'I've always got things to do. Close your eyes and sleep.' She rips open the door. 'And teach him more quickly.' She raises her hands in the opaque light. 'Just do it. No more argument.'

But Fien can't sleep. She has visions, imagined, she

thinks, of what Lindsey did to her father before setting fire to the house, terrible, blood-ridden visions. And she knows, she's certain, that Lindsey stole the watch, the emerald, the ticking jewel, her father's keepsake from his marriage, his only love. Even when, especially when, she closes her eyes, she sees nothing but a bloody grimace from a tall, aristocratic face, an arrogance of murder. The moon fades into sea fog until the sun burns it away and shines onto her face, too hot, too soon.

'Lil told me to come to you as soon as the sun rose,' Ben says, an apology in the tone of his voice.

'Yes, I can imagine.'

'She says you can forget about cooking for the next few weeks.'

'Is that right?'

Ben nods.

'Well, she's wrong.' Fien pulls a sheaf of paper across the map desk. 'I want you to write a short story for me. At least two hundred words. I don't care if you use any of these books, but if the story doesn't make sense, I'm going to make you drink ink. Understood?'

Ben nods, tenses in his chair, and says nothing.

'That should take you a few hours. I'll bring you some breakfast when all the others have had theirs.'

'She'll get angry with you.'

'I don't care.'

'You should.'

'I'll get angry with you. Do you care about that?'

Ben shrugs.

'In other words, yes. So I'm getting through to you at last.'

'I don't understand why she wants me to do this. I can think well enough.'

'Neither do I. But she wants it, and quickly. That's what she told me.'

'I'll do my best.'

'Thank you.' Fien feels a surge of affection for the tall youth sitting there like a child, his skin soft with brown, his arms too muscled to be thin, and his eyes wide with apprehension. 'She does love you, you know.'

'And I love her,' he says, so quietly she almost doesn't hear him. 'But I can't let her know.'

Chapter 8

In the galley, Fien, still tired but wide awake, slams pots and pans around on the stove, and mutters to herself. She drinks two cups of coffee while she cooks.

'I told the boy to tell you there'd be no cooking duties for you for a while.'

'I know.'

'So what are you doing in here?'

'What does it look like?'

'Why are you disobeying me?'

Fien turns and faces Lilian. 'Because you're wrong.'

'How dare you?'

'Because …' Fien turns back to the sizzling pan.

'Out with it.'

'I want to know what it is with you and that boy. He's afraid of you, and he doesn't understand why you're in such a hurry.'

'He doesn't need to understand. Nor do you.'

'He loves you.'

'I don't want to be loved. Not by anyone.'

Fien shrugs. 'That makes no sense. I thought we all needed to be loved.'

'What about the pain?'

'We can't just hold back because we think we'll get hurt.'

'Is that why you can't cry for your father?'

'It's the need for revenge that's keeping my tears away. I'll cry when I've done him justice, I'm sure.'

'What's Ben doing now?'

'I told him to write a story. I'll go and check on him when I've finished cooking.'

'Maybe we were sisters, in another time.' Lilian's voice softens.

'You saved me. Let me save you.'

'You don't know what you're talking about.'

'Fine. Now have some breakfast.' Fien empties the pan onto a plate. 'A pirate ship with fine crockery. Why's that, I wonder.'

'Lucky there was any left after that storm.'

'I don't think that was luck; it was judgment. You know exactly what you're doing and when to do it. If you weren't so horrible you'd be quite nice.'

'How kind of you,' Lilian says, her mouth full.

'You'll let me carry on cooking, then?'

'I suppose so.'

'And I want to practice with my knives.'

'The deck is yours, if you find the time.'

'The moon's full. There's no better time, is there? The time for ambush.'

'When you're good enough in the moonlight, you'll have to practice in the dark. That's the best time to turn defence into attack.'

'Thank you.'

'Don't mention it.' Lilian drops the plate into a tub and walks away.

One after another, the men come in to get their food. Hairy Harry is the last. He leans against the stove while he eats.

'She wasn't half angry this morning,' he says, looking at his plate.

Fien shrugs.

'I didn't hear you,' he says.

'I didn't say anything.'

Harry grunts.

'What?' Fien says.

'Nothing.' He forks in another mouthful. 'Just thought you might know why.'

'Why? You know her better than I do.'

'Aye, that's true. But then I'm not a woman.'

'And I'm just a girl.'

'Same thing,' he says. 'Unfathomable, that's what.'

53

'I could say the same about men.'

'P'raps. But it wouldn't be true. We're just greedy bastards. You can see through us right away.'

'Is that right, Harry?' Fien says. 'Except you're too fat for me to see anything.'

Harry rubs his beard and then his belly. 'Well, a bit of a layer for when it gets cold.'

Fien shakes her head. 'I don't know how she puts up with you.'

'Because we're harmless little pussy cats when it comes to her,' he says.

'Well, wipe your whiskers then, because you've got food in them.'

'Better food in my beard than no food in my beard.'

'Is that all you pirates do, eat and sleep and fight against the storms?'

'Oh, we're not pirates, girl,' he says. 'That's just your imagination running away with you.'

'So what are you exactly?'

'Now that would be telling.' He belches. 'Thanks for breakfast.'

She pretends to slap him as he walks out past her.

There's no wind, and the ship lies still in the water as she walks back to the cabin to check on Ben. The water laps against the old wood. She stares out across the sea. There's nothing to be seen for as far as her eyes can reach. She walks into the cool of the wooden room, closes the door quietly behind her.

'Have you finished?' she says, trying to put some intimidation into her voice.

Ben doesn't even look up.

She puts her hand on his shoulder and looks at the table. Under his right arm there's an untidy sheaf of papers.

'Let me see,' she says.

'It's bad,' he whispers. 'You'll be angry.'

'No, I won't. You've only just started, so how could I be?'

'Can I go now?'

'Stay here while I read it.'

Ben blushes. 'Do I have to?'

She nods. 'If there are any mistakes, I need to show them to you.'

'We'll be here till sundown then.'

'We'll see.'

'And you'll throw me into the water.'

'I don't think so.' She sits down and starts to read, her mind ignoring the crossings-out and the jumbled letters.

I can think of nothing to write. The ocean is deep. I don't know what's in the deep. If I turn the world upside down, the deep is high, and the water is the sky. I have no memory of the world, this way up or that way down. Here is where I have always been, and where I want to stay.

The woman with the red hair shines in my dreams. One day she was there. I don't know when, and I don't know why. Who was I before? She won't tell me.

When it rains, the up is the down, and the sea falls onto us. Some day we'll all drown and no-one will find us. And no-one will miss us. I will miss us.

What will I be when I grow up? A commandant or a slave? Commandant – it's the longest word I know to spell. There was a princess, a long time ago, who could spell the longest word in the world with her hair. She lived in the ocean, in its deepest deep, to keep the word a secret. No-one knows where that deepest water is. Should we try to find her? Perhaps she's drowned already, when the sea becomes the sky, because she can't breathe air. Or perhaps she has red hair and has come to save me and the world. I don't know. Is that enough?

Fien has tears in her eyes when she looks up at the boy who's almost a man. 'You're so sad,' she says. 'And I wish I could make you happy.'

He walks across to her and puts his arms around her. 'Don't cry,' he says. 'I didn't mean to make you cry. It's all I could think of. I'm still hot from the effort.' He lets go of her. 'Are you going to make me drink ink now?'

'No,' she says, and swallows the lump in her throat. 'But I'm going to make you write it out again with no mistakes, and with nothing crossed out.'

'You're not going to show it to the Commandant, are you?'

'No.' She shakes her head, hating her lie.

Chapter 9

Lilian paces the cabin, from one wall to the opposite and back. Again and again. The night oppresses. There is no air. 'Why couldn't we have saved some of the wind from that damn storm? Why can't we have a box we can store it in to use when we need it?'

Fien watches her, the candle light dripping from her hair like scarlet wax. She says nothing, keeps reading her book, Ben's corrected and tidy story folded up and tucked in behind the last page.

'Say something.' Lilian almost screams without slowing her paces.

'What do you want me to say? I don't know the sea. I don't know what you're planning, where you want to be and when.'

'That'll do,' Lilian says, throws herself into the seat opposite Fien. 'Can't you invent a machine for the wind?'

'I'm still a child. You're an adult. Can't you?'

'I wish I could.'

'The fresh water's starting to run low.' Fien remembers how low the level of water in the galley was that morning.

'Guess why I want some wind.'

'Oh.'

'I need us to be further along before we pick up more water.'

'We'll just have to go without.'

Lilian laughs. 'In this heat? And go mad?'

Fien closes her book, pulls out the folded piece of parchment, spreads it out on the table, the rustle an edge into the silence. 'He wrote this,' she says. 'I promised him not to show it to you.'

'And yet you are.'

'You wanted to know how quickly he's learning.'

Lilian puts the palm of her left hand on the parchment on the table, holds it down flat. 'Have you told him who you think I am?'

'No. But he's not a long way from guessing, I think.'

'Hm.' Lilian takes away her hand, picks up the parchment between thumb and index finger, brings it close up to her face, her cheekbones flaring with the blood of her quickening heart. She reads, puts it down again, leans back, and picks up the sheet once more. A smile, faint, plays around her eyes and her lips. 'That's what he thinks, does he? That I'm a mermaid become human.' She shakes her head.

'Are you?'

'What do you think?' She laughs. 'There's no such thing as a mermaid.'

'There are such things as princesses.'

'And there are such things as princes who fall in love with those who are supposed to be below them.'

'Is that what happened to you?'

Lilian rubs her face, her eyes bloodshot now, and tired. 'A long time ago, in a faraway land …' She stops, leans backwards in her chair, stretches her narrow body, and sighs. 'No.'

'What happened?' Lilian is on the edge of her chair now, her hands clasped together, her legs shaking. 'Tell me.'

'No-one knows.' Lilian's voice is a long-lost breeze.

'I won't tell anyone.'

'Not even the boy?'

'Not even Ben, no.'

'Do you think you know what love is? I mean love for someone other than a parent or a sibling?'

'I've no idea. I can't imagine it, if that's answer enough. Like you keep telling me, I know the words, but I don't know what to do with them.'

'A young girl, not much older than you, couldn't feel

the words either, however much she weighed them in her head or tried them out loud. She thought it was all nonsense, that her parents were just acting out a play or something like that when they kissed and smiled at each other, when they said nice words, when they called their love by name.' She pours herself a glass of wine, takes a mouthful, and wipes her lips dry. She stares into the darkness beyond the window.

'But they weren't acting, were they?'

Lilian doesn't move, doesn't stop staring. Then, suddenly. 'No. They were just living, living with all the passion they had, holding on to life as if it was the most precious thing, as if they were afraid it would be gone tomorrow. The girl, of course, thought she was immortal, thought they were immortal, too.'

But no-one is, Fien thought, but said nothing, and waited.

'So.' Lilian takes a deep breath. 'So the parents decided to travel from England to India with their girl, to make the most of the growing trade, to settle in the warmth and not have to put up with the damp. A new life, it was meant to be. Better, richer, healthier. They even made it there without being shipwrecked, like others had been before. They lived in a house that was almost grand, in Calcutta. Yes, almost grand, it was. They could almost believe they were royal now. Such a foolish notion, such a foolish thing, to be royal. What does it even mean?' She shakes her head. 'You see, even in the cleverest mind there is a weakness, a desire to be something you think is better than what you are, and when you're there, you suddenly realise it's just a sham, just a show, and that with it comes evil, evil just like Lindsey.'

'Was this a very long time ago?'

'It's half a life-time away, and more than half a memory.' Lilian kicks at the floor with her boots, willing herself away from this conversation. The floor sways and creaks. She jumps out of her seat. 'Here comes the wind.' She rushes to the door, rips it open, only to see the men already scampering up the rigging. 'Full sail,' she shouts. 'Full sail.'

'Aye aye, Commandant,' Ben calls from the top of the main mast. 'We're on our way again.'

The sails unfurl with a drop of canvas. To Lilian, it sounds like the short sharp purring of a big cat. The wind catches in the huge curtains, ruffles them, and pushes them into rounded shapes. The ship stutters momentarily, before picking up speed. She climbs up to the wheel, puts her hand on Harry's shoulder, and he gives way to her, one hand at a time.

'Keep her steady now,' he says, with a grunt and a slap on her back. 'Just a straight line, and she'll find where we need to be.'

'She's a good old girl, isn't she?'

'You chose wisely, Lil,' he says. 'Wood black as the night. Sails best then, too.'

'Get the boys some wine,' Lil says. 'Just keep an eye on them. Don't want them too tired to work in the morning.'

'Whatever you say, Skip.' She hears his grin. 'You want some up here, too?'

'And my pipe. I like a smoke when she gets her nose into the water. And bring the girl up here with you. She could do with a bit of sailing.'

'Right you are,' he says, scratches his bald head. 'Keep your eyes peeled.'

'Always do. That's why you like me so much.'

He laughs. 'Course it is.'

The wind's in her hair now. That's why she has it short, or tells herself that's why. She can feel it better this way, its long fingers running their way along her scalp, their softness on her most sensitive skin, at one with the elements that help her. She closes her eyes for a moment, breathes in the gathering speed.

'Here they are,' Harry says. 'Wine, pipe, girl.'

'Thanks. Now, off with you, and don't forget to treat the boys to that drink.'

'I won't forget,' he says.

'And change watches every hour so they can all have a drink and know they have to stay half-sober.'

'Always a popular decision,' Harry says, and jumps down the steps.

Lilian watches him, waits until he's out of earshot. 'The thing that's always fascinated me is the way the wind drives us, and in driving us creates another breeze to blow into our faces. Can you feel it?'

'Yes. It's nice and cool after these dead days.'

'Isn't it just?' Lilian doesn't turn her head, just looks out forwards into the direction they're traveling.

'So, are you going to finish your story of that girl in India?'

'Where was I?' She sucks on her pipe, and the smoke blows away behind her. The rush of the water along the side of the ship is almost a lullaby.

'The grand house.'

'Oh yes,' Lilian says. 'The almost grand house, filled with things no-one needs, like servants and tutors. Yes, all the illusions of wealth. Anyway, one day, the girl comes across a palace of sorts, up on the hills, out walking with her parents who want to show her how the other half of the world lives, showing off what they think is real wealth. And then she sees him, and her world changes. This prince, wrapped in silk, a turban of bright colours wound around his head, standing, watching, waiting. And things are never the same.

'He has these dark brown eyes, and long eyelashes, a colour she's not familiar with, and naked forearms, so tense and taut, even though he's resting, doing nothing else than sitting in the shade, watching people walk past the palace. And she suddenly understands, or thinks she understands, what love is. Every part of her wants him. Her mind, her body. Feelings she can't understand, emotions she can't decipher, draw her to him.'

Fien says nothing, listens to the sounds of the sea, the wind, the sails, the ship murmuring.

'The next day, the girl walks up there with one of her tutors, under some pretext or another. And he's sitting there again, in the shade, looking like he owns the world, like everyone walking by belongs to him. And she walks into the garden, as if by accident, walks up to him, and tells him her name. He raises an eyebrow, and talks back to her in a voice she's never heard, a voice so round and smooth she'd never tire of listening to it. And he speaks her language.

'Now she goes there every day, tells her tutor she wants to walk every day. And every day she snatches a few moments with him, comes to realise he's two or three years older than her. And after a while, he comes to expect her visits, looks forward to them, because they somehow let him escape from the golden cage he's been forced to live in.'

Fien sighs into the breeze, feels the ship push hard into the sea, cut through it, as if it really knows where it's headed. She shakes her head. 'Some wine?' Lilian says.

'I'm too young.'

'You're never too young for a drink.'

'I don't have a glass.'

'Share mine.'

Fien takes a short sip, the redness raw and bitter on her tongue.

'You'll get used to it.'

The next sip is smooth and dry. 'Perhaps.'

'Trust me.'

'So, this boy, this man, was he really a prince? Did your friend ever find out?'

Lilian's laughter is dragged behind her across the sea, and down into the ship's wake as soon as she opens her mouth. 'Oh yes, my friend, yes, she found out soon enough that he wasn't lying. That he was the son of the man who ruled some part or other of Calcutta and the lands around there. But she didn't care how rich or poor he was. All she wanted was to be with him. To hear his voice, to feel his hands on her, to put her hands on him. To have with him what her parents had with each other.'

'And did she?'

There is a long silence. And then a cry from the Crow's Nest at the top of the main mast. 'Pirates!'

Chapter 10

'Take your places,' Lilian shouts.

There's no chaos, no screaming, no panic. Just the clinking of half-empty bottles being put back into crates, the shuffling of eager feet across the deck.

'Bearing?' Lilian calls up to the Crow's Nest.

'A light north-north, closing quickly, Commandant.' Ben's still up there, and his voice sounds suddenly deep to Fien.

'Thanks.' Lilian's voice carries a smile. 'Man the rear cannons. And the starboard ones. And all the lights out. Now.'

Fien hears the candles being extinguished. There's nothing but darkness now, and the sound of the ocean around them. She goes to the rear railing, listens to the water passing under the ship and churning out into an invisible wake. She searches for the light Ben says he saw. She sees nothing.

'His eyes are very sharp,' Lilian says. 'They're out there alright.'

'What are you going to do? Kill your own?'

'They're not my own. They're pirates. And I'm not a pirate.'

'I don't understand.'

'You will. Just get ready to see death up close.'

'You're all so calm.'

'It's what we do.' Lilian grabs the wheel tight. 'Are you ready down there?'

'Oh yes.' Harry's voice. 'All loaded and primed.'

'Let the bastards come then. Go get your knives, Fien. You might need them.'

Fien feels her way down to the cabin, finds her knives despite the dark, straps the holster tightly around her. She feels the ship slow. What is Lilian doing? She rushes back up the steps. Beneath her feet, the cannon rumble into place. And in the distance, she sees a grey shape pushing through the night, gaining on them.

'Aren't you going to try and run?'

Lilian laughs. 'Why should I?'

'So no-one gets killed.'

'Oh, but the spoils of war are death. Nothing more, nothing less. One less murderer to think about.'

'What?'

Lilian shakes her head. 'Now's not the time. Are you ready?'

Fien nods.

All at once, a grey ship noses its way out of the dark. It's so close now, so close she can discern its shape better, even at this hour. It's bigger than Lilian's ship, and there are ghostly figures on its deck. The glint of a sword.

'Rear cannon! Water line!' Lilian yells.

The cannons of *The Odyssey* roar, and yellow smoke blisters the night. The whole ship shakes, pushed forwards by the force of the deafening explosions. The air whistles, and plumes of water erupt around the base of the chasing ship, and then the rending sound of splintering wood. The hunter become the prey begins to list almost at once, towards its port side, its bow digging deep into the water already.

'Again.' Lilian, not shouting this time, her voice steady above the tumult of the noise.

The cannons fire anew, and larger dark holes tear into the grey shape, its nose even lower in the water now.

'Perhaps you won't need those knives,' Lilian says. 'Looks like they won't even manage to get off one shot, never mind try to board us.'

'Perhaps they weren't who you and Ben thought they were. Maybe they were coming to us peacefully.'

'Look very carefully, girl, then you'll see what we see.' Lilian starts to turn the wheel towards starboard, as hard as she can. 'Turning.' Her call is bright and clear.

The Odyssey turns, much more quickly than Fien would have expected such a ship to turn. The other ship is heading off down into the ocean portside first, with the underside of its starboard side rising out of the water. A vulnerable belly.

'Broadside!'

The explosions are even louder than the first two volleys from the rear cannon. Bright white flashes carve crazed shapes into the black, and the other ship is mortally wounded in its most exposed part, as the cannon balls hit what must have been the armoury, and the entire structure is rent apart by an enormous blast, a brief fire, and then nothing but bubbles.

'Hm. That was too easy,' Lilian says. 'Torches, please.'

'You're going to look for survivors, aren't you?'

'Naturally.'

'And then she'll kill them one by one,' Ben says, now descended from his lofty nest.

'Oh, Ben, don't you ever give it a rest?' Lilian says. 'Those who survive become part of us.'

'Haven't any of them tried to kill you?' Fien says.

'There haven't been that many survivors in the past, truth be told,' Lilian says. 'They're grateful to be free. Most of them weren't on those ships by choice.'

'Doesn't that make it worse?'

'It's not up to me to judge myself,' Lilian says. 'I'll let others do that. It's not something I lose sleep over.'

The torches are lit now, and two boats put down in the water littered with wreckage. Each boat has two men rowing it, and two men standing up, one at either end, bending forwards and shining the light into the breaking water, broken yellow reflections spinning. *The Odyssey* slowly circles the carnage, Lilian one hand on the wheel, and a glass of wine in the other. The golden light reflects back into her face, her eyes full of emotions Fien can't understand – rage and melancholy wrapped in metal, hard and unyielding.

'You don't have any sympathy for those you kill, do you?' Fien says.

'Why should I? They'd have done the same to us.'

'Just as brutally?'

'Just as brutally, girl,' Lilian says. 'Just not as quickly and painlessly.'

'That's quick?'

Lilian shrugs, holds the wheel steady.

'Nothing,' one of the men in the rowing boat calls up.

'Then start dredging,' Lilian calls back.

The two boats are now next to each other, and the men unspool a net from one of them, reach one end of it across to their companions, heavy weights already dropping it down into the now still sea. The boats drift away from each other, and the net scuttles even deeper below the surface, away from the shadows the moon throws onto the silver ocean.

'Let's see what we get today,' Lil says, and rubs her hands together. Her eyes burn brighter.

'You're fishing for dead men?' Fien says, her hands grabbing the railing so hard her knuckles shine white and bloodless.

'No. We're fishing for immortal treasure. I only want what doesn't perish.'

'And what happens to it when we're all dead?'

'It'll pass on,' Lil says. 'Someone will have it, of that you can be sure. Someone I choose. And someone else after that. It never stops.'

The sails flap in the uneasy breeze, oars slap into the water, holding the boats steady under the weight of the nets.

'And how long will this take?'

'Patience, girl. It'll take as long as it takes.'

'And the bodies?'

'It'll be weeks before they come up to the top. And we'll be well gone by then.'

'I don't understand why there aren't any floating already.'

'It all happened too quickly for them. They weren't ready for me.'

Fien leans against the railing. 'Tell me more about the prince.'

'You're not interested in watching my fishermen?'

'I'm more interested in your story.'

'I'll finish it later.' Lilian turns away. 'I need to watch the boys.'

The net comes up empty again and again, and the moon begins to fade away into a colourless dawn.

'Three more goes,' Lilian calls into the empty air.

The boats draw a wider circle, their wakes making whirlpools in the water so deep Fien doesn't want to imagine it. How far down, how dark and cold down there. To lose your life to the ever-moving, ever-suffocating water. It must be a terrible way to die.

And, suddenly, everything stops, the water lies immobile and the boats upon it, and the oars stopped and pulled in. The men stand up, start pulling up the net again, only harder this time, slower, until the beads of sweat roll across their faces, and into their eyes and mouths. The boats glide towards each other ever so slowly, almost imperceptibly, toy figures on a polished mirror, until the dark, soaking net lifts out of the water, and in it a roughly-hewn chest large enough for half a man, green water pouring from it as it lifts out of the ocean.

'Bring it on board,' Lil says, no excitement in her voice. 'Let's see what we've got.' She jumps down the stairs onto the main deck, helps her men drag the dripping chest up over the edge of the ship onto the deck. She grabs a cutlass and smashes open the lock, pulls the lid open.

The men, in a circle around her, whistle quietly when the torch light catches the glitter of diamonds and gold. A murmur, stilled as soon as Lil stands up straight, her skin and red hair fierce against the dark wood of *The Odyssey*. She has a crown in her hand, a simple wreath of white metal, spliced with white and red stones, cut into uncountable facets, elegant and fragile. She raises it into the air and places it, deftly and tenderly, on her short hair. It's like it was always meant to be hers.

'Behold your queen,' she says. She laughs harshly. 'But we don't need a queen or a king, do we, boys?'

'Hell, no,' they shout as one voice.

'Very pretty, Lil,' Harry says. 'You were born to it, weren't you?'

'Very good, Harry,' she says. 'You still don't stand a chance.'

'None of us do, and we'll kill the lucky bastard who does.'

'Not much chance of that,' Lil says. 'And better that way.' She adjusts the crown a little. 'I'll add this to my collection. You boys put what's left in that crate with the rest of the stuff.' She climbs back up the stairs to Fien. 'Does it suit me, or was Harry just flattering me?'

'What do you think?'

'I don't think much,' Lil says. 'I just do.'

'Who did it belong to?'

'Does it really matter?'

'Perhaps a king or a queen won't be crowned because you have it.'

'Oh, rest that guilty conscience of yours. If you don't, you'll never get your revenge, even when you're old and strong enough to take it.' She pulls the crown from her short hair. 'Here, take it, and see if you still feel guilty when you're wearing it.'

'I can't. It's yours.'

'Who cares about kings and queens when beauty is all that matters?' Lil puts the crown on Fien's head. 'My, my,' she says. 'It fits you even better than me.'

'Stop playing games,' Fien says and rips the crown from her head. 'I don't want it.'

'We'll throw it into the water then, shall we?'

'Don't be stupid. You only just found it.'

'Then keep it. Let's say it's a loan, just so you don't feel too bad.'

'What would I want a crown for?'

'You never know. Maybe you'll need to pretend to be a queen or a princess one of these days. Or you can paint soot over your face and pretend you're a prince. And Lindsey will be flattered and let you up close so you can twist one of your pretty little daggers into his squirming heart.'

'Is that what you did to your prince?'

Chapter 11

'I wish I had. I wish someone had before I met him.'
She pushes the crown back into Fien's hand.

'Finish the story then.'

'The story's not finished yet. It never will be.'

'What happened?'

'We met every day, in secret I thought. Silly little girl
that I was, I thought he was as innocent as me. I
thought he felt the same way I did. He kept telling me
he'd never seen red hair before, never seen curls of
blood around a face as pale as the moon. And my need
of him was so physical, tearing rifts into my muscles, it
made me weak to my stomach.' Lilian looks out across
the sea to the endless horizon, the world in slow
motion. 'And then, one day, months after I'd first seen
him, I couldn't control myself any longer, and I
touched his hand, took it and put it against my burning
face, and asked him to kiss me.'

'Did he?'

'Of course he did. Who could resist?' She sighs. 'It
was as if the world had ended, as if a force from
outside was driving me. I could feel what I was doing,
but I couldn't stop myself. I didn't want to. I didn't
want him to stop either. I should have known, I should
have known that he'd done it before, when he took me
so gently it didn't hurt, and all I could do was to hold
him tight and cry because I loved him so much, and he
was all I wanted.'

Fien says nothing, just crosses her arms and waits.

'I'd never felt anything as intense before, never ever.
It was like the veil before my eyes disappeared. I
suddenly understood my parents, understood what
bound them together, understood how they'd do
anything for each other, why they would leave where
they'd grown up and met to try to make a better life for

themselves, for each other. And I believed passion to be boundless, never thought passion could hide a lie, be a lie. I couldn't see how a feeling that heavy could make anyone say anything but the truth.'

'He lied to you?'

'That's what men do. All men. I know that now. But I didn't know it then.' She brushes imaginary specks of dust from her shirt. 'He said he loved me every day, and every day we made love in a hidden grove in his garden while my tutor thought I was having tea. His skin was so smooth, so perfect, and my hands so white on it. And his body. I couldn't believe that someone who didn't seem to do any work, who just sat around all day, could be so strong, have so much muscle.'

'I know nothing of men.'

'Keep it like that. … I was in heaven. A few months, that's all. And then, and then … I didn't start bleeding when I should have. I waited and waited for the blood to come. I waited for two weeks, and then I knew. But I didn't tell him. Not straightaway. Perhaps I had an inkling, perhaps I knew I'd push him away with it. But then I had to, because I felt my body change, and knew he'd notice sooner or later when my belly would come between us rather than caving in under him.'

'Was he married?'

Lil shakes her head, her lips tight, but the fire of anger in her eyes. 'I should be grateful for small mercies, I suppose. I told him, and asked him to marry me, asked him to make my life even more perfect. And I really expected him to say he would, hoped he'd finally take me to his mother and father and tell them that here was the woman of his dreams, the woman who would be his princess.'

'You were just a girl.'

'My thoughts were girlish, certainly. But that changed the minute he laughed at me, when he called me a common bitch, when he said he could never marry someone who wasn't his equal, that he'd have to marry the right sort of woman to carry on his family's name. When he said I was just one of many and that I'd been lucky he'd spent some of his precious time with me. And he told me if I ever bothered him again, he'd have my parents thrown out of Calcutta. When I looked at him then, I saw that his beauty was nothing but a front, that he was arrogant and hateful, that he'd just been playing a game, and that he was a most dreadful and cruel man.'

'So Ben … is he your son?'

Lilian nods. 'The one good thing to come from that.'

'And yet he doesn't know.'

'I can't tell him. None of the men know either.'

'But, how did you get here?'

'Anger does the most wonderful things to you, you know, if you only believe in yourself. Forget guilt, just like I stopped blaming myself when I walked away from his garden. I wouldn't let him beat my parents with my treason, wouldn't let them be held hostage to their daughter's mistakes. However superficial and ridiculous their striving for greatness might have been, I didn't want their illusions destroyed because of me. So I ran away, with no money, nothing. Just like you. Dressed up as a young man. I was lucky. And I still have the rage and discontent, and some day I'll have my revenge.'

'Are you strong enough yet?' Fien says.

Lilian smiles. 'Well met, my girl. Who knows when any of us will be strong enough?'

'And yet you tell me to wait.'

'You've had a few weeks. I've had eighteen years.'

'Maybe you'll have eighteen years more.'

Lilian shakes her head. 'No. I can't wait that long. I could be dead before then. Robbing pirates is dangerous.'

'So that's what this is all about,' Fien says. 'How stupid I am.'

'I did tell you we weren't pirates.'

'It never crossed my mind to think of anything else.'

'That's the art of deception. Let others deceive themselves rather than telling lies about yourself.'

'Is life really that simple?' Fien holds her breath.

Lilian laughs. 'Nothing's simple.'

'But you make it sound like it is. Treasure and revenge, nothing else.'

Lilian shrugs, shadows creeping across her face as the torches gutter. 'It's been a long time coming.'

'What about your parents?'

'What about them?'

'Do they know where you are, who you are?'

'I've not seen them since that day. And he works for the enemy.'

'What does that mean?' Fien says.

'The East India Company.'

'How are they your enemy?'

'They try to steal my trade, everyone's trade. And they exploit the poor, plunder country after country for profit.'

'And you plunder them in return, do you?'

'Sometimes. … You think I'm just as bad, don't you?'

Fien nods.

'I give away most of what I take, to those who need it. What you saw in the hold is only a fraction of what I've made.'

'And yet …'

'What?'

'Aren't you just as bad as your parents? Thinking richness or notoriety makes you equal to princes?'

'That's just an illusion,' Lilian says. 'I'm not interested in that sort of equality. I have my independence now.

Everything I do is on my terms. As it should be for everyone.'

'And we're not going to India.'

'No, we're not going to India.'

'So when do you get your revenge?'

'He'll be in Gombroon when we get there. It's the trading season.'

'And then?'

Lilian's shoulders barely move. 'I'll kill him, or just take everything he has.'

'Haven't you got a plan?'

'No, no. They tend to spoil the fun.'

'You're mad.'

'Only a little.' Lil drains the last of the wine from her glass. The wind freshens, the sails fill again, and the torches pucker out. 'Harry,' she shouts into the darkness. 'Wheel.'

'Yes, Lil,' he calls back, his voice deeper than ever.

'Wake me in four hours,' she says when she hands over to him.

'Aye aye,' he says.

Back in the state room, Fien hands the crown back to Lilian. 'Keep it safe for me, please. I'll ask for it when I need it.'

'Very well.' Lil unlocks a drawer in the map table, puts the crown on top of a scattering of more tiaras, earrings and chains.

'You collect crowns then, do you?'

'Just like I collect dead princes and princesses, kings and queens. These are the real spoils of my war.' Lilian locks the drawer and pulls the curtains across the row of windows at the stern. 'We need to sleep now.'

'When are you going to tell Ben?'

'When his father's ruined or dead.'

Chapter 12

The rattle of the anchor chain wakes Fien. She jumps out of bed, rips the curtains away from the windows. The sun's halfway below the horizon, a full twelve hours since she came down here. She swears at herself.

'Why didn't you wake me?' she says to Ben in the galley.

'She told me not to.'

'Do you do everything she tells you to?'

'She *is* the Commandant.' He waves his arms at her. 'And you could have woken yourself.'

'I know. That's why I'm so angry.' She bangs around with plates and cups.

'Don't worry,' he says, grinning. 'There'll be no sleep tonight. That's probably why she told me not to wake you. You might have travelled a lot, but you've never been part of a ship.' He coughs awkwardly, grin gone. 'And you've still got other things on your mind.'

'The thing is,' Fien says. 'I don't really miss him. And that feels even worse.'

'I'm sorry. I didn't mean.' He takes a step towards her.

She shakes her head. 'No, don't.' She looks at him. He looks older, suddenly, different. 'I'm not ready to cry.'

'Come with me,' he says. 'I want to show you something.' He walks past her, careful not to touch her, and she follows.

They reach the bow of the ship, within touching distance of the bowsprit, the sun now behind them, what remains of it. In this, the ship's narrowest space, their shadows fall long and thin, far ahead of them, into the blue sea.

'There's an island out there if you look carefully,' Ben says. 'Once it's dark, we'll sail into a deep bay there, and go ashore to collect fresh water and fruit. And if we're really lucky, we'll come back with some fresh meat, too.'

'Under cover of darkness? Isn't that a bit risky?'

'The Commandant's been here often. She knows the waters like the back of her hand. And she won't leave the ship if it's still light. Not anywhere.'

'Does anyone live on the island?'

He shakes his head. 'But even so. Others must know about it, must use it for the same reason we do.'

'And I guess we have to drag anything we collect back to the ship,' she says.

'Of course. But then you didn't think this would be easy, did you?'

'I'm not complaining. It's exciting. And I need some exercise.'

'And you can finally do some proper practice with your knives.'

'That's what I was thinking.' She leans against him briefly, before she knows what she's doing, and pulls away again at once.

'Just don't kill me with one of the damn things,' he says, ignoring the touch her body's left on him.

'You can write an essay about the outing when we get back,' she says, distant again, and in control of herself. She hates her weakness, and turns sharply to make her way back to the galley.

'Don't go. Stand here and enjoy the sunset while we've got time to breathe.'

'You're all poetic of a sudden.' She stops.

'Not really. I just know how busy we'll be, and the sun is lovely and warm just now.'

'What do you do with your life, Ben?' she says. 'How could you enjoy it without being able to read?'

'You don't need to be able to read if you can watch and listen.'

'But you can write down your memories now.'

'Perhaps I will. Perhaps I won't. But what's the use of

writing them down if it makes you forget them? Isn't it better to keep them alive in your mind?'

'I see you've only been playing the fool for these past weeks.'

'You've never asked me a serious question before.'

'And that story I made you write?'

'It was a story.' He shrugs. 'Nothing more. And I just used the words I knew how to spell.'

'I don't believe you.'

'Would I lie to you?'

'Probably.' She laughs, at ease again.

'Never.' He lowers his eyes. 'Just like I could never lie to her.'

'Is that because we're women?'

'No. It's because you're you, both of you. It doesn't matter if you're man, woman or goat.'

'That's a silly thing to say.'

He shakes his head. 'Everything's equal.'

The sun drops away behind them, and they remain still, in the warmth of shade. They say nothing, leaning against the tactile wood, and watch the ripples of the endless blue. And then, despite herself, she starts to talk.

'My … my father had a beautiful watch, a green watch. He bought it for my … my mother. When she died, he kept it, and hung it around his neck on a piece of string. It was like something out of this world.' She sniffs, still looking down at her feet, and doesn't notice the excitement in Ben's face. 'He had it round his neck, still round his neck, when … when they came. I should've taken it with me. He should've given it to me. But there was no time, no time.' Her face is red, her eyes red, her hands shaking.

Ben doesn't move. 'Tall Face has it, has he?'

'Probably.'

'It's the only one in the world, you know.'

'What?' She lifts her head, too quickly.

'Didn't you know?' He takes her by the shoulders. 'Didn't he tell you?'

'Tell me what?'

'We need to talk to the Commandant.'

'Talk to me first, Ben, goddammit.' She pushes him away. 'I'm not a baby.'

'I didn't say you were.'

'So, come on, tell me.'

He sits down on the swaying deck, darkness imminent now. 'Why didn't your father tell you? I don't understand.'

'If you talked some sense, I might understand.'

'No-one knows when the clock was made, or who by. There's a story that a watchmaker discovered the secret of keeping life in the mechanism of his clock, and that whoever owned it would be immortal as long as the clock was kept wound up.'

'That's just the sort of story you would believe.' Fien snorts. 'It's a fairy tale. That's why my father never said anything. I'd have known about it from all the books he gave me to read.'

'So tell me, dear Fien, did he always wear it? Did he always have his hand on it, holding it near to his heart?'

She can only nod, the last picture of her father at the table with her alive in her mind. Only she can't hear it ticking, can't remember it ever ticking.

'Do you believe me now?'

'He said it was because he wanted to keep it close to where he held my mother forever. In his heart.'

'That's only what he said, not what he was doing.'

'How is this thing supposed to work?'

'You can't hear it ticking because its ticking is the beat of your heart. And when it stops, so does your heart.'

'Are you saying the watch killed my father?'

'No, no.' He reaches his hand out to her, but not far

79

enough to touch her fingers. 'It can't stop you from being killed by violence.'

'That's not much use, is it?'

'Well, no.'

'And what makes it worse is that if it is true, people will come and try to kill you just so they can live forever hiding away and being safe.'

Ben blushes. 'I don't think I'm explaining it very well.'

'I think you're an idiot.'

'But it's true. That's why we need to tell the Commandant.'

'And what will Lil do?' Fien says, deliberately using the name the boy could not bring himself to say.

'She'll tell you it's true. And she'll explain it better. And she'll try to get it back for you.' He ran out of breath.

'Oh, for me? Not for her?'

'I thought you trusted her.'

'I do.'

'Then act like it.' He jumps up, grabs her by the hand before she can stop him, and drags her back to Lil's cabin. 'Commandant, Commandant,' he calls as he barges through the door without knocking. 'Fien has something she needs to tell you.'

'How often have I told you to knock?' Lil snaps. She is sitting at the map table, reading a book, shirt open to the waist.

'S ... S ... Sorry.'

'You'd better be,' she says, buttoning herself up. 'The heat gets too much sometimes.' She coughs. 'Now piss off out of here, close the door, and knock. Both of you.'

It's Fien's turn to drag Ben along behind her. 'You idiot,' she hisses. 'How can you just storm in like that?'

'I forgot she's a woman,' he says, his composure restored. He turns, pulls his ragged jacket into a shape resembling order, turns, and knocks on the door.

'Come in.'

'Commandant, Fien's just told me something you have to hear.'

'Something I don't know already?' Lil says, leaning back in her chair, smoking her pipe.

'Yes, I think so.' He turns to Fien. 'Or have you told her already, and are just making fun of me?'

Fien smiles and shakes her head slowly. 'No,' she says quietly. 'I haven't told her.'

'Out with it then, girl,' Lil says.

'I ... I ... I'm not sure there's anything to tell,' Fien says, suddenly intimidated by the woman twice her age, twice as beautiful, hardened through battle and grief.

'Oh, come on,' Lil says. 'Don't be shy. Ben does get overexcited sometimes, but not excited enough to barge in on his Commandant when she's not decent.'

'Her father had a watch, Commandant,' Ben says, sitting down opposite the red-haired fawn. 'And not just any watch. A watch made of one emerald.'

'*That* watch? Surely not?'

'You mean what he's been telling me isn't just made up?' Fien lets herself sink to the floor. 'Not just a fairy tale?'

Lilian pulls open a drawer in the map table, lifts out a piece of paper, pushes it down onto the table top with the palm of her hand, and pulls the quill from the inkwell so hard the ink blotches all over the desk. 'Draw it for us,' she says. 'Every detail you remember.'

Fien takes the feathered pen and begins to sketch a picture of the clock, rough at the edges at first, but, as the other two remain silent, her confidence grows, and the lines she puts down onto the plain white sheet sharpen and become more certain. She forgets the other two are watching, and draws the watch as she recalls it behind her eyes, the black ink and the white spaces turning into green, gold, blue and red. She etches the intricate clasps into the pale cream, the perfect hinge, the exquisite numerals and the elegance of the leather strap her father used to hold it around his neck. She remembers, to her surprise, the shape and direction of the facets, the cut and gleam of the diamond, the faint light and the strong, the power of the precious stone. Finally, she stands back, looks at the finished drawing, and throws the pen back into its well.

Ben reaches out for the paper, but Lil stops him before he can touch it. 'Let it dry,' she says. ' Be patient.' Her eyes shine.

Fien pulls a wooden stool across to the two chairs by the table. 'And?' she says. 'Does this mean anything to you?'

Lil stands up, walks around the table, not once, not twice, but three times, clouds of smoke trailing behind her. 'Let me think.'

Fien and Ben sit in forced silence as Lil carries on walking, as she pauses to look out of the window at the weather. 'We need to move soon,' she says.

Fien stares at the drawing, finds nothing she can improve, tries to lean back and nearly topples from the stool without a backrest.

'You can be patient, too,' Lil says. 'We've waited this long without knowing we've been waiting that another minute or two won't matter.' Finally, she sits down, draws the sheet of paper towards her, holds it up to her face, one eye closed, then at arm's length. 'Are you sure you're not just making this up, or that you've got this from one of your books?'

'That's how it looked the last time I saw my father,' Fien says.

'It is the watch, then,' Lil says. 'That watch. Ben wasn't wrong.'

'And it's supposed to give you eternal life, is it?' Fien

says.

'So they say.'

'But you can still get killed for it.'

'Ah, now that's not quite right,' Lil says, looking at Ben who doesn't look back at her. 'That's one reason he needs to learn to read properly, so he can tell hearsay from reality, so he can read about things rather than just listening to what's said and getting it all jumbled in his head.'

'What does that mean?' Fien says.

'It means that, yes, they say it doesn't protect you from violent death,' Lil says. 'But what many don't know is that you can't take the watch and benefit from it in that way.'

'I don't understand.'

'The watch has to be a gift for its power to work on the one who has it. It can't be stolen, or burgled, or ripped from someone who's just been killed. For it to work, it has to be given of free will, as a gift, a present, a reward.'

'How does it know?' Ben says.

Lil shrugs. 'How does anything work that we can't comprehend?'

'It sounds just like the myths about alchemy,' Fien says. 'People just make things up to make themselves and ordinary things seem mysterious when they actually have no meaning or power at all.'

'You're a cynical young thing, aren't you?' Lil says.

'My father's been killed for it,' Fien almost shouts.

'D'you think Lindsey knew about this?' Lil says. 'Did your father advertise the fact that he had it?'

'Well, he wore it all the time, everywhere, and he was forever putting his hand into his shirt to hold it. ... Oh, he was always telling me how warm it was to the touch, how it comforted him.'

'How did he get hold of it?' Lil says.

'I don't know. He always said he bought it as a present for my mother for when he asked her to marry him.'

'He can't have bought it. That doesn't work either,' Lil says.

'Unless he didn't know its power,' Fien says.

'I thought you said he was a very well-educated man.'

'He was.'

'Then he must have known about it. Someone he knew, or someone who owed him his life must have given it to him.'

'And then he gave it to my mother. So why did she die when I was born?'

'Perhaps she forgot to wind it up,' Ben says.

'That would be pretty careless,' Fien says.

'But not impossible if she wasn't well when she was pregnant,' Lil says.

Ben blushes at the talk of pregnancy and says nothing.

'But she shouldn't have died,' Fien says. 'Not if the watch was protecting her.'

Lil throws the drawing back onto the desk. 'The thing is, no-one actually really knows how it works. There are some people who even say that it can take you through time, into the past or into the future.'

Fien shakes her head. 'That's even more ridiculous then.'

Lil takes a deep breath. 'Actually, you're right. And it's irrelevant. The thing is, though, that Lindsey has it now, and we need to get it back for you.'

'Why?'

'Even if it's only of sentimental value to you, I'll not have that long-faced bastard own something that belongs to a friend of mine.'

'I'm a friend now, am I?'

'I think you became our friend the minute Ben found you,' Lil says. 'Let's get ourselves fresh water tonight and turn the ship round.'

'You can't do that,' Fien says. 'You have other plans.'

'Oh, that can wait,' Lil says.

'No, please,' Fien says. 'You have to do what you planned first.'

Lil nods. 'And then we'll get that English weasel.'

Chapter 13

The night is complete now, the ship alive with low voices, soft steps and the rustle of ropes uncoiling and straining, the sails filling with the tender wind, and the wood barely creaking. Lil's at the helm, staring into the absolute blackness, her hands barely touching the wheel, guiding it with her fingers. She sniffs at the air as *The Odyssey* noses across the last few shallow miles towards the unnamed island. She has men stationed at the bow and all along the sides of the ship, although she's sure she won't need them. She's lost count of the number of times she's been here, remembers the first time she found it, when she had a much smaller vessel, and hardly any crew, and they were close to death from thirst and hunger. And every time she comes here, she's elated and frightened, driven and relieved, all at the same time. It's never not dangerous. She pushes her right hand softly down on the wheel and the ship turns almost imperceptibly.

Fien can only feel the boards beneath her feet. She can't even see her hand in front of her eyes. What the men are looking for she doesn't know, because surely they, too, can see nothing. She reaches for Ben, next to her, on the port side. 'How can she do this?'

'She just can. And she won't let anyone else do it.'

'Harry's up there with her. He must know how.' Her whisper is swallowed by the gloom.

'Its not just knowing how. It's taking the responsibility for everyone. She won't burden anyone else.'

Fien thinks her eyes are getting used to the dark, although she can see no distinct shapes. She hears the water flow past the hull down below, not the surge of full speed, but just the placid gurgle of it gently parting to let the ship make its way. 'How long does it take?'

'An hour or so. It depends on the water, the tide, and on her. Be patient.'

Fien says nothing, stands still, her hand on the invisible wood. She listens to all the sounds, magnified in the overriding silence. She smells the salt in the water, feels the wind blowing them shoreward with its light touch. The ship turning this way and that with what feels like absolute certainty, as if it were fixed to a rail. And yet she knows there are only Lil's hands guiding it. Gradually, she feels the swell around the island shifting, the salt in the air receding, and thinks she can sense something different, warmer somehow, heavier, a scent not of the sea's wide open space, but the musk of trees and the moss beneath them, of fresh grass and dew and glades and safety, of being enclosed rather than exposed to all sides on the mirror of endless water. The sounds around her change, too. Instead of floating harshly out into nothingness and away, they take on new weight, a mellow tone, a resonance emptiness could never give them. They're round now, all the notes she hears, not harsh and edgy any longer. You could talk here and never be heard.

'All set, boys?' Lil's voice drags Fien out of her fascination.

There's a quiet murmur all round.

'I'll try to put her right next to the rocks,' Lil says. 'So there's not too much lugging to be done. The tide's about right.'

Fien tries harder now to see something. A dark shape appears in front of her face, to the side of the ship, something solid, a wall of rock, she thinks. She's about to shout a warning.

'Easy does it,' Lil calls. 'Ninety yards. Drop the sails.'

The men run, on their tip-toes it seems, to obey the command. The sails float lightly down, a mellow bustle of material and rope against wood. And another sound that Fien can't decipher, a rustle high up, beyond her sight. The ship slows, more quickly than she thought it could, and stops. Around her, some of the men jump off the side with ropes in their hand, to land level on hard ground. She can see them dimly, dragging the ropes around what look like massive tall rocks. Only now, the men back aboard, torches dimly lit, does she recognise them as trees, huge huge trees, like nothing she's seen before. And they're all around the ship. They have landed in a cave of trees.

'Six hours,' Lil says, her voice clear as crystal. 'That's all we have tonight. Fresh water and fruit. That's what we need. Go and bring them back for us.' She beckons Fien and Ben. 'You two, with me.' She turns to Harry. 'One-hour watches, as usual. I'll see you later.'

Harry smiles his usual smile, and nods.

Lil takes the two down to the cabin, opens a tall cupboard and pulls out two bows and two quivers full of arrows. 'Time for hunting,' she says. 'Let's go.'

They clamber over the side of the ship out onto a promontory of rocks and bushes and trees. 'Be careful,' she says to Fien. 'Stay with us. You don't know this place as well as we do.'

'There must be others who've found this place,' Fien says.

'Oh, there are,' Lil says. 'But no-one's found a hiding place as perfect as ours. I've scouted around here for years, and there's nowhere better to hide a ship, even one as big as *The Odyssey*. And I'd know if there was anyone else here. And right now there isn't.' She wipes the sweat from her forehead with her arm. 'The secret is not to use it too often. That way there's always plenty of prey, and plenty of harvest.'

'No hidden treasure then?' Fien says.

'That would be foolish.'

'I know. It was a stupid question.'

'Not really. It's what people might expect pirates to do, to bury treasure on a remote island. Careless is what I would call it.' She hurries up the green slope. 'No more talking. Let's hunt.'

Fien feels the weight of her knives under her jacket. It's not a burden, more of a comfort. Her eyes are used to the low light now, and she's full of wonderment for the lithe way in which Lil charges noiselessly through the undergrowth, at home on solid ground as much as she was on the water. It feels like hours before they come to a halt again. Fien is out of breath.

'You need more exercise,' Ben whispers.

Lil turns sharply, puts a finger to her lips. Then she points two fingers to her right and nods at Ben. One finger to her left, and she nods at Fien.

Can I do this? Fien thinks. She watches Ben take an arrow out of his quiver, load it into this bow, and creep forward, one small step at a time. *Focus.* She looks in the direction Lil pointed and sees an indistinct blur of a shape. She needs to get closer, crouches down, fingers light on the ground and only her toes. Everything around her disappears. She's on her own in the forest with an instinct for hunt she understands but the source of which she can't fathom, a city-dweller all her life. The shape sharpens into a body and four legs. She holds her breath as she pulls one of her knives from her belt. It lies in her hand, a beautiful weight. The wood handle is warm in her palm. She takes one last look at the living thing, a deer of some sort, and releases her breath as she lets go of the knife. It makes no sound as it slices through the air, no sound until it hits its target. A gentle thud, nothing more. And the shape collapses in on itself. The world around her reappears, and she waits to see if Ben has let off his two shots. She feels a soft touch on her shoulder, a warm hand through her thin jacket.

'Go get it,' Lil says. 'Ben has one of his. The other one ran off when he hit the first one.'

Fien crawls out towards the dead animal. Its eyes are still open, instant death. The blade is embedded in the still-warm body up to its hilt. Hardly any blood.

'A good kill,' Lil says. 'Well done.'

'Beginner's luck,' Fien says.

'Then carry on as you begin. It will save your life one of these days.'

Ben says nothing. He's brought his kill back to the small clearing they've created, retrieved and cleaned his arrow. 'We need more than this,' he says.

'On we go then,' Lil says. 'We've only just started.'

The moonless night is beginning to fade when they finish their hunt. Fien has made six more kills, all to the heart, and Ben six more, too.

'We're equal,' Fien says, trying hard to keep the relief out of her voice.

'I should've beaten you,' he says. 'I've been doing this for an age.'

'It was luck, honestly.'

'Seven knives to the heart in the dark, from distance?' Lil says. 'I think not. Have you been practising much?'

'Not before you took me on board,' Fien says. 'And even since then, I've not been able to make much time, in between cooking and teaching Ben.'

'When, then?' Lil says, genuinely curious and surprised.

'When you've been asleep, both of you, I've been trying to hit the main mast from as far away as I could.'

'Any success?' Lil says.

'Not as much as I'd have liked.'

Lil shakes her head. 'I've never seen this before. You must like to kill. That's the only way I can explain it.'

'I don't, actually.'

'Listen to me, Fien. You may think you don't, but a

hunter does not kill that precisely if she doesn't enjoy it. It's the enjoyment that makes the skill. Be thankful you have it. You can keep yourself fed.'

'And us,' Ben says.

Lil grunts. 'Thanks, young man. Now go and get some of the others to help us get these creatures back to the ship before the sun comes up. They can start cutting them up and preserving them while we sleep.'

He disappears off between the trees.

'How does it feel to be so talented?' Lil says.

Fien shrugs. 'I'm glad I've helped get us some food. I don't really feel anything else.'

'It'll be interesting to see how you do if you're ever confronted by enemies who are trying to kill you. I wonder if then you'll understand how much you really enjoy killing.'

'I hope it doesn't come to that.'

'It will,' Lil says. 'It will. Especially if you want your revenge on Lindsey. Especially if you want that watch back.'

'Do you really believe what's said about it?'

'Does it matter? It's like anything else people choose to believe in. If it works for you, believe.'

'And what do you believe in?'

'Just myself. That'll do for now. It means I don't have to rely on anyone else. And I don't have to force myself to trust anyone else.'

'You trust all your men. And your son.'

'Watch those careless words, girl,' Lil snaps. 'Or they may be your last. You never know who's listening. … And as for trusting them, it's mutual, and not forced. We all depend on each other. We can't do everything on our own. Remember that.' She reaches across and ruffles Fien's hair. 'You're a brave girl.'

Before Fien can say anything, Ben reappears with three of the crew. They drop long wooden poles to the

91

ground and wordlessly begin to strap the dead animals to them. A few minutes later, they lift the poles and carry the catch back to *The Odyssey*. Lil and Fien follow behind, hands empty.

'I'm lost,' Fien says. 'How do you find your way round?'

'Memory. Age. Knowledge of nature.'

'Are we anywhere near?'

'You tell me.'

'I honestly don't know.'

'What can you see?'

'Trees. Bushes.'

'Any broken branches?'

'No.' Fien is tired of the game.

'Good. That's what I teach them. If we break anything on a tree we'll give ourselves away.' She laughs a short sharp laugh. 'I wouldn't expect you to know where we are. She's so perfectly hidden that only those of us who know this place would be able to find her.'

The men have stopped, laid down the catch, wait for Lil and Fien to catch them up. Lil nods, passes them, and pushes aside, carefully, slowly, the low-hanging branches, holds them to one side and gets Fien to do the same opposite her. As the men march through between them, Fien and Lil let the branches come back down with a rustled whisper.

Fien turns to Lil to ask her how much further they have to go, but has no time to get her words out. Just as the rays from a fully-risen sun push their way through the curtain of leaves, she hears, from somewhere close ahead, a quiet clink of metal on metal, and a sibilant hum of moving water, subdued voices. And then, as Lil lifts yet one more patchwork of leaves, branches and twigs, Fien sees the ship, within touching distance, rocking in the swell, jammed into a narrow channel of sea that seems now, in daylight, to extend into the heart of the island.

'It only looks like it,' Lil says. 'I know what you were thinking. The rest of the water flows underground. It's deep here, but thirty yards further in, there's nothing. The water just disappears into the rock. Or, should I say, the water just appears out of rock. Talk about getting water from a stone. It's a miracle of sorts.'

'You love it,' Fien says. 'You love it a lot.'

'It saved my life, once upon a time.'

'You were lucky to find it.'

Lil shrugs. 'Or destined to find it.'

'Such a modest woman.'

'An honest woman.' She holds her hand out to Fien. 'Come. We need to sleep while it's hot and light. No matter how hidden we are, sound can still find its way through those leaves.'

'Has anyone ever got close?' Fien says, feet now back on the familiar wood of *The Odyssey*.

'Not really. Within half a mile, maybe. And that was just bad luck.'

'How do you know so precisely?'

'Do you really think I'd only guard the ship and not what's around her? We have people five miles out in all directions. It's imperative. I may not plan, but I do have strategy.'

'You're too modest all the time.'

Lil shakes her head. 'Like you said, I've been lucky.'

'People make their luck.'

'Enough.' She turns to Ben and the men carrying the catch. 'You know what to do. Within an hour. Or it'll go rotten. And then sleep. Harry knows not to include you in the watches.'

The men nod.

Lil puts her arm around Fien's shoulder. 'There's a lot we need to talk about, but not now. Sleep and dream, and then we'll talk. And dream about learning to fight with a sword. You might be as good at it as you are with the knives.' She throws herself onto her bed, the curtains in the cabin already drawn. 'Sleep well.'

Chapter 14

Fien can't get to sleep. The heat here is different and weighs heavily on her. Despite the closed curtains, specks of light dance across the room. She closes her eyes and shifts on her bed, misses the feeling of space she had when she was at sea, misses the breeze, even if it was sometimes imagined, that kept her cool out there. She feels the boat shift under her, but being hidden in a bay isn't the same as being rocked to sleep by an open ocean. She shifts again, tries not to make a sound, which, to her ears, only magnifies every sound she does make. She tries to lie still, opens her eyes and imagines the dark as cool, but her body knows the time of day, the brightness outside. She pictures the guards sitting in their trees, in a circle of safety, wiping the sweat from their brows, baking under the leaves, trying not to fall out of the branches, listening, hearing, watching.

Why didn't you tell me about the watch? She starts talking to her father, his face smudged by the passing of a few months. *Why didn't you tell me what Lil and Ben told me?* His mouth doesn't move. He doesn't answer. He retreats, becomes shapeless, disappears until nothing is left but the blackness and the knowledge of the sun.

Naked feet pad across the room. 'Here,' Lil says quietly. 'Take this and tie it over your eyes. It might help.' She folds a cut of silk into Fien's hand.

To Fien, it feels red. The darkness is complete now and the specks of light are gone. 'Thank you,' she says, but Lil has gone again already. Fien hears the creak of the older woman's bed, wonders how she can live this life of depending on no-one, wonders how she can move on and on without having anyone to lean on when she has doubts. Perhaps she no longer has any doubts. Perhaps she has a lover in every port she visits into whose ears she can whisper about whatever she chooses. Perhaps that's where the silk came from, from one of her lovers. Perhaps, perhaps, perhaps.

The silk calms her eyes. She drifts into that place between waking and sleep where nightmares and visions reside. Her breathing slows until her breaths are like a baby's, reaching down into her belly, calming her.

'Ben, why have you got the watch?'

'Just showing you how it works.'

'It's mine now.'

'I know. Here.'

The watch is heavy in her hands, too heavy. It burns her. She doesn't want it. It has her father's blood on it. And the man with the tall face is coming to get it back.

'Leave me alone.'

'I'll have what's mine.' He grabs her, holds her arms behind her back with one hand while he rips the watch from around her neck with the other. 'You'll never get it back.' A lecherous look, a lick of the lips. 'You are a pretty one, aren't you? Shame we didn't catch you when we killed the old man.' He lets go of her, tries to fondle her.

She pulls one of her knives out of her belt, sticks it in his throat. The blood spurts onto her face, hot, gushing, endlessly.

He falls onto the ground, squirms, blood now oozing from his mouth.

She screams.

'It's ok, it's ok.' Someone is stroking her hair, holding her, keeping her safe. 'Just a dream, girl, just a dream.'

Fien opens her eyes. Lil, her eyes worried, her lips tight, is sitting next to her, rocking her. 'It takes a long time for grief to come out of us.'

'I'm not sure it was grief,' Fien says, and tells Lil about her dream.

Lil sits up straight. 'I guess you'll need more practice

in killing so you don't scream when you get him.' Her smile is back. 'You wouldn't want his men to get you just after you've got him.'

'Did I wake you?'

'No.'

'Has Lindsey tried to rape you?'

'He thought he could seduce me once, but I didn't care for him.'

'So he tried to rape you?'

'He tries to rape every woman he meets. He thinks it's his right to have any woman he wants.'

'It seems all men are like that.'

'There are some good ones,' Lil says, softly. 'Ones who expect nothing in return for kindness. A few anyway.' Her smile is one of faraway places, distant from the sounds of war.

'Who might they be?'

'Oh, just the odd one, here and there. ... And who expect nothing in return for my legs around them.'

Fien blushes.

'Sorry.' Lil laughs. 'I forget how untouched you are by that world.'

'I'm not sure I want to be touched by that world.'

'You're going to be a nun then, are you?'

'Perhaps.' Fien stifles a laugh.

'See. There'll be a good man somewhere for you if you want one. I'll show you how to get what you want without having to give anything of yourself away.'

'And what if I want to give myself away?'

'Make sure he loves you completely. That's all.'

'And you never loved Lindsey?'

'That's a ridiculous question. He's evil.'

'Who do you love then?'

Lil sighs in the dark. 'Your guess is as good as mine.'

'You just don't want to tell me.'

'No, I don't know. There are more important things

than love.'

'And they are?'

'Ask me a simple question. ... Looking after you.'

'Don't be stupid.'

'It's not just the watch, girl. There's something about you.'

'There's nothing about me. I'm just another orphan.'

'Who's beautiful, who's been wronged.' Lil stamps her foot on the ground. 'Lindsey doesn't even know you exist. Hell's teeth.'

'What's that supposed to mean?'

'He doesn't even think anyone's out to get revenge.'

'And that's relevant, how?'

'You can take him by surprise,' Lil says. 'Now or in ten years, or whenever.'

'He'll find out, surely.'

'He's a man who never looks back.'

'What makes you think you know him so well?'

'I just do.'

'I wish you'd tell me everything.'

'Everything is nothing, always. ... Go back to sleep.' Lil moves away.

'What time is it?'

'Twenty minutes later than when I gave you the blindfold.'

'Is that all?'

'Time draws strange curves.' Lil's voice from the other side of the cabin.

'Maybe I should get up and leave you to sleep in peace.'

'Maybe that would be a bad idea.' Lil's voice has the texture of the old wood around her.

'Why?'

'You need to sleep. And tomorrow, tonight, you need to fight with a sword. You have to become a warrior, not a blonde girl subject to the Fates.'

'But I want to talk.'

'There'll be plenty of time for that. Another day.'

Fien slides the blindfold back over her eyes. It's still cool, despite the wearying minutes she's already worn it for. She hears Lil's breath, slow and low again. *How can she sleep so easily, so deeply, and wake so quickly?* Day passes quickly to turn into night. Too quickly. And then it's over.

'The watch brings death, not life,' Fien says as she eats alongside Lil.

'That's nonsense.'

'Then why did my mother die? And my father? And Lindsey in the dream? Where did my father get the watch from? Did he kill someone to get it? It's like I don't know anymore who he was. That's why I didn't want the watch, why I don't want it. It brings death, I tell you. We shouldn't try to get it back.'

'I think you're seeing the wrong signs.' Lil's face flickers with the candles.

'How long are we staying here?'

'Just tonight and tomorrow. We'll leave in twenty-four hours.'

'And then Gombroon.'

Lil nods. 'And then Gombroon. It'll be a while till we get there.'

'It can't come quickly enough.'

'Are you tired of our company, girl?'

Fien shakes her head. 'Tired of waiting, and tired of thinking about things that are really not important.'

'You'll change your mind.' Lil pushes her chair back. 'More hunting, I think.'

'Whatever you say.'

There's no time for swordplay, no time for anything but hunting and sweating and getting their hands covered in blood, and lifting dead animals onto sweaty backs, trying to find the way in the dark, trying to leave as few signs of intrusion behind them as possible. And in the beating of a heart, the wink of any eye, the night that is day is gone, and they find shelter again from the light in the dark innards of *The Odyssey*. They've neither seen nor heard anyone else on the small island, have covered their tracks, have skinned and gutted the prey, and thrown its dismembered limbs into vats of salt, bloody but saltwater clean fur now hanging across the deck.

As night comes again, Lil gives the order to cast off, and the boat lurches slightly, allows itself to be pushed, by the reversing tide, out of its hiding place, Lil's soft hands on the wheel, those familiar veins entwining the familiar grains of wood, a tiny encouragement here and there. *The Odyssey* might almost be sentient, and her communing with her captain a perfect symbiosis of wood and flesh. As she hits the open water, she bucks joyfully, her bow drilling into the white crests of the waves, nosing her way to where she next wants to go, out towards the East, a well-trodden path for her, a tiny speck on a massive planet, spinning, turning, racing through an unfeasible and endless universe, the moss of stars a shimmering canopy.

Chapter 15

They don't speak of the watch again. Fien tries not to think of her father, of the monster he's threatening to become in her mind, this vision of a murderer, not a gentle, kind philosopher father. She throws herself into her lessons with Ben, surprised and elated and moved by his sudden enthusiasm, his quick learning, the passing of his childish phase, and his growing maturity in the spoken and written word. Has the island changed him, or has it changed her?

When her birthday comes and goes in their second week back at sea, she tells no-one. It's not something she needs or wants to share. All she knows is that she's eighteen and an orphan without a home. There are other things that are more important, other things that need her attention. Like the early-morning coffee, like making sure the men keep the galley clean, that they don't just eat and drink, but cook as well. She stays on deck at night often, sometimes to practice with her knives, sometimes to get a feel for the sword Lil has given her, sometimes just to sit and watch the wake of the ship under the moon, to listening to the ocean racing away beneath them. And sometimes she sneaks a look at the diamonds and coins her father left her and wonders just how much of it is blood money, and if she can ever feel happy with it burning in her hand.

Time slips away without her knowing it, and then the day has come. Land to the left and to the right, and straight ahead. Piping hot. Early, early morning.

Lil comes on deck, her head covered in cloth, her trousers loose, boots up to her knees, a plain white baggy shirt. If Fien didn't know she was a woman she'd have taken her for a particularly pretty man. Lil hands her a similar contraption.

'Put your hair up and roll that round it. Securely,' Lil

says. 'We're men from here in.' Her voice bears no contradiction. She climbs the stairs to stand next to Harry at the wheel. 'We'll drop anchor on the south side of Hormuz,' she says.

'As usual,' Harry grunts.

'I'm nothing if not predictable,' Lil says. 'Are you still happy with that?'

'Always happy with you, Lil,' he says, and the smile makes him look younger than Fien thinks he can be.

Perhaps he's one of the kind ones, Fien thinks as she wraps the white cloth around her bound-up hair. It feels tight and uncomfortable, but if she is to be a man, this is what she must do. She's glad of her small chest.

'Don't look so nervous,' Lil says. 'We're just going to go out for a small look see.' Her eyes tell a different story.

You've not told anyone why you're here this time. Fien stares at Lil. *Why not?*

Lil stares back at her, silencing her unspoken question. 'Drop the boat,' Lil says. She never has to shout. 'Come on, Fien.' She jumps down the stairs, lithe and full of life. 'It's time we had some fun.'

They climb over the starboard side of the ship, down the rope ladder, drop into the small shell of a rowing boat ready for them down there, and push away. Fien looks up and sees Ben standing up there, his face a frown. She can't tell if it's concentration or concern.

They row around the island of Hormuz, its strait already bustling with ships, and then across a wide bay, the sea flat and shiny, a vacant face, towards the city of Gombroon, dominated by a large white fort, its walls almost lapping up the ocean. They each have an oar, and pull hard and wordlessly through the few miles that separate Hormuz from the mainland. They pull together, against the current, against the receding tide, pull and push the small vessel close into the rustling pebbles, the whispering sand, the ages hidden amidst the stones and sunshine, until they feel the crunch of keel against solid land. One more pull, one more stroke of the oars, and they're fast, anchored, wood against land, land against wood, and the ocean still around them.

Lil jumps out first, her boots into the water above her ankles, starts pulling the boat right out of the water.

'What if someone takes it?' Fien says, pulling next to her now.

'They won't. Traders are honest in most things except trade. They can't afford to steal.'

The boat firmly perched at the top of the shore, Lil walks off towards the crowds, towards the colours that grow brighter and more frantic as she and Fien approach, boots dragging through the shallowing water, the fort of pearl.

Fien struggles to keep up with Lil. 'Slow down,' she pants.

'Why?'

'Why have you brought me with you?'

'You know the story.'

'What about Ben?'

'He'd get too excited if I told him anything.'

'I'm a novice. I can't help you if there's a fight.'

Lil stops. 'Who said there'd be a fight?'

'You said you want to kill or ruin whatever his name is.'

'Sachin,' Lil said, and the name came over her lips too softly.

'You want to make him love you again, don't you?'

'No, not really. I just can't say his name angrily.'

'This is not a good idea,' Fien says. 'You're putting yourself in danger when you don't need to.'

'I want to do some trade as well. It's not just him I'm here for.'

'Why not just go home with all that loot, find yourself a nice house and one of those kind men of yours and settle down, away from fighting?'

'Because nowhere would be peaceful, because everywhere will be at war sooner rather than later, especially here, especially in England. Anywhere, in truth. So why wait for death? Why not go and find it and rejoice every time we escape it?'

'And your son? What about your son?' Lil has to work hard to keep her voice deep and quiet, to not start shouting. 'He deserves a life, too, you know.'

'He enjoys being on the ship, and thinking he's an orphan who was rescued by me when he was a baby.'

'What if he wants to settle down, start a family, be a father?'

'Then he can go and do it.'

'While you drag him around the world, from one place to the next, always looking for the next fight?'

'That's why I wanted him to start reading, so he'd understand there's another world out there.'

'Reading's not living,' Fien spits.

'Says the girl who says she spent most of her time reading.' Lil puts her arm round Fien's shoulder. 'I know this place. I wouldn't have brought you here if it wasn't safe.'

'I've been here before. I know how safe or not it is.' Fien shifts, the unfamiliar weight of the sword on her hip. 'But then I'm just a girl,' she says.

'You're a woman already,' Lil says as they start walking again. 'You've learned so much in four months. You're taller, you're stronger. You're a natural hunter. And you've taught my son to read and write. I have much to be grateful for.'

'And I.' Fien widens her strides. 'I dwell too much on things. Let's go and be men amongst men.'

'That's my girl.'

104

'My boy to you now.'

Lil laughed, a deep belly-laugh. 'Yes, Master Finn.'

'I like that name. I'll call you Will.'

They stride towards the city walls, through rows and rows of fire and the scents of cooking meat, hands on their swords, legs wide with the swagger of seafaring men.

Inside the city, the stone buildings have open fronts, like they've been built with only three walls, and canopies hang over the narrow pathways between them. The breeze ruffles the bands of cloth into place, showers slivers of sand onto the crowds wandering through the crisscross of alleys. Colours, colours, bright and fluttering. Red and green and purple and lilac and yellow. A ripple of canvas between the sun and the city.

Lil ducks into a side alley even narrower than the others. It takes them away from the masses, where the loudness of the crowd subsides a little, where there's a semblance of fresh air for them to breathe. They stroll, silently, for hours, never even looking at each other, until the sun reaches its highest point, and they have to stop for a gasp of water, beside a primitive well, where men and women of all colours and languages stand in a loose line waiting for a mug of clear, translucent wetness. They drink fully and slowly.

The day falls away almost without them noticing. Stallholders start to collapse their canopies, the crowds drift away, the noise comes to an abrupt halt, and darkness settles over the city. The warmth remains in the empty alley, the stone walls whiter in the light of the rising moon.

'I don't suppose you've seen him yet,' Fien says.

Lil shakes her head. 'Too many people. But I know where he might be now.'

'We could have come across later.'

'No. I needed to feel my way back into this place.

105

Even a month away from it is a long time. It's like it's always changing. Don't you feel the difference from when you were last here?'

'That's so long ago I can't really remember it. Just the language.'

'It's beautiful, isn't it?'

'It can be.'

They creep through the silence now, interrupted only now and again by a low shout or a movement behind the now lowered canopies, towards yellow lights shining into the night from an indecipherable location further up the hill. Lil knows where she's going. As they get closer to the lights, they hear laughter and voices.

'Were you ever here with your father?' Lil says.

'I don't know.'

'This is where the real trade happens.' Lil pushes aside the curtain covering the door opening and walks into the building, the heat and the smell of burning tobacco rich in her face. 'You'll like it here.'

Inside, the noise is almost suffocating. The long room is full of men and women in all kinds of different clothes, of all kinds of different colours, waving their arms, gesticulating, calling across to each other, small packages changing hands, coins leaping from one palm to the other. And, up against the walls, and in the dark corners, there are others, leaning towards each other, faces serious, mouths moving slowly, earnest conversations to be had, and surreptitious passing of money, behind a sleight of hands, silence under the volume of the bear market at the centre of the floor.

'It's like an exchange,' Fien says under her breath.

'That's exactly what it is.' Lil pushes her way through the crowd, nods at people she doesn't know, to all appearances a buccaneer travelled from far with his sidekick, desperate for a drink or a trade or both, until, she reaches the bench from which men and maids alike are decanting beer and wine from barrels into mugs. She points at one of the barrels, holds up two fingers, a small coin balanced between them, takes the full mugs, passes one to Fien, and signs to her to find a vacant spot by the wall furthest away from the windows, furthest away from the flickering lights. She leans against the wall next to Fien. 'And now we watch and wait and drink.' She lifts her mug up to Fien's and taps it. 'Cheers.'

Fien wonders if she's been here before, with her father. Wouldn't she remember it? And if they were, what were they doing here? And then she realises he could have been here before, before he was her father, before he became who she thinks of as her father, when he was just plain Piet, just a man trading, buying, selling. Is this where he got the watch, is this where he was given it or stole it? Lawlessness isn't always on the surface of life. It lives underneath, burrows its way, like woodworm, into the grain of it. Maybe this is what Lindsey wanted, not just to steal Piet's collection, but to make anyone who knew him wonder if he really was the honourable man he made himself out to be. Even if Lindsey doesn't know she exists, everything he's done is targeted at her, at destroying the image, the face, of the man she loved, admired, worshipped. If only she had those last moments with him again. She'd never have got up to get that coffee. She would have sat down, looked at him across the empty cups and asked him who he really was, and where the watch had come from.

'What are you thinking?' Lil's voice echoes into her wondering.

'About my father.'

'If you think he was a good man, that's what he was.'

'I don't know any more.'

'Stop thinking about it.'

'I can't.'

'Help me find Sachin instead.'

'I don't even know what he looks like.' Fien takes a mouthful of the beer. 'Do you know what he looks like now? He may have changed a lot.'

'What I omitted to tell you was that I cut his face the day he betrayed me. And I don't think it's possible yet to have a scar across your left cheek and eye magicked away.'

'How many more secrets do you have?'

'Enough to keep surprising you.'

'And won't he recognise you?'

'I had hair then, long hair down to my waist.'

'Is that why you cut it? Part of your reinvention of yourself?'

'Many reasons, girl,' Lil says, still scanning the room, not looking at Fien. 'If I didn't change myself all the time people would know who I am.'

'Including Lindsey?'

'I had black hair then, and still long. There are many ways to fool a man, and faking is just one of many.'

'Faking what?'

'Everything.'

'Did he lose the eye?'

Lil shakes her head. 'I don't think I cut him deeply enough.'

'And brown eyes?'

Lil finishes her mug of beer. 'An initial impression of kindness. Never be deceived by brown eyes.' She gets up. 'Time for another.'

'I'm nowhere near finishing mine.'

'You need someone to keep you company, then, don't you?' Lil disappears into the crowd.

Fien watches the curtain open and close, looks at every newcomer from her place in the dark. None of them look like Lil's prince. *This is a fool's errand.* She leans back against the wall, takes another draught of the beer, a longer one this time. She could get used to this. She watches Lil push her way back through the thickening throng.

'Won't Harry worry?' Fien says. 'If we're not back soon?'

'He knows we might not come back tonight. I told him.'

'We'll never find your man here.'

'Be patient.'

'Don't you ever feel like you're wasting your time?'

Lil shrugs. 'What else would I do? Sit at home knitting? Or breeding? Being told what to do?' She nudges Fien. 'Can you really see me doing that? Or you, for that matter?'

'No. I suppose not.'

'And I'm sure it's not what your father educated you for.'

'Wait.' Fien's voice is a gasp. 'Look, by the door. Is that him?'

Lil doesn't turn round. She takes a sip from her fresh mug, beer foam around her mouth. 'Describe him.'

'Tall, taller than most men, and skinny. No sign of a beard. Dark skin and bright eyes. And a slice of white from above his left eyebrow down to his cheek bone.'

'Clothes?'

'He's coming this way.' Fien's whisper drops. 'Yes, he's wearing clothes.'

'What are they like, you fool?'

'Oh, red, looks like silk, and yellow. … He's right here.'

Lil chooses this moment to turn, accidentally bumps into the man Fien has been describing, drops her mug on the floor. 'Watch it.' Her voice unfeasibly low.

'Sorry, sir. Let me buy you a replacement.' Guttural, soft, like a lion's purr.

Lil doesn't know where to look and decides it's best for her to look straight at him.

'And you, sir,' Sachin, because it has to be him, says. 'Can I get you another drink, too, at the same time?'

Lil nods, says nothing, raises an eyebrow.

'You're a long way from home,' he says.

'We all are,' Lil says. 'Are you buying or selling?'

'Looking,' he says. 'It's too soon to decide what I want to do. So early in the year.'

'Looking for girls first?' Lil says.

'Oh, no, my days for such frivolities are long gone.'

'You surprise me.'

Sachin shrugs, pushes his way on to the barrels. Lil follows him, her hands loosely down by her side, her right hand dangerously close to her sword.

Fien feels for the security of her knives, sure they'll never get out of this place alive if Lil decides to kill him right now, sets off after them. She never used to like her tallness. It used to make her feel awkward, but now she's glad of it. Is this really what the world does, let men feel invulnerable while women have to cower in a corner? Her hand wraps round the grip of her sword even tighter. By the time she reaches the barrels, she's finished her beer and almost forgotten she's a woman.

Sachin gets his beer, their beers, hands them over, turns away from the servers, retreats out into the middle of the room, neither welcoming nor dismissing Lil and Fien. There's an arrogance, an uncomfortable certainty, about the way he carries himself. 'And you two,' he says, without preamble, 'are you buying or selling, or are you just innocent bystanders like so many of you Europeans claim to be?'

'Buying, mainly,' Lil says. 'What do you have?'

'Oh, I'm not sure you'd be able to afford what I have.'

He seems unaware that whatever he says sounds like an insult.

'You should let me be the judge of that,' Lil says. 'Don't judge a book by its cover.'

Sachin raises his scarred eyebrow. 'I don't think I could ever be accused of such a carelessness.' He empties his mug in one drag. 'I merely meant that I tend to deal in the finest merchandise, and not many have the funds to make it worth my while.'

'So what brings you to this godforsaken place? Most of the people here probably haven't got enough to make the simplest of trades.'

'Now it's my turn to tell you not to misjudge those around you.' He laughs, a high-pitched laugh that ill matches his deep, smooth voice.

'What do you have?' Lil pushes him.

'Are you impatient by nature, or is your ship waiting to cast off with the next tide? Or is it too hot for you, and you want to get back to your frigid European climate?'

Fien is just waiting for Lil's temper to snap. It doesn't.

'None of those, my man. I just don't like the eternal back and forth of bartering, of keeping secrets you have no need to keep. I just like honest and quick trading.'

'Honest trade?' He laughs that irritating laugh again. 'There's no such thing. And you should know that.' He waves his empty mug in the direction of the servers.

'They know you that well?' Lil says, feigning surprise.

'Don't you know who I am?'

'Should I?' Fien drains her mug, too. 'Let me pay for this one.'

'You really don't have to.'

'You have me intrigued about your wares, sir.' She throws a silver coin over the heads of the crowd between them and the bar. One of the servers catches it, looks at it nestled in the palm of his hand, and smiles. He brings three beers to them, the only group Fien has seen getting such special treatment. 'You see,

111

my friend, I can make myself known here, too, without anyone knowing who I really am.'

'Now you intrigue me,' Sachin says, the long fingers of his hand draped around the plain mug. 'Tell me what you're looking for.'

Lil looks around, and although Fien recognises she's only playing a game, Sachin doesn't seem to. 'Have you ever heard of the Immortality Clock?'

Sachin's face hardens for a split second, his mouth a thin line for a moment, before he hides his surprise. 'The emerald clock?' he says. 'It's been lost forever, so I hear.'

'Is that so?' Lil wipes the beer from her mouth with the back of her hand. 'I'd heard that some English mercenary had found it and was looking to sell it.'

'Why would he do that? It makes it worthless.'

'I think his king needs the money.'

This time Sachin's laugh is a roar that makes others turn and look at him. 'Those damn English,' he says. 'Always wanting to make war on someone or other. I'd like to see them try here in the East.' He shakes his head. 'They never learn.'

'I guess that means you don't have it,' Lil says.

'I'm afraid not.'

Why did she even mention it? Fien thinks, hiding her face in her mug in case it gives her away.

'Perhaps you don't have anything that interests me then,' Lil says, and goes to turn on her heel.

'A shame you should have travelled so far on a rumour,' he says.

'One has to speculate to accumulate, don't you think?' Lil's face is so close to his. 'Perhaps you'll manage to persuade me you have something I want. If I don't walk away.'

'Plenty of other buyers here.'

'People who could afford to buy the Immortality

Clock?'

He shrugs, the muscles in his face rigid, holding back either a smile or genuine rage. 'Prove it.'

Lil pulls a small pouch from her trouser pocket, leans even closer to Sachin, and opens the pouch. The light of a hundred diamonds sprinkles his face. 'And there are more where that little lot came from,' she says.

'Who are you?' he says.

'No-one important. Just another buyer. I'll be in touch.'

'But you don't know who I am.'

'Oh, I know alright,' she says. 'It's just best to keep the smallest secrets till last.'

Chapter 16

'What are you doing?' Fien says when they get back out onto the street. The night has cooled.

'Baiting him. Keep walking. He'll follow.'

'What if he doesn't?'

'He will. Anything for a profit.'

'Where will we stay tonight?'

'Somewhere.'

Heavy footsteps behind them. Rushing. Panting.

'I think you misunderstood me.' The voice, still as smooth as the silk he wears.

'In what way?' Lil stops and turns.

He inclines his head. 'There may be some trade to be done.'

'Worth my while?'

'Only you can decide that.' He bows. 'Will you accompany me to my camp?'

'No ship?'

'The camels don't like the sea.'

'But the expense.'

'Not as expensive as losing camels.' He leads them along a street up the hill, away from the harbour.

'Don't you fear bandits?' Lil says. 'I hear there are many of them these days.'

'No more, no fewer than ten years ago,' he says. 'And I have plenty of men to protect my cargo.'

'The expense,' Lil says again, mockingly. 'You must make hardly any profit.

'Let me worry about my profit.' His voice sounds rough all of a sudden, like sand on paper.

The climb for the best part of an hour. It's cooler up here, a blessed relief after the closeness of the city.

'How do I know you're not planning to rob me with your men?'

'I've seen your sword.' He bends towards Lil. 'Does

114

your companion not speak?'

'Only when he needs to. He tends to ask questions after the fact. But he's not slow at all. The very opposite, in fact.'

'I understand.'

'Good.'

They're at the top of the hill now, and the city is spread out before them like an encampment, only a few golden light finding their way through the thickness of the night, some of them, down in the harbour, rising slowly up and down, undoubtedly ship lights moving with the swell. Ahead of them they see the minor flickers of small camp fires, catch the scent of animals, the low murmur of camels at rest. A guard steps out of the dark, a curved sword ready in his hand. Sachin stops him with a simple gesture.

'My guests,' he says.

The guard bows and disappears into the dark again.

'Very good,' Lil says. 'A shame we saw him some way back.'

'I meant you to.'

'Without doubt.'

They walk through the camp, which appears enormous, small tents on the outskirts, larger ones, and then, at what appears to be the very centre, a huge, circular tent, high enough for a tall man like Sachin to stand upright in. At the entrance, two Moors, scimitars slung carelessly over their shoulders. They stand to one side as Sachin approaches. He pushes the tent flap to one side, beckons Lil and Fien. 'Please, make yourselves at home.' He sits down on one of the cushions on the carpets covering the ground, and claps his hands. Two women appear, carrying trays of decanted wine and glasses, and fruit. They demurely bend their knees to place the trays on the ground, bow to Sachin and walk backwards away.

Sachin pours three glasses of scarlet wine, takes a big sip from his, and smiles. 'See,' he says. 'No poison.'

'That's always good to know.' Lil raises her glass.

'I have a hundred more of those,' he says.

'Wine decanters?' Lil says.

'Women,' he says. 'You white men like our dark women, don't you? Just like the Moors like your white girls. Valuable exchanges.' He sniggers. 'Or do they have no interest for you?' He leans back, waits for an answer.

'They're too expensive to keep alive on the way back,' Lil says. 'So much food, so much argument amongst the crew. I could end up at home with half the crew dead, half the women dead and half the remainder pregnant.'

Sachin shakes his head. 'Not pregnant. We've prepared them for you.'

Fien senses Lil shaking, but can't risk reaching out to her to calm her.

'How very thoughtful of you. It makes them worthless in their own country.'

'A small sacrifice, don't you think? For inconveniences avoided.' He picks up an orange, rips off its skin, throws it over his shoulder.

'Our men like them pure, and to have had a surgeon's knife down there is as good as selling second-hand goods.'

Sachin nods. 'That's why we've found a new way to do it. It only leaves a little scar in their navels. They can cover that up with a semi-precious stone.'

'How many of them die while you're ripping out their insides?'

'Only about twenty out of every hundred. As I say, a small sacrifice.'

'And how much do you want for your hundred women?'

'Two hundred of your diamonds.'

'That's not cheap.'

'Nor is it expensive.' He peels another orange. 'Do I have your interest now?'

Lil grabs a banana, peels it roughly, bites it in half, chews for an age, and shrugs. 'A hundred diamonds.'

What's she going to do with them? Fien empties her glass of wine with one gulp, and coughs.

'You think even that's too expensive, Mr Finn?' Lil says. 'Would eight-five be better?'

Fien nods, breathing in through her nose.

'That's craziness,' Sachin says. 'I thought you were a serious trader.'

'I am,' Lil says. 'But, you know, the inconvenience of finding something to put in their navels, and the long trek home. Don't you have anything more valuable?

He shakes his head. 'I can always take them somewhere else.'

'And make your trip even longer and more wearisome? I notice your guard hadn't shaved in some weeks. I think you've been holding out for too high a price.'

'A hundred and seventy-five.' He fills up the glasses with more wine.

'Getting me drunk won't make me any less of a haggler,' Lil says. 'I'm back to a hundred.'

'A hundred and sixty.'

'A hundred and fifteen.'

'Have a heart,' he says, but he doesn't mean it. 'A hundred and fifty.'

'But you have no heart either,' Lil says. 'You stole them in the first place, so all you've had to do was make sure they'll stay childless and feed them scraps.'

The veins in his neck start to bulge, and he throws another mouthful of wine down his throat. 'A hundred and forty.'

'How about a hundred and thirty?' Lil says. 'Throw in a couple of the Moors, and I'll round it up to a hundred and forty. I can take them off your hands straightaway with that arrangement.'

'You don't want to wait till daylight?'

'Why would I? I'm assuming they're all still hobbled except for those two.'

'You're right.'

'You're a fine businessman,' Lil says, and drains her glass, too. She stands up, and steps across the carpet to him to shake his hand. 'Deal?'

He stands up; too slowly, Fien thinks. 'Deal,' he says, one hand behind his back. 'You have all the diamonds with you?'

'Of course,' Lil says, a step closer to him, her left hand reaching for the pouches in her pocket, her right hand extended for the traditional handshake.

'Good,' he says, falls towards her in a smooth curve.

Fien jumps over the trays. Too late.

Lil has a bloody knife in her left hand instead of the diamonds. 'Thought you could fool me, did you?' she hisses. 'Do you recognise my smell now. Do you?'

He tries to say something, but only bubbles, not words, come from his mouth. The thin line of blood from his throat spreads as he falls down, silent, his eyes fixed on Lil.

'I told you,' she says, and kicks him. 'I will have my revenge. Only a woman, am I? Only women, are they? You would rob your own kingdom to make yourself rich?' She pushes him. 'You have a son, and you'll never see him.'

He can only gurgle in response, then his body jerks once, and slides towards the trays. Fien catches his feet, guides them past the decanters and glasses, all sound averted. He vomits blood.

'The guards with the girls,' Lil whispers. 'We need to

get them now.'

They creep run to the back of the tent, a small rent in the fabric the signpost to the harem.

Fien puts her finger to her lips, puts her eye to the rip, reaches under her shirt, lifts two fingers, and, without waiting for Lil, pushes through the fabric. The blades, one from each hand, flash through the gloom, followed by two dull thuds as metal slices through flesh. 'Bring a light.'

Lil carries a single candle through to the charnel house. The two guards have knives sticking from their throats, their eyes ripped wide open in surprise at the speed of death. The women crouch, mouths open, in dark recesses. Not one of them has screamed.

Lil, her voice guttural now, speaks to them in low tones as she unhobbles them. A small thing, no older than thirteen, tugs her shirt. her vowels are strange, her consonants distorted.

'She's not one of them,' Fien says. 'She's from here.'

'I did understand.'

'Language can breed confusion,'

'I know,' Lil says, her arms around the girl.

'The back of the camp isn't protected,' the girl says. 'Towards the mountains. We can slip out that way.' She wipes her nose. 'Maybe.'

Fien pulls her knives out of the guards, wipes them clean, red smears, on her trousers. Then she takes the guards' swords, and their knives, from their dead bodies. 'Not enough to go round,' she says.

'We must crawl,' the girl says. 'Then they won't see us. They never look down.'

Lil explains to the women what they must do. Some shake their heads, too afraid to understand, and she has to explain it again. She cuts a hole in the back of the prince's tent, down at the grass line, and one by one, they crawl out, caterpillars into the cool night.

119

Chapter 17

The grass smells of better things than death. Fien's nose is buried in it as she follows the last woman out of the tent. The sounds of her hands and feet on the ground are magnified to her, but she ignores them as she follows the line of women, two by two, through the unlit camp. There are no guards this way. Was Sachin really all bluster? Was he really that arrogant, to leave the back door open and unlocked, to post all his strength at the front? She's surprised and grateful when the lights recede in the distance, when they reach rocky ground, and the grass and its scent are behind them. They keep crawling until the they can see no lights at all. Only then does Lil call all the women into a tight circle around her. They are nothing more than spectres.

'I know you're all hurt and damaged,' she says. 'I know you can no longer have children, and understand your pain. But you're not without value. You are not helpless. But you have nothing, and I have something.' She walks amidst them, her hands busy. She hands each one a gold coin and a diamond. 'This should help you,' she says. 'I can't protect you against men like the dead prince, but I can give you something that might protect you. You can get passage on a ship from here, or you can go back to your own country, into a different kingdom than the one he took you from, and start again.' When she has finished and her hands and pouches empty, she says one last thing. 'I can't take you all away on my ship, but if some of you want to come with me, you're welcome to.'

The little girl puts up her hand. 'Me, please,' she says, from under mane of wild hair, her face dirty and almost invisible in the dark.

'What's your name?' Lil says.

'Ishtar.'

'And why should I take you?'

'Because my parents are dead. Because I am clever.'

Lil smiles. 'That's good enough for me.' She looks around at something she can hardly see. 'Any more?' No-one moves or says anything. 'Really?' She doesn't sound disappointed. 'You're all brave women, very brave.' She turns away, then back again. 'Braver than I.'

The chattering starts, and, one by one, the women crowd around her, hug her, kiss her cheeks, and slope off towards the north, towards the mountain. Some change their minds and turn right, eastwards, towards India, where they came from.

'Will they really be able to do something with what you gave them?' Fien says, her arms aching, but her mind curiously free of guilt at the first human deaths she has wrought.

'I don't know,' Lil says. 'I hope so, but I can't do any more than I have done.'

Ishtar scrabbles around at their feet.

'Get up,' Lil says, in her broken Persian.

'I owe you my life.'

'Not yet. We have to get back to the ship first.'

'Wait until just before dawn,' the girl says. 'They'll be drunk by then.'

'They'll notice that he's not moved,' Fien says.

'No, they won't,' Ishtar says. 'They always leave him alone with the women when he comes back. They know what he's like, and they don't want to see what he does.'

'Blood runs quickly,' Lil says

'And carpets are thirsty,' Ishtar says.

'You're a wise one,' Lil says.

'If truth is wisdom.'

'Have you read a lot?' Lil says, and lifts the girl into her arms.

'Only picture books,' Ishtar says.

121

'Then you've learned a lot from those pictures.'

'Maybe.' Ishtar puts her arms around Lil's neck. 'You smell nice.'

'Of death and fear maybe.'

'Of home,' Ishtar says. 'How I remember it.'

'My poor girl,' Lil says.

Fien says nothing, just revels in the warmth, the temporary safety. 'You have two children now.'

'Perhaps,' Lil says.

'What will Ben think?' Fien says.

'Who knows?' Lil strokes Ishtar's hair. 'Does it matter?'

'Perhaps he'll fall in love with her.'

'I don't think so,' Lil says. 'He's already in love.'

'Who with?'

'You, you fool. Totally, utterly, absolutely.'

Fien staggers. 'But ... but.'

'What? You can't tell? You've got a lot to learn.'

'He's only eighteen.'

'So are you.'

'How do you know? I didn't tell you.'

'You didn't have to.' Lil leans back against a rock, ignores the abrupt shapes it cuts into her back. 'Do you really think I sleep through whatever it is you choose to do when I'm not on watch?'

'I ... Your breathing doesn't change.'

'That's because I won't let it.'

'That's like spying.'

'No, it's not. It's looking after you.'

'Do I need looking after?'

'You were a bit slow tonight when he jumped me.'

'You knew he was going to.'

'That's not the point.' There's laughter in Lil's voice, and a touch of relief. 'You need to watch people more closely, because that's what they do. Profit, that's all that counts. Murder is irrelevant. Those are the times we live in.'

'I'm sorry.'

'Don't be,' Lil says. 'I got my revenge. I killed him, and that's what I wanted.'

'And you don't think that was too high a price for him to pay?'

'I might have done before he started telling us what he'd done to those poor women.'

By now the last of the women has disappeared, and the three of them are left on their own on the rocky plateau.

'You didn't know?'

'No.' Lil shakes her head in the dark. 'I had found out that he came to Gombroon once a year, but not what he traded in. And even if I suspected what it might be in, I had no idea he mutilated them before selling them on.'

'Are all men really like that?'

'Most of them, yes.' Lil sounds sad now. 'We're not important to them. They think they own us. That's all. And they'll breed with their wives, wherever they might be from. But they want others, courtesans they'll call them, and they want to do anything but breed with them. They just want to possess those women, put things into them, but never breed. Why else do you think women are traded?'

'It's horrible. I never thought about it.'

'That's because your father protected you from that reality.'

'I wish he hadn't.'

'I think that's a wish you want to take back.' Lil blows out a sharp breath. 'Did you notice Sachin's face when I mentioned the clock?'

'Yes.' Fien doesn't know what else to say or think.

'Do you believe me and Ben now? That there is something about it?'

'It doesn't mean that what people say is true. Or what they believe is true.'

'There's no smoke without fire,' Lil says.

'Oh, come on. That's a platitude.'

'Oh, come on. Platitudes mask the truth.'

'But I don't want it. It brings death.'

'I think you're wrong,' Lil says. Ishtar has fallen asleep against her shoulder.

'Is it really worth finding out?'

'You want to go after Lindsey anyway.'

'You said it would be years until I was ready.'

'That was before I saw how you handled your knives.'

'That's foolish talk,' Fien says.

'And it will take us almost four months to get to England.'

'He may have gone by then, somewhere else.'

'Not unless the King has told him to. There's a civil war brewing there, you know. I don't think the King will want Tall Face to go anywhere.'

'And if you're wrong?'

'Maybe I'll have a rest, for once,' Lil says. 'I could do with one.'

'We've got to get out of here first.'

'Oh, we will, we will.' She gets up, Ishtar still in her arms, nods towards the southwest. 'We need to go that way.'

'What if it's not safe?'

'I've got you to protect me.'

They feel their way over the scree, onto grass again, Sachin's camp now far away, and back into the outskirts of Gombroon. There's still life in some of the inns they pass, drunk shouting inside and kissing couples outside. No-one takes any notice of them. They keep their footsteps slow and quiet.

Ishtar wakes up. They can smell the sea. They can hear it rolling up against the land, the pebbles shifting, the sand sighing. The city is a dark mass behind them, only a few desolate torches now, flickering in the distance. They feel the dampness of the sea on their faces, the coolness of the ocean's breeze on their hands.

'Left, left,' Lil whispers. 'Almost there.'

They dance around the rolling pebbles. Their feet sink into the sand in between.

'I've found it.' Fien stops and touches the wood of the boat, sure it's theirs.

Lil comes to her side, reaches out, caresses the shape, finds an oar. 'You're right. How did you know?'

'Must be the hunter in me.'

'So now you believe me.'

Fien grunts.

The three of them, Ishtar strong for such a tiny thing, lift the boat out of the ridge it carved when they landed, carry it, step by painful step, until they're knee-deep in the water.

'Tide's coming in,' Lil says. 'That'll be hard rowing.'

'It'll feel like a gentle walk,' Fien says.

'Hop in, then, you two,' Lil says. The boat sways when she gets in after them. 'Sit in the back, Ishtar, and guide us to the island.'

An hour later, their boat pushes its way past the southwest curve of the island, the promontory which hides *The Odyssey* from the mainland. They row on, towards where the ship should be. There's nothing there but ocean.

Chapter 18

'We're in the wrong place,' Fien says.

'No we're not,' Lil says. 'They are.' She pulls her oar into the boat. 'Stop rowing.'

The boat is a pendulum on the tide, back and forth, back and forth, water splashing lazily against the side.

Ishtar leans back, her arms crossed.

'Aren't you two going to panic, or something?' Fien says, her heart beating up into her mouth.

'Quiet,' Lil says. 'I'm trying to listen.'

Fien clamps her mouth shut, sits still, closes her eyes. Moments pass like years. The silence becomes a sound. And the longer the silence goes on, the louder it gets.

'Can you hear that, too?' Lil says.

'What?' Fien is confused by what she can and cannot hear.

'Masts creaking.'

'I thought I heard a hum.'

'That, too.'

'It's the masts I'm interested in.'

'I can't hear any creaking,' Fien says.

'Close your eyes again.'

Fien does as she's told. Her hands are aching. There's just blackness where she expects sound. 'Nothing,' she says.

'That's what comes from living in a town for too long,' Lil says. 'Our ears go mad.'

'Where can they be?'

'Either they've sailed off because there was danger, or they've been attacked and captured.'

'Yet you seem unconcerned.'

'I can't think if I'm concerned.'

'So what do we do?'

'We go ashore on the island and wait till first light. And then we decide what to do.'

'That's more time lost.'

'Any better suggestions?'

'No,' Fien says.

They row towards the island.

'Careful now,' Lil says. 'Nothing but rocks here. Hold her steady.' She pulls Ishtar to the oar, and stands up, her hands outstretched. 'That's it. I've got it.'

'What?' Fien strains to hold the boat in one place.

'The island. There are caves along here somewhere. I just need to work out ...' Knocking sounds, bone on stone. 'Ah, yes, this way.' Lil mumbles to herself.

The boat shudders and shakes.

'Heads down,' Lil shouts, and throws herself down.

With a gush of water and wind, the boat shoots into a hole in the rock, the echo a clap of thunder, the water a circular roar, until the wave recoils and the water is smooth again.

'There,' Lil says. 'We're in. Just let her drift.'

Within a few minutes, the keel finds sand, and the boat quietly scrapes to a stop. Lil jumps out, and the other two with her. They push the boat up onto the hidden shore.

'We could do with a torch,' Lil says. 'I can't see a bloody thing.'

'How high do we need to be to keep out of the water?' Fien says.

'If we find rocks, we'll climb them.'

After some stumbles and falls, they do find a gentle slop of rocks, and crawl up it on all fours, Lil at the front, followed by Ishtar, and then Fien. They follow the slop upwards until they find a level platform. Even here, under the island, it's warm, comfortably warm.

'It won't be long before it's light,' Lil says. 'And then we'll know where we are, and where they are.'

'You hope.'

'I hope, yes, I suppose. There's nothing else to do. If

The Odyssey's been taken, it's not safe out there for us. If they've moved on because of some danger, it's not safe for us out there now. I'd rather fight in the light where I can see the enemy, or a place to run to.'

'Let's take it in turn to watch.'

'I can go first,' Ishtar says.

'You'll do no such thing, young lady,' Lil says. 'You need to sleep, so lie down.'

'I'll do first watch,' Fien says.

'And how will you measure time?'

'I'll count to three thousand or something like that.'

'And make yourself fall asleep while your numbers turn into sheep, eh?'

'I'm not that tired.'

'You will be.'

'We can't all sleep at the same time.'

'Fine. Keep watch until you think you can't keep your eyes open any longer. Then wake me, and I'll do it.'

In the end, Fien manages to stay awake until the first, uncertain rays of the sun sneak their way into the cavern, turning the green water blue. She almost expects the small footsteps of light to make small splashing sounds as they wander across the water. She prods Lil. 'It's time.'

Lil, wide awake straightaway, stands up and starts to scramble back down the rocky slope. 'Here we go, girls, here we go.'

They're rowing out of the cavern less than a minute later, stealthily, carefully, Ishtar at the front, looking left and right, forwards and upwards, for rocks they could run aground on, and for anything that might attack them. The horizon is a blue speck of nothing. And beyond it, even more nothing.

'We'll row round the island on a north-easterly course,' Lil says. 'And then we'll find them.'

'And if we don't?'

128

'We'll steal another ship and go looking for them. …
Now look up.'

The cliffs are higher than any building Fien has even
been close to, towering so high above them she thinks
they must be touching the sky.

'Amazing. We should climb up. We'd be able to see
for miles from up there.'

'And we'd be a perfect target, too,' Lil says.

'We can't do anything from down here.'

'That's why we'll row round the island.'

'And people will see us. Aren't we less suspicious on
land than off it?'

'Maybe. But the only fortification on here faces the
mainland. We'll stop before we get there. There's a
cove about a mile and a half from here where they
might have gone to hide.'

'And whoever was after them is still here somewhere.'

'They may just have noticed something unusual going
on on the island.'

'Let's get going then,' Fien says. 'Before it gets too
hot.'

They row. The sea is calm. *How beautiful it would be if we
weren't at war with everything,* Fien thinks. She says
nothing. It feels like she has blisters growing blisters on
her hands. *Keep going.* She loses track of time, rows
without thinking about what she's doing. The sun is hot
on her face.

The cliffs start to shrink, as if Fien's rowing away
from the island. But it's an optical illusion. The island's
harsh edges are softening, smoothing themselves into
hills and slopes. There are tinges of green on the slopes,
sparse but visible nonetheless. And then the illusion is
broken by a massive rock tower, arches through which
the sea flows uninterrupted.

'Just round here,' Lil says.

They round the sharp tip, and there she is, *The Odyssey,*

anchor chain taut, a thin dark line against the pale blue of the sea, about a mile off the shore.

'Thank God for that,' Lil says. 'One last hard push.' She starts to count their strokes, speeding them up until they are alongside the ship.

They all look up from the boat to see Harry's familiar shape gaze down at them.

'Had no choice,' he calls down. 'All sorts of people showing too much of an interest, for that side of Hormuz.'

The rope ladder drops down the side of the ship.

'You first,' Lil says, lifts Ishtar up onto the first rung. The girl shows no fear and scrambles up the rocking ladder.

'You next.' Lil pushes Fien towards the ladder.

As soon as Fien is three steps up, Lil grabs the rope and starts climbing up, too.

Ishtar tumbles over the railing onto the deck, Fien close behind. Fien bends over, reaches a hand out to Lil. There's a puff of smoke in the distance, at the edge of Fien's vision. As she grabs Lil's hand, she's covered in a spray of blood. And then the sound of a gun reaches her. Fien screams.

Lil's shirt is a tatter of red and bone, her back broken open by whatever's been fired. Harry and Fien drag her over the railing and lay her down on the wood. Her eyes are still open.

'Ben,' Lil mouthes.

'I'm here, Commandant.' Ben bends down over her. 'We'll soon have you fixed up.'

Lil smiles at him, blood already dripping from her mouth.

Chaos around the dying.

'Anchor up,' Harry shouts. The crash of masts and the clanking of the chain.

Lil tries to lift her arm. Blood is now running freely

from her mouth, and her chest is a mess of shirt and flesh.

Ben holds her hand. He's crying.

She shakes her head. 'Don't,' she sighs. 'Son of mine. All I love.'

Ben sobs.

Fien holds Lil's other hand.

'I'll have that rest now,' Lil says, still smiling.

'No, no, no.' Ben, screaming. He puts his arms around her, smothers her pain in his. 'Please.'

There is nothing more. Lil's smile is fixed, her eyes open, looking straight into the sun. The ship begins to move, sails already shredding under a fusillade of shots. Lil's blood soaks into the deck. There is nothing more.

Chapter 19

Harry at the helm, Harry screaming at the crew. Lil's body where it fell. Fien and Ben and Ishtar dragging cannon balls to the firing stations. Explosions and screams. The smell of gunpowder and sea. *The Odyssey*, after a slow start, hurtling forwards, away from the island, away from the mainland, southwards, southwards, to the open sea. A flotilla of ships, led by a black warship in pursuit. Dropping back one moment, gaining the next. The crack and splinter of wood as *The Odyssey*'s cannons find their targets. Lil's body, all alone, still leaking blood, arms spread wide, her golden face untouched, her white shirt red.

A cannon ball whistles through the air, smashes into *The Odyssey*'s stern, a shower of wood falling into the sea from her. A volley from the stern cannons booms out a reply, and two of the pursuing ships halt in mid-gallop, capsize and disappear. The gap widens, and now only the black ship is visible, with its black sails. Harry, his knuckles white on the wheel, stares ahead to the empty sea, his eyes deliberately avoiding what lies on the deck below him. He doesn't want to see her like that, doesn't want to believe someone's got the better of her, finally, and forever. The stern cannons fire again. Harry looks over his shoulder. The black ship's bow takes a hit, and the gap widens. 'That's that,' Harry says. They sail on past the sunrise, and land is soon out of sight.

Harry hands the wheel to one of his men. 'Keep a steady course,' he says. 'And don't let the speed drop.' He walks slowly down the stairs to the blood-stained deck, drops onto his knees at Lil's side, takes her right hand. 'Oh, Lil,' he whispers. 'You old fool. Why'd you have to go leave us now?' He bends forwards, and kisses her, gently, lovingly, on her red mouth. 'We had some good times, didn't we, you and me?' And then he picks her up, like the ragdoll she is now, and carries her into her room.

Fien and Ben try to follow him, but he's barred the door already. 'Go away,' he bellows. 'Make coffee. Just leave us be.'

Ben collapses on the deck in front of the door. He curls up, screams, kicks his feet, lies still.

'Come,' Fien says, puts her hands under his arms and pulls him away. She almost carries him to the galley, her tears forgotten. As soon as she lets go of him in the heat of the kitchen, he lets himself drop down again.

'Why didn't she tell me before?' he says. 'Why did you let her climb that ladder last?' He spits as he talks.

'I don't know why she didn't tell you. ... And you knew, you knew a long time ago. You just didn't' think it could be true.'

Ben groans.

Fien's tears are all over her face. 'A gun shouldn't reach that far. It can't reach that far.'

'Why didn't you tell me you knew?'

'She told me not to. Threatened me. She wasn't a woman to say no to.'

'It's your fault,' he says, and doesn't look at her. 'I thought you were our friend.'

'Everything's my fault,' she says, accepting.

'I don't want to live without her.' His sobs are uncontrollable, his body out of control.

'Neither do I.' She grabs him. 'But we have to. Otherwise everything she's done is wasted, all this.'

'They all listened to her. They won't listen to Harry. They'll desert us as soon as we reach the next port.'

'Harry loved her.'

He tries to speak in between crying. 'That means nothing. She's dead. She's gone. There's nothing left of her.'

'Except for you.'

'Nothing.'

'You're the Commandant now,' Fien says quietly, certainly.

'There is no Commandant now, and there never will be.'

'You are the Commandant. You're her son.'

'Then why did she bring that girl?'

'She saw someone who needed her.'

'Why couldn't she ever think of herself?'

Fien shrugs, suddenly cold, despite the stove, despite the sun outside.

'Tell me. Why?'

'I don't know. ... I do know. ... She didn't care about herself.'

Ben takes a deep breath. 'What do you mean about the gun?'

'How far from the shore were we?'

'A mile, at least.'

'Do you know of any weapon that can reach that far?'

He shrugs, starts to sob again.

'So, how did they kill her?'

He shrugs again, still caught up in his sobs.

'Who was it? Someone on that black ship?' Fien says.

'How should I know? And if I did, would it bring her back, would she walk in that door now and tell us to stop being idiots and get on with our work?'

'She was always telling me about revenge, you know she was, when it's ripe, when your blood is cold again. We have to find out who killed her and with what.'

'If it's a weapon you say shouldn't even exist, how can we?'

Fien tells him about Sachin, about his slit-throated father, about how Lil was humiliated, how she took her revenge.

'That doesn't matter to me,' Ben says. 'All this

coincidence, all this made-up life. I don't know it. I don't want to know it. I don't want to understand it. It's all madness. She'll never walk this earth again.'

'The clock.'

'What about the clock?'

'If what you and Lil said is true, we could use it to go back in time and stop her from being killed.'

'That's stupid.'

'You said you believed in it. And now you say you don't.'

'I can't believe in legends any more.'

'Why?' Although she sees he's broken, she pushes him.

'How can you even say that? We have nothing without her.'

'You are the Commandant now.' She grabs the hot kettle, pours him a cup of coffee. 'Drink.'

He does as she tells him, although the dark liquid singes his tongue. 'All that blood,' he says, puts his hand to his stomach, jumps up and rushes out into the unmoving air.

She hears him vomit. There's a pain inside her she's never felt. Not even when her father died. She leans against the hot stove and ignores the burning on her back. It would be so easy to let the fire consume her.

Ben walks back into the galley, wiping his chin with his bloody shirt. 'Maybe you're right.' He tries a sad smile. 'But she's still dead.'

'Feel better?'

He nods unenthusiastically.

'So we need to find Lindsey,' Fien says.

'He found us,' Harry says from the door.

'What do you mean?'

'That's his ship, the black thing with the matching sails.'

'That doesn't mean he killed Lil,' Fien says. 'He

doesn't know what she looks like now.'

'He knows most things,' Harry says. 'Unless he found out that your father had a daughter who got on this ship.'

'So you're blaming me as well?'

Harry holds up his hands. His face and beard are blurred by the wetness of his tears. 'I didn't say that.'

'You meant it, though.'

He shakes his head. 'I meant nothing. Maybe he meant to kill you.' He puts his hand on his chest, wringing for breath. 'She's ready now.'

They follow him. Ishtar, from nowhere, face black with gunpowder, grabs Ben's hand. 'Brother,' she says, and nothing else matters.

Harry stops in front of Lil's cabin. 'Anchor,' he yells. 'Gather.'

The Odyssey stops dead in the water. There is nothing around her but horizon. The crew, faces so familiar and unfamiliar to Fien, form a half circle around her. The last man glides down from the Crow's Nest on the single strand of a spider's web.

Harry wipes his eyes. 'I didn't want this,' he says into the hushed crowd. 'But it's the way it is.' He points at Ben. 'The boy is her son.' He looks at Ben. 'Walk up to the wheel.'

Ben hesitates, ignores his fear, walks up the steps slowly, his head down. When he reaches the quarterdeck, he turns, looks down at the assembled crew, the marks of war and grief etched into their faces and clothes. He steps across to the huge wheel, grips it with his left hand and raises his right. His face is pale. 'I swear, by the spirit of this ship, by the will of this wood, by the blood of my mother, that I will lead you as she did, that I will think of you with every breath I take, that I will keep you safe, that this ship will always be your sanctuary, that we will always be of one blood, of one family.' The tears run down his face, sobless.

The men don't cheer. Instead, they bow their heads, each and every one of them, and those who still have hats, take them off before bowing. There is a collective murmur. 'We swear.'

'And we'll find who killed her. And we'll make the murderer pay, with life, with blood, with money, with whatever we choose. Because we can. And we will.' Ben's voice is suddenly an octave deeper, a man's voice. And he looks taller, and stands taller, and thinks taller.

'We will.' The men speak in chorus.

Ben moves away from the wheel, to the top of the stairs. 'I want you all to say your good-byes to the Commandant first. I was only a boy yesterday. All she did she owed to you.'

Harry pushes open the double door to Lil's cabin. The men drift in, one by one, and come out crying, drift away to their stations. The anchor chain is would up, and the ship is under way again.

When the watch has climbed its way back into the Crow's Nest and one of the crew has taken the wheel, Harry calls Ben down from the quarterdeck. 'I know I'm not your father, but I loved her. I'll be here for you.' He opens his arms, and Ben falls into them and the bear hug. 'Do you want to see her?'

Ben nods. 'And Fien with me.'

Ishtar tugs at his hand.

'And the girl.'

'Ishtar,' the child says.

'And Ishtar,' Ben says.

They walk into the stateroom, wrecked on the port side by the one cannon ball that hit them, damage to be repaired. The map table has been cleared, turned into a bier. Fien and Ben walk towards it.

Harry's cleaned the body, and bandaged the deadly wound so there's no blood. He's dressed Lil, not in a dress, but in clothes she would have worn every day. Her eyes are closed, but the smile is still on her face, the smile of a woman with nothing to regret. Her short hair seems sumptuous now, under the tiara Harry has chosen to adorn her. She looks alive asleep.

Fien stumbles, grabs at the table. This is too much. How can someone look so real and alive and not be there? She touches the now cold face, strokes the cold hands, already rigid, says a good-bye in her head that she can't compose into spoken words, turns away.

Ben just stands there, looks down at the body. 'It's not her, is it?' He looks at Harry. 'She's not in there, is she?'

Harry shakes his naked head.

Ben turns and look out of the wide window at the sea. 'I don't want to remember her like this,' he says.

'But Harry did the right thing,' Fien says. 'The way she would want to look.'

'Of course he did,' Ben says. 'Thank you.' He bows towards Harry.

Harry, still gazing at Lil, tears still running down his face, nods. 'We need to bury her today,' he says. 'We can't take her home.' He swallows. 'We can't even take her back to the island.' He shakes his head, doesn't want to say what he has to say. 'We need to let her go now.'

Ben crumbles. 'Already?' He leans on the table for support.

'There's no other way,' Harry says. 'The heat.' He shrugs. 'I wish it were different.'

'How?' Fien says.

'I was going to get some of the ballast from the hold, and wrap her tightly into a sheet with it,' Harry says. 'And then we let her go over the side.'

'That's terrible.'

'She'll be at sea. It's what she loved.'

'It doesn't seem real.'

'It *is* real,' Harry says. 'We need to be practical.'

'And then?' Ben says.

'And then we decide where we're going to go,' Harry says. 'You decide.' He looks like a very old man now.

Ben looks at Lil again, holds his hand out against her silent lips. 'Good-bye, Commandant.' His body stiffens. 'What do I need to do?'

'Leave it to me,' Harry says. 'I'll let you know when I'm ready.'

Ben walks out of the door with Ishtar by his side.

'You have a lot of grieving to do, don't you, Harry?' Fien says.

'It was never going to be forever,' Harry says. 'I was lucky. She … she was very kind to me, to let me be part of her, to love something of me.' He runs his hands along where he once must have had hair. 'I'm not much to look at, I know, but she looked at me.' His lips quiver. He takes a deep breath. 'Enough,' he says. 'We need to move on.'

'Do you want me to stay with you?' Fien says.

Harry shakes his head. 'The boy needs you more than I do. My race is run now. Yours is just starting.'

'Why does everyone think Ben and I will be together?'

'Because it feels right, because he's mad about you.'

'I think he has other things on his mind right now.'

'And you need him,' Harry says. 'To remind you of how strong you are.'

'I'm not just a little girl, you know.'

'That's exactly what I just said. Let the other little girl be his sister. You're like Lil, you know.' He comes across to her, puts his hands on her shoulders. 'Whatever you do, do it for yourself,' he says. 'Do it because your guts tell you to, and don't ever let anyone tell you any different.' He plants a bristly kiss on her cheek. 'Now go. Let me do this last thing for Lil on my own.'

Fien kisses his hairy cheek, hugs him. 'Thank you.'

Dusk is approaching when Harry emerges from the cabin. He jumps up the stairs to where Ben is holding the wheel on the quarterdeck. 'She's ready,' he says.

Ben nods. 'Anchor,' he calls, his voice a little tremulous.

Harry smiles at him. 'That's the way.'

When *The Odyssey* has stopped moving, Harry and Ben disappear into the cabin. Fien rings the ship's bell. The men gather, form two lines each side of the door. Harry and Ben come out again, carrying between them a final funeral bier fashioned from some of the oak shelves that hung from the walls in Lil's room, and on top of it, a sheet of bright white linen, wrapped around a human shape. Nothing adorns the sheet. This is simplicity. They carry the bier to the ship's edge, rest it on the railings, still holding it tight.

'We're here to say farewell to our Commandant,' Ben says, his voice now strong. 'Farewell to Red Lil, to our friend and leader. May we always remember her rages, her kindnesses, and her honesty.' He nods at Harry.

'We are wedded to the sea, all of us,' Harry says. 'With these last words, let us rejoice in Lil's union with the oceans. With our hearts and minds let us commit her to the sea forever.'

Ben and Harry gently incline the bier, and Lil's body begins slowly to slide from it. And then it's gone, with a swift drop to the waterline and a subdued splash. The crew line the side of the ship, and make salutes of their own. The sea closes over the white sheet, and it's done.

Fien thinks she can see Lil's shape spiralling down through the blue water. And then her tears come. For Lil, for her father, for everything she's lost. She clings to the railing, wants never to leave this spot, wants to be dead, wants to stop feeling. She closes her eyes. When she opens them again, the sun has disappeared.

Chapter 20

Harry taps Fien on her shoulder. 'There's something I need to show you and the Commandant.'

'Can't it wait?'

'No, it can't,' he says. 'Ben's already waiting for us in his cabin.'

'I need to find somewhere else to sleep,' she says, not moving.

'We can fix that later.'

She follows him into the cabin, where Ben's standing next to the map table, all scrubbed and clean, and covered in maps again. The damage to the cabin has been repaired, roughly, and the shelves that were Lil's bier have been replaced, and the books put back on them. And still the cabin feels strangely empty.

Harry opens the table's top drawer and lifts out something wrapped in a cloth.

'What is it?' Fien says.

'That's what I want to know,' Harry says. 'I've never seen anything like it before.' He unfolds the cloth. A glint of gold, a nugget, its pointed end flattened. 'Bullets are round,' he says. 'Not sharp. But this is what I found inside her. A knife shot by gun powder.'

'Why didn't it go right through her?' Ben says.

'Muscle, distance, and her spine' Harry says. 'And if she hadn't stopped it, the ship would have.'

'Is it really a bullet?' Fien says. 'It looks like something from another world.'

'That's what worries me,' Harry says. 'What if it is?'

'Sorry?' Fien says. 'How could it be from another world?'

'The clock,' Harry says. 'It's not just about immortality, is it? It's about travelling through time. And Lindsey has it.'

'For God's sake!' Fien's grief disappears under her

rage. 'Those are all just fairy tales. No-one's ever seen this watch take someone from this time to another. It's impossible.'

Harry stares at her. 'You can't deny this is a strange thing. You can't ignore that none of us have ever seen something like this before.'

'It could just be that someone has a very clever gunsmith who's been working on this forever, and who's finally found an answer to making a bullet travel a much longer distance than ever before.'

'Then why was that Lindsey's ship? And why did they kill Lil? And with a bullet that hasn't even been invented yet?' Harry picks up the bullet, runs his finger along the circular ridges that frame it. 'And one that rotates in the barrel before coming out?' He holds it between his thumb and his index finger, and frowns. 'That would make it fly straighter. And make it easier to hit the target.' He throws it onto the table. 'We have to go back. We have to get that clock. That's what this is all about. There's no other explanation.' He's at the door now. 'Think about it.' He closes the door gently and walks away outside.

Fien sinks down onto her bed, and holds her head in her hands. 'Say something,' she says to Ben, who's standing next to the table, fingering the bullet that killed his mother.

'I've been thinking,' he says, and sits down next to her. 'I might be her son, but I'm not her heir.'

'What do you mean?'

'I can't do this. I can't lead. This is a woman's ship, it always has been. This is your cabin, not mine.'

'This is Lil's cabin.'

He shakes his head. 'In the morning,' he says. 'We'll tell the crew that you're the Commandant, not me.'

'I know nothing about sailing ships or telling people what to do.'

'Me and Harry'll do the sailing. You just tell us where to go and what to do. And we'll do it.'

'I'm a coincidence.'

'Isn't that all we are, all of us?'

'You know what I mean.'

'I know exactly what you mean, and I'm glad you stumbled on us.'

'If Lindsey can travel through time, he could be anywhere.'

'Really?' He leans back against her legs without realising, and doesn't recoil. 'If Lil was what he wanted to get rid of, he still doesn't know you exist, so why would he leave this time again? He's got what he wants. And now he can gather all the riches he needs to keep his king happy.'

She likes the pressure of his back against her legs, and doesn't move away. 'It can't be that simple, can it?'

'I think it can. He thinks he's eliminated the one person who could beat him, and now he has free reign. He'll be sailing back to England.'

'And where are we headed?' Fien says.

'Back to the island. We could go anywhere from there.' He sits up straight again, and misses her warmth against him. 'We could either drift around the oceans waiting for more pirates to rob, or we could find Lindsey and take the clock back, and stop him from using the future to make him stronger.'

'I still don't believe that a simple clock can do that.'

'Then the best thing to do is to get the clock and prove to yourself it's nothing more than an overpriced lump of emerald and mechanics.'

She reaches for his hand. 'Is that really want you want? Not to own your mother's ship, not to lead a crew of good men, not to be in charge?'

He returns her touch and nods. 'I can think of nothing better. I've never been very forward.'

'What if I'm useless?' Her heart's beating faster, and she's not sure if it's because of the gift he's making her, or because of his hand in her hand.

'Then Harry will tell you that you're being useless. And he'll teach you to be better.'

'Then we'll go to England,' she says. 'But not London. That's where Lindsey would expect us to go, where he'd expect Lil's revengeful crew to go to find him. We need to find another way in.' She gets up and walks to the map table, shuffles the papers that are piled on it now. She thinks of Lil lying there a few hours ago and has to stop herself from feeling ill, from letting the grief infect her thinking. She spreads out a map of England, flattens it down with her hand. 'Come here,' she says. 'Explain these markings to me.'

'What do you need to know?' He's next to her now, watches the veins in her hand move as she points at the east coast of England.

'Water depths,' she says. 'I need to know which of these ports *The Odyssey* can land at. And I need to know how long it'll take us to get there.'

'I'll get Harry,' he says. 'He'll know better than me.'

While Ben's gone, Fien wanders around the room, her shadow huge against the walls in the light of the burning candles. She touches Lil's books, caresses the covers on Lil's bed, and finds a decanter of wine and a glass. She pours herself some of the red stuff, savouring its taste on her lips, down her throat. Tears run down her face, without sobs. 'I'll miss you,' she says into the vacant space. 'I already miss you. I'll always miss you.'

There's a knock at the door.

'Come in,' she says. 'There's no need to knock.'

'There is now,' Harry grunts. 'After what the boy's told me.'

'Stop being silly. We're equals, all of us.'

'Some of us are more equal than others,' Harry says.

'That's the way it is.'

'Whatever you want,' Fien says. 'There's no point arguing.'

'He says you want to know about water depths,' Harry says.

'Yes,' Fien says. 'There's no point trying to get in through a locked front door if the back door's wide open.'

Harry laughs. 'Quite right, girl … er … Commandant.'

'Fien will do, Harry.' She rubs her tired face. 'Girl will do, actually.'

Harry puts his big hand on the map. 'East or West?'

'East,' Fien says, pushes his paw to one side. 'Here. Aldeburgh. It's straight across the North Sea from Antwerp.'

'Ah,' Harry says. 'Lost birds always try to find their home.'

'I didn't know you were a poet.'

'I'm not. It's just the truth.'

'Can we land there?'

'Yes, we can,' Harry says. 'They build ships there. Lots of fishing, too, so we won't starve.'

'You don't think Lindsey would expect us to go there?'

Harry shakes his head. 'He needs somewhere close to London, so he's at the king's beck and call. Aldeburgh's too far away.'

'How long for us to get there?'

'Two months.'

'We'd better get a move on then,' Fien says. 'And let the boys have double rations of booze tonight, and three-hour watches.'

'Aye, aye,' Harry says.

146

Chapter 21

Two months don't ease grief. Time never heals.

The Odyssey trudges on in her journey across the oceans, around the continents, the tip of Africa, on the way to the island she visited on her outward journey for replenishment. The daily routines are the same as they ever were, as is the readiness for poor weather, attack, and salvage. Voices are subdued, jokes are fewer, reflection never far away from everyone's mind. The Commandant's cabin is the Commandant's cabin, and when she talks, everyone listens. There have been no grumbles about Ben withdrawing after less than a day in the post. In fact, a big cheer went up when he announced he was handing it over to Fien, because these men are used to being led by a woman, used to respecting a tall, wild woman, even if this one is almost still a child. But her eyes, those cold, blue eyes now, frighten them all, and they're sure, and Harry knows, that her temper is as short as Lil's was.

She hasn't had the courage, though, to talk to Ben about what everyone is saying, about how he's supposed to be in love with her. And he, similarly, has said nothing. They're been companionable, as they always have been, since that first day in Antwerp, though none of the levity of those first few weeks has remained. They've helped each other with their grief, have spent much time together in her cabin when their duties have allowed them to. But they haven't touched hands again since that first night after Lil's burial, have kept their distance, physically, and have kept their counsel. It's been easier that way.

Today, Fien's out on the quarterdeck, in the sun, a map in one hand, her other hand on Harry's shoulder. 'How much longer?' she says. 'We've not exactly got much water left.'

'A day,' Harry says. 'If the wind keeps driving us.'

'We'll stay there for a week this time.'

'Are you sure?'

'You and the men all need a rest. Time to be able to think without having to fight against the elements as well.'

'We're always happiest at sea.'

'I know that, Harry. But these months have been difficult for us all, and I want you all to be able to rest up. You're exhausted.' She squeezes his shoulder. 'And heartbroken.'

Harry shrugs. 'I'll have a long time to sleep when I'm dead.'

'Which I hope won't be for many years yet.' She takes the wheel. Since Gombroon, she's taken the wheel for at least four hours a day, always with Harry or Ben by her side, to try to learn to steer the ship as sensitively as Lil did, to try, not to become Lil, but to become at least as accomplished a sailor, so she can share the responsibility for safety with her men.

'Just keep that course,' Harry says. 'If the wind changes, shout.'

Fien manages to smile. 'Aye, aye, Harry. I'll do just that.' She stretches her neck into the breeze of travel, breathes it in deeply, the scent of sea and wood and freedom. Even before they reached Gombroon, she'd grown to love being at sea, being able to sense the endlessness of the water below and of the skies above in a way she never appreciated when she travelled with her father. She was a passenger then, she supposes, nothing more than a passenger, with no responsibilities, with nothing to do all day but read and look and listen. It's different now. The ship's company is her family.

That evening, just as she's about to hand the wheel over to one of her men, a cry comes from the Crow's Nest. 'Land ahoy. And smoke, straight ahead.'

'Say again,' she shouts.

'Land ahoy. Smoke dead ahead.'

'Anchor,' she calls. 'Stations.'

The ship explodes into a flurry of activity, now familiar to her, and comes to a stop almost as soon as she has called the commands. Harry and Ben rush up to the wheel. Fien grabs a telescope, looks dead ahead. Her face hardens as she takes the telescope away from her eye.

'We made good time,' she says. 'Since this morning. But it seems someone has beaten us to it.'

'What do you mean?' Ben says.

'The whole island,' Fien says. 'It's been on fire. That's where the smoke is coming from.'

'It can't be the whole island,' Ben says. 'You can't tell that from here.'

'Look for yourself.' She hands him the scope.

'I can't see the far side of it from here.'

'If a fire started there, what would you expect it to do?' she says, no emotion in her voice.

'Burn.' He lifts the telescope up again. 'But the river divides the place in half almost, and the fire'd be hard pushed to jump across it.

'I've got a bad feeling about this,' Fien says. 'We stay here until it's pitch black, and then I'll get the ship within rowing distance. I don't want us to land there until I'm sure it's not a trap.' She leans over the railing and looks down onto the lower deck. 'Have a rest, lads,' she says, in a low but crystal clear voice. 'We'll not do anything till after dark.'

The men disappear into the various nooks and crannies of shade *The Odyssey* offers, some just sitting down where they are and leaning against the ship that's their backbone, swaying with the swell. Others take off below deck, to catch up on some sleep in their hammocks, or to play cards or dice. The tumult of the sudden stop gives way to peace. The boards creak, in time with the ship's breathing.

Dark now, black now, the ship inching forwards without a single torch being lit. Fien, the wheel light in her hands, Harry behind her. Her first test. A real test. She doesn't have time to be nervous. The smell of burning reaches her before they're anywhere near the island. She trusts herself to take the ship further. The smoke is acrid, the stink of things being burned alive. But there are no flames.

'It's an old fire,' she whispers. 'Almost gone.'

Harry grunts his agreement. She's pushing on further than he'd have done. But he says nothing. This is her ship now, and she must know what she's doing. And he can't risk doubting her, or the whole crew will begin to doubt.

'Anchor,' she hisses, and turns the wheel hard to starboard.

The crush of the chain sounds violently loud in the silence.

'Wheel, Ben,' she says. 'Harry, with me, and Franz and Dirk.' She allows herself a smile of pride that she's memorised all their names, and knows all the faces to accompany them. 'Put the boat down.'

Ben wants to contradict, but he doesn't.

'You're here for insurance,' she says, guessing his thoughts. 'Someone to take over if …'

'No ifs,' Ben says.

She clambers down the rope ladder without effort, lets herself slip into the boat without a sound, kneels down in the bow. 'Nice and slowly.' She can feel the island there, somewhere ahead of her, somewhere close. She just can't see it. She stretches her arm out. There's no sign of any glow, no sign of anything still burning. Her gut aches with the intuition of something.

She wishes she knew what it is. She listens to the small sounds the oars make. The water's getting shallower. Her hand feels out ahead of her, and she holds her breath. There. That's land. 'Stop.'

They sit in silence for an age. Nothing. Not a single sound.

'There should be something,' Harry says into her ear. 'Some signs of life.'

'Not if it's all gone to hell,' Dirk mutters.

'He's right,' Franz says.

'I know that,' Harry says.

'Depends on whose hell,' Fien says. She levers herself over the side. Her feet touch the ground, and the water rises above her knees and seeps into her boots. She shrugs to herself.

They wade onto the shore, wet step by wet step, as slowly as they can, trying not to create a wake that will cause a splash. Once they feel sand under their boots, they crouch down.

'We stay together,' Fien says, the sweat running down her face. 'All the way. No separating. Understood?'

Three grunts in a different tone.

She thinks. If anyone was here, they'd expect her to stick to the shore, to circumnavigate the island, not to aim straight for the heart of it, through where the trees were, through the undergrowth, if there's any left. If her suspicions are right, there won't be any vegetation left to leave broken tracks on, just ash in which their footprints will be obvious, wherever they go, whichever direction they choose.

She leads on, into the strange silence, one of her knives in her hand, ready. Even though she's only been here once, she feels, like Lil once told her, what direction is the right one. The ash is soft under her feet, spongy almost. They reach the river too soon, no sign of anyone else on their way. She puts her hand into the water. It doesn't feel right, as if it's become thicker, as if something's been added to the water, to make it sluggish and warm, too warm to be fresh. 'This is bad,' she says, not sure if she's only thought it, and says it again.

'Heard you the first time, boss,' Franz says.

'Thanks for that.' She flops down onto the ground. 'It's a dead place.'

'Don't you want to search the rest of it?'

'There's no point. This wasn't the weather. Someone's done this. But we'll have to wait till the morning to find out what exactly they've done.'

'You don't want to go back to the ship till morning?' Harry says.

'That's a waste of time,' she says. 'We might learn something in the dark by just staying in one place.'

'Like dying of breathing smoke?'

'We won't,' she says. 'That's dying, too. We're a couple of days too late.'

'Too late for what?'

'To have stopped whatever it is that Lindsey's done.'

'You think it was him then?'

'I don't just think it. I know it. But how the hell did he beat us to here? We hit the bow of his ship.'

'Didn't sink it, though.'

'Maybe we should've turned round right then,' she says, although she knows they wouldn't have had the heart to, with Lil sprawled dead and broken on the deck while they were running for their lives.

'That's silly talk,' Harry says.'

'Aye,' Dirk and Franz say.

'Might as well get some rest,' Harry says. 'The boys will take first watch.'

'Sounds fair,' Dirk says. 'Two hours?'

'Yes,' Fien says. 'Thanks.' Even so, she doesn't sleep and is wide awake when her it's time for her and Harry to keep watch. At least the ground has been soft enough for her to rest.

'You really think Lindsey did this?' Harry says.

'Can you think of any other explanation?'

'No.'

'How did you meet Lil?'

'Oh, that's not a story for a burned-out island. That's a story for a long night in an inn and several casks of wine.'

'Give me the short story, and save the details for another day.'

'A long time ago. The boy was only about three.'

'Fifteen years ago? I didn't realise that.'

'I was on one of those ships she, erm, salvaged.'

'You were a pirate.'

'Well, sort of, I suppose.'

'And?'

'And I got pulled out of the water, and had to stand in front of the most fierce beautiful woman I'd ever met. She had long hair then, down to her waist. Glorious red. I knew then I wasn't good enough for her.'

'But you were, obviously.'

Harry scratches his beard. 'Well, erm, that took a while. I think she'd got a bit bored of finding something new everywhere we landed, so she just picked on one of us.'

'That sounds awful.'

Harry coughs. 'Not really. She was a free spirit, like you know. She chose what would happen when. We men do it, so why shouldn't she?'

'You give yourself no credit at all.'

'There's no credit to give an old bald man.'

'What happened?'

'She called me into her cabin one night. The boy was asleep behind a wall she'd built of books. We were at anchor somewhere far down south. Cold it was, cold as the devil. And she said to me that we had something in common. And I said, what do you mean? We're both too kind, deep down, she said. I remember it like it was yesterday.' He sniffs. 'And I asked her what she meant. You spend a lot of time with the boy, she said, and he needs it. I thought she'd rescued or stolen him from somewhere at first, you see. And then she told me he was hers, and that she was going to have to bring him up like he wasn't.

'And it's cold tonight, she said. And that she liked a beard she might keep her hands warm in. That was it, really.'

'Didn't any of the boys ask any questions?'

'You didn't ask the Commandant any questions if you knew what was good for you. She'd stop being nice then, you see. And, like she said that night, it wasn't anyone else's business, and no-one else would ever know or dare say anything.'

'And you never had a child of your own?'

'We were too clever for that. It would've been a really bad idea.'

'And I stopped you from being with her when I came aboard.'

'No, Fien, no. Ways and means, ways and means.' He chuckles.

'You should have married her.'

'Ah, not the marrying kind was our Lil. Faithful, though. I'd trust her to the end of the world and back.' He sighs. 'I'll kill the bastard.'

'Not if I get him first.'

'You take the clock. I'll take him.'

'We need to get to him first,' Fien says. 'If we're still alive.' *If there's any water*, she thinks.

Chapter 22

When Fien wakes, she realises she must have fallen asleep against Harry's shoulder. She mumbles an apology.

'It doesn't matter,' he says, gives her a quick hug. 'The boys are still asleep.'

First light is creeping through the smoke that lingers like fog. Fien's eyes take time to adjust. She gasps, stands up, and turns a full circle. 'Impossible,' she says.

The forest has disappeared, in all directions. There's nothing but a black remnant of what once was luxuriant and dense foliage. Even the thickest tree trunks have been reduced to blackened stumps. She falls onto her knees and looks at the water. It's slime, thick black slime with strands of red drifting along it. 'We have to find the spring,' she says to Harry, goes to wake the other two.

Close together, the four of them move against the slow, almost non-existent current of the stream. Finally, the sun high in the sky beyond the drifting smog, they find the source of the stream. Piled high around the place where the water exits the earth, are the charred remains of dead animals; deer, wild boar, birds. Nature raped and mistreated. Harry uses his sword to push the bodies to one side. He stops, suddenly.

'He's stooped low,' he growls.

'Let me see,' Fien says.

'He's killed some of his own and let them pour their fester into the water, too.'

'How do you know he killed them? They might have been ill.'

'I've not heard of people removing the heads of the accidentally dead before,' Harry says.

Fien looks over his shoulder. It's like a butcher's been at work, and has started stuffing all his work's limbs

155

into the smallest mincer he can find. She retches, breathes deeply to recover herself. 'Poor bastards.'

'Don't feel too sorry for them,' Franz says. 'They decided to be with him.' He picks up a scrap of red uniform. 'All for the king.' He laughs bitterly. 'We got away lightly.'

Fien's mind is racing. 'We need water,' she says.

'Well, we ain't finding it here,' Dirk says. 'We've got about two weeks' worth left on board. We'll have to find somewhere else to get some.'

'There isn't anywhere else,' Harry says, glum. 'Not till we're much closer to England.'

'Then what about just hauling in to the coast?' Dirk says.

'Too risky.'

'How about not going to England at all?' Franz says. 'There must be somewhere else we can put into.'

'We need to get to England if we're going to catch Lindsey,' Fien says. 'Don't you want to pay him back for what he did to Lil?'

'We won't be able to do anything if we're dead,' Franz says.

Fien sticks her booted toe into the morass of ash and blood that's now running into the stream. She rubs her cheeks, runs her hands through her hair. 'Would this work? Digging into the ground further back, behind the bodies and the hole, to see if we can find the stream underground and get water from it before it even gets to this charnel house?'

'I don't know how long that would take,' Harry says. 'Or if it would work. And we're not exactly overloaded with food.'

'We can fish, can't we?' Fien says. 'If we give ourselves two days to dig, we'll have twelve days' water left, some meat, and whatever we manage to fish. If we don't find anything after two days, we sail on and try to find somewhere else, as long as it's not on the mainland.'

The men shrug. It's not their decision.

'And another thing,' she says. 'We take one of the sails down and use it to catch rain water. That should help us, too.'

'If there's any rain. It's nearly May.'

'Worth taking the chance, though, even if we only get one more cup of water from it.'

They walk the entire island. Nothing but dead trees, dead animals, thick ash.

'He was going to make sure, wasn't he?' Fien says to Harry. 'He knew about this place.'

'We were never the only ones.'

'So he's decided to destroy it for everyone including himself.'

'He's got half an army with him, so he can put in anywhere he wants without having to worry about word spreading or about getting ambushed. He's on the king's errand anyway, or at least that's what he'll say.' Harry crashes his right fist into the palm of his left hand. 'We're going to have to be a damned sight cleverer than him.'

'We are,' Fien says, softly. 'Just too slow in our grief, and that's what he's been counting on.'

'That clock must be helping him, somehow.'

'There's nothing I can do about that until we've caught up with him.'

They get back to where they left the rowing boat the night before. No sign of any other human presence. Fien can just make out the silhouette of *The Odyssey* in the far distance.

'Go get the other boat and some more of the crew with tools we can use to dig out the stream,' she says. 'I'll wait here.'

Harry raises an eyebrow.

'One of the boys can stay with me if you think that's safer,' Fien says.

Harry nods. 'Dirk, stay with her, eh?'

'Aye aye.'

'Harry,' Fien says. 'Thanks. We'll go back and start moving those bodies.'

'No,' Harry says. 'Just stay here. I don't want anyone else touching them. God knows what's in 'em now. That's why I used my sword.' He pulls it out of his belt, holds it under water for some time. 'We'll start digging at least 10 minutes walk east of them.'

'We might miss the stream then.'

'We'll see, Fien, we'll see. Let's be safe first, eh? Not as foolhardy as Lil could be sometimes. Yes?'

Fien nods. 'How did she put up with you always being right?'

'She didn't.'

The two days they've given themselves to find fresh water fly by in a blur of digging, changing shifts, letting one team of men go back to the ship to wash in the sea and find shelter and shade on the ship while the other carries on the search.

'It's useless,' Harry says. 'It just comes from nowhere.'

'That's impossible,' Fien says. 'And you know it is.'

They are the only two to have spent the entirety of days and nights on the island, and their faces are black, as are their hands and Fien's hair, their eyes white beyond white in that mess of dirt.

'We're twenty foot down, and the trench is fifty feet long, if not more.'

'Why haven't we gone deeper?'

'Where would we do that? It's like finding half a needle in a thousand hay stacks.'

Fien jumps up. 'Hang on, hang on. Is it soil all along the trench? Or have you hit any rock yet?' She starts walking back to the start of the trench. 'Ten minutes walk from those dead things is too far.' She puts her hand against Harry's chest. 'Stay here,' she says. 'Don't you dare follow.'

'Fien.'

'It's an order, Harry.'

She stomps off until she can see the pile of death, and draws a mark in the ground with the heel of one of her boots. She can hear the slime crawl into the stream from here. She lies down on her stomach and watches the ground rise until it flattens again towards the beginning of the trench. *It has to come from somewhere*, she thinks. *Underground. Rock splits. That's it!* 'Harry!' she yells. 'Harry! Get here now.'

Harry's out of breath when he reaches her. 'Dear God, girl, I thought something had happened.'

'Go back to the ship. Bring as much gun powder as we can spare, and lots of spare cannon fuses.' She points at the dome of ash. 'There'll be rock under there,' she says. 'That's where we'll find it, where it splits the rock.'

'It's all gibberish to me.'

'Trust me,' she says. 'I'm just sorry I didn't think of it before.' She calls the team of men across, and helps them clear the ash and soil from the raised land. They have to dig a yard down before they hit rock. 'Look for cracks,' she says. 'Some hole we can make deeper by chipping away at it before Harry gets back.'

'Here,' Franz calls. 'The hole's at last a foot deep already, and there's cracks all around it.'

'Good man,' Fien says. Let's see if we can chip away into it.'

By the time Harry gets back, the hole is a few inches deeper, and slightly wider than a man's fist.

'Now, this is the advantage of never having seen the real world,' Fien says. 'Reading about gun powder and explosions. Let's stuff that hole full of pebbles and gunpowder while someone joins all these fuses into one long one.'

Soon afterwards, they have finished, and Fien sticks one end of the new fuse into the hole full of powder, unfolds it a full thirty feet, to the furthest edge of the trench. 'You lot,' she says. 'Get as far away as you can. Go lie in the water. You, too, Harry. Go, go.'

When she's sure they're where she told them to be, she gets a firebox from her pocket, strikes it and watches the spark jump away along the fuse. She lets herself fall into the trench. Five seconds later, the island is rocked by a massive explosion. Fien lies there, covered in dust and rubble, and the gentle mist of falling water.

When the cheering's over, when Harry has wrapped her into his bear hug, and his beard has tickled her face until she's collapsed laughing, she orders them to bring the ship as close to the shore as they can, to bring every container they can find and fill it from this new fountain of water, gushing from a hole they can't now stop, saturating the burned ground with clear, sweet wetness, maybe the promise of new life.

For two days, they search the island, to see if they can find something other than them that's alive, hoping to find at least a pair of birds that can mate to keep the island breathing. But they find nothing.

'It's depressing,' Ben says. 'Whoever did this knew what they were doing.'

'Four bonfires; one at each edge,' Fien says. 'Yes, he knew what he was doing. Killing us.'

'He didn't reckon with your reading.'

She shrugs. 'Who knows? Maybe all he wanted was to delay me, not kill me.'

'What will we do about this place?'

She takes his hand without thinking, and puts it

against her cheek hot from the sun. 'When all this is over, we'll come back with some birds, and some deer. Maybe a couple of pairs of wild boar, too. And we'll live here until everything is plentiful again.'

'You're joking, aren't you?'

She shakes her head. 'Why should I be?'

'We'd need to live on something.'

She punches him in the chest. 'We'll work that out when the time comes. God, you're so bloody unimaginative.'

'I was just being practical.'

'I know. That's the problem.' She kicks at the ash. 'For both of us.'

'Meaning?'

'Everything and nothing.' She walks away from him, her arms busy. 'You know what I mean.'

'I can guess, but I don't want to guess.'

'We'll talk about it when I've got the clock.'

'Oh, so now you do believe us.'

'It's not a question of believing,' she says. 'It's a question of being practical and narrowing down the possibilities.'

'So you do think Lindsey has got it and that it's giving him some sort of advantage.'

'That's about it. I'll leave the superstitions to you and Harry.'

'It's not superstition.'

'There's no proof until I have the watch. That's all.'

'Fien.' His call is almost plaintive.

She turns, her hands on her hips, her hair bright in the sun, almost blinding, almost a halo. 'What?'

'What do they say to you about us?'

'Harry keeps telling me you're in love with me.' There, she's said it, and she wishes she hadn't.

Ben blushes. 'He keeps telling me the same about you.'

'Oh, really?' She clenches her fists.

'Don't go shouting at him.'

'Why not?'

'He's not trying to match make.'

'He wouldn't be able to anyway,' she says. 'I know my own mind.'

'And what does your mind say?'

'It says that it doesn't know what to think.' She spreads her arms. 'What if all this only makes us think we're in love with each other, because there's no-one else to fall in love with? Adversity throws people together, and then they throw each other apart when there's nothing else to fight against.'

'So you do think you love me?'

She looks at him, stares at him with those blue eyes that can be cold one moment and hot as liquid sapphire the next. 'What do you think?'

Chapter 23

The watch is in his hands. He can hardly bear to hold it. Some of his fingers are broken, and the blood from his wounds seeps through the straw onto the wooden floor he's lying on. The cage he's in is at the very bottom of this rocking ship, and he can hear the rats scurry across the boards in the darkness. He hopes for death, but he's sure it won't come. Because of the clock. Why did she have to give it to him? Why, when she could have survived, when she could have lived, did she wrap it in a letter and bequeath it to him, and, with that simple act of love sign her own death warrant? He shakes his head. She would have been much more capable of looking after their daughter, of protecting her and keeping her from harm. Now he doesn't know where she was, not after he'd pushed her down the stairs into the cellar of their house when they'd both seen Lindsey and his men outside. At least Lindsey hasn't got her, at least he has no idea of her.

This latest beating has been the worst of them all. Lindsey still hadn't dared touch the clock, superstitious man that he is, and focused instead all his brute force and violence on the man who held it. Perhaps he should just have let him smash it, so that its blessing and its curse would be broken forever. But he knows that Lindsey wants it as a gift, that Lindsey hankers after the immortality the watch is supposed to give. And that's why Lindsey won't just stick a knife in his heart and take the watch, because then it would be useless.

The pain in his chest grows worse. More broken ribs. He sighs and tries to move himself into a more comfortable position on the straw sodden with blood and sweat. He regrets using the clock to give Lindsey a vision of the future, to let him gather enough knowledge to make that gun that carries a bullet further than any gun should, the knowledge to make a pointed bullet that rotates in the barrel to allow a true aim. He regrets allowing himself to be dragged on deck to watch Lindsey shoot that pirate in the back, wishes he'd shaken his head away from the sight of the pirate's back exploding and showering blood on the ship's crew helping him aboard. He should just have closed his eyes. Too late now, too late for everything.

In the darkness, the warmth of the clock is even more noticeable. The strap around his neck has broken so many times now it's just a collection of knots where he's mended it, and about half as long as it was the day Lindsey came to get him. He's just about to nod off and forget his pain when the clock begins to vibrate. To begin with, it's just a slight shiver of movement. Within seconds it gathers enough force to fully wake him, to make him sit up, despite the hurt, to undo the strap and hold it in his hands again. There's a light shining up against the translucent lid that covers the clock's dial. Streams of light from the emerald numbers converge into a whirlpool at the very centre of the dial. He shivers.

He hesitates before he opens the lid, and the light shoots up and fills the whole room. At the same time, a spiral of colours rises from the whirlpool of brightness and anchors itself to the floor, a twisting column, a puzzle of an image, until it settles. His mouth hangs open as he begins to understand what he's seeing. His daughter, her hair hanging free, a dazzling yellow, with her arms around an olive-skinned man, her lips on his lips, an undeniable look of love on both their faces. He reaches out to the image, so real he feels he should be able to touch it, but his hand goes straight through it. The clock has never done this before. Not shown him the present. How does it know his daughter? He starts to cry, wipes away the tears, looks for anything that might tell him where she is. But there's nothing except for a blue sky, and a few black, burned-looking tree stumps. It could be anywhere. At least she's alive.

He hears heavy footsteps coming down the ladder outside the cage. He snaps shut the lid of the clock as quickly as he can, hopes the light disappears just as quickly, ties the strap back around his neck as well as he can in the dark, hides the clock back in his grubby shirt, and lies back down on the hard floor, curls up into as small a shape as he can, the position of a man in pain.

A flickering torch throws its guttering light in a small circle around the man carrying it. 'You awake yet, Brants?' the voice behind the light says. 'You should be. I've got some more work for you to do.'

Chapter 24

Never before has Fien felt like this. She shivers when Ben kisses her, and kisses him back, hard, to escape those shivers and the feeling of guilt at being alive. Tears run down her face.

Ben pulls away. 'What have I done?'

'It's not you. I'm thinking about my father. And Lil. And I feel bad for being happy, for wanting to kiss you.'

He says nothing, just strokes her face. 'We'll get through this, all of us.'

'We're going to have to keep this secret, you know that, don't you?'

He nods.

'And no creeping up into my room at the dead of night.'

'There'll be a watch on the quarterdeck anyway.'

'You know what I mean.'

'I know what you mean.'

She blushes at the thought of what she's going to say. 'I don't know anything about love and all the things it involves. Lil laughed at me about it, said I should find out sooner rather than later.'

'I'm no different.' He smiles. 'When you have the clock.'

'When *we* have the clock.'

A gentle cough interrupts them. 'We should be going,' Harry says. 'Tide's at its best, and it's a long way home.'

Fien, for once, doesn't blush. 'And you boys can learn to make nets and start fishing,' she says. 'Because we're not stopping on the way.'

Six weeks without storms. This surprises even Harry.

'I don't like it,' he says.

'Why?' Fien says.

'It's just not right,' he says. 'There's something brewing.'

'Do you mean Lindsey or the weather?'

'The weather, mainly. I'll worry about Lindsey when we've made land safely.'

'You worry too much.'

'Someone has to.' He has dark rings under his eyes by now, although Fien has told him he should take more than his fair share of rest.

'Are you sure you're alright?'

'That question's never helped anyone who worries, girl,' he says. 'Best just to let me get on with it. Plenty of rest ahead.'

'But nothing to make up for the emptiness.'

'Oh, I dunno,' he says. 'Maybe I'll find myself some empty-headed country wench.'

'You don't mean that, and you know it.'

He smiles a tired smile. 'I can always pretend.'

'You can,' she says. 'But I'll know you're lying.'

'Aldeburgh in two weeks. We'll see land in one. And then we need to have our wits about us.'

'We will,' she says. 'We will. I want us to anchor out of sight of land for two days so we can all be fresh, and so we've got all hands on deck when we need them, and not a tired one amongst them.'

'Aye aye,' he says. 'You'll make a great captain yet.'

'You mean I'm not one already?'

'Too much cooking, teaching, and nursemaiding for that.'

As if she'd heard them, Ishtar grabs Fien's hand, starts pulling her towards the steps down to the lower deck.

'What is it, girl?' Fien says, sounding to herself like Lil did all that time ago.

'I want to show you something.'

'Can't it wait?'

Ishtar shakes her head, hair even wilder than when

167

they rescued her.

'Alright, but only a few minutes.'

Back in the room she now shares with Ishtar, Fien sits down, puts her booted feet up on a table. 'Show me then.'

'Close your eyes first.'

Fien does as she's asked. When she opens them again, Ishtar has put an old book on a table about two yards from the far end of the room, on a table, spine facing forward. Ishtar walks to the other end of the room, swings her arms around until she is red in the face.

'Is that it?' Fien says.

'No. I'm just getting warm.'

'Ah.'

'I've watched you with your knives.'

'Yes?'

'And I found some.' She pulls two curved daggers from her belt.

'Are they from the galley?'

Ishtar shakes her head. 'It's a secret.'

'You haven't stolen them, have you?'

Ishtar shakes her head again.

'I think I know who's behind this.'

'Don't be angry.'

'I'm not,' Fien says. 'Just tell me you're not going to use that book as a target.'

'Not really.'

'What does that mean?'

'Watch.' And she throws the first dagger in a way Fien's never seen a knife thrown.

The silver blade hurtles at the book, misses it by a fraction, but, instead of smashing into the wall behind it, curves around in the air, flies round the book and flashes back towards Ishtar who catches it by the handle.

'How the hell did you do that?' Fien says. 'It's

impossible.'

'It's taken me a long time to get it right. I had to wear gloves to start with.'

'You could have killed yourself.'

'Not really,' Ishtar says. 'I can always get out of the way.'

'Not if you throw the knife too hard.'

Ishtar shrugs. 'It works.'

'How long for is what worries me.'

'Trust me.'

'Knives round corners. Whatever next? Tell Ben I'm very impressed.'

'It wasn't Ben who gave them to me.'

Fien laughs. 'Aha, now I see. So much for me doing too much nursemaiding.'

Back on the quarterdeck, she elbows Harry in the side. 'Nice knives,' she says. 'Very nice. And I guess you taught her that trick as well, did you?'

Harry points at himself. 'Me?' He laughs. 'What trick?'

'I'll let her show you herself.'

'Land ahoy.' Ben likes it in the Crow's Nest. He can see the cliffs in the distance. The south-westerly is driving *The Odyssey* nicely into the narrow gap between England and France north-eastward. They need to stay right in the middle of it, try to, anyway, and try to avoid contact with any other ships. They just look like a trading vessel, anyway. He clambers down the mast, making way for the next watch, and heads into the Commandant's cabin.

'So what do we think Lindsey is doing right now?' Fien says to Harry. 'If he knew we were going to go the island, where does he think we'll go next?'

'The island was an obvious guess for him. The only thing I don't understand is how he got there before us.'

'Maybe he invented something else new, just like the

gun that killed Lil,' Ben says. 'Something to make him go quicker.'

'Or he bent time,' Ishtar says.

They all look at her.

'What are you talking about?' Harry says.

'There are legends about time benders in our country. People who can make time go more slowly for themselves but move at normal speed, which really makes everyone else go much more slowly.'

'Oh God,' Fien says. 'Immortality clocks, guns that shouldn't exist, time benders.' She stares at Ishtar. 'Shouldn't I have read about these somewhere in all that reading my father got me to do?'

'Maybe he didn't get you to read enough,' Ishtar says.

'Or just the wrong books,' Ben says.

Fien shakes her head, suddenly serious in all the laughter. 'None of those. What I read taught me about all those things. I just couldn't believe they were real. I still can't believe they are. When we touch things ...' She puts her hand heavily on the armrest of the chair she sits in. 'When we touch things that are part of our lives every day, physical things, we can't believe there's any force other than science that governs them. Everything else is supernatural, spiritual, imagined.'

'Didn't the book teach you anything about believing in things that lie outside this world, things there's no explanation for?' Ben says.

'Not really. When you're reading in an empty space, with nothing else to compare with what you're reading, it's all abstract, it's make-believe. Everything becomes a fairy tale.'

Harry thumps his massive fist down onto the map table. 'And while you're all busy philosophising, the clouds are gathering.'

'What's that supposed to mean?' Ben says.

'It means look out of the bloody window and see why

we've not had a storm for seven weeks. It means get the hell out of these chairs and onto deck and get those sails down.' He's already out of his chair and out of the door, and shouting at the crew.

Fien rushes up to the wheel, pushes Harry out of the way. 'I'll deal with it.'

'Then stop thinking about things you can't touch.'

'I wasn't. I was trying to say exactly what you think.'

'There's never any time to talk, girl. You have to be doing instead.'

'That's not as easy as it sounds. It's not what I was brought up to do.'

'Poor excuse. Lil would tell you exactly the same.'

'I know. But I can't find my way between the two as easily as you.'

'I never had to choose. Maybe that's to my advantage.' Harry runs his fingers through his beard. 'And now Mother Nature's choosing to push the wind between that bloody island on your left and that great rock on your right. And to stick it right up your arse.'

'That last bit was unnecessary.'

'Sorry.' Harry turns and looks up at the sky. 'Here it comes.'

The sails are down, but the wind catches *The Odyssey* nevertheless, tries to turn her side-on, tries to catch her unawares and vulnerable, so it can turn her over, drive her, keel uppermost, against the rocks that line both sides, the island and Europe, separated only by the narrow gap in between that probably didn't exist when the world was made. The waves heave their weight against the ship, and she tries to resist, creaking and groaning.

Fien spits and shouts, the swirling wind driving the rain into her face, her hair, finding the gaps in the clothes she's wearing, soaks her right down into her bones, until she almost can't remember what it is to be dry. She remembers the way Lil steered the ship, not with her hands clutched around the spokes of the wheel, but nothing but fingertips on them, gentle, understanding, sensing the ship's emotions, drawing its spirit out of the wood into her very being.

Wave after wave thrashes her from behind, throws hundredweights of water over her head. Visibility is almost nothing, too dangerous to drop the anchor. Too risky to call a halt to their advance, in the middle of this channel, where any ship could be one of Lindsey's, where any ship could be that of a pirate, out for a quick profit and some other quick pleasures. Being an independent woman isn't simple, never an easy path to tread, even if it's not a badge she chooses to wear. She is, in her own mind, just a person, the same as everyone else. And, as the wheel turns, she can't understand why it should be any different.

Each and every one of the crew is on deck now. The wind is so strong, the ship is skittering from one side to the other. Fien hears the cargo shift and strain against its restraints down below. Is it time to throw all those riches over the side to save the ship and its company? Her fingers sense another huge wave coming behind them. There's nowhere to hide from this storm, no way to protect her family from this one singular wave. She closes her eyes and lets go of the wheel. There is nothing more she can do. *I trust you*, she whispers to *The Odyssey*, to Lil, still alive in every grain of this bending, hissing, groaning, shattering wood. She holds her arms open wide. *If this is what you want.*

The wave hits and the world starts spinning. Up is down, and down is up. The pictures of Ben's words spring into her mind, wherever those words are, probably buried with Lil, sinking still, somewhere in the Southern Ocean, for the fish to feast on. The world is nothing but a spiral of confused shades of grey; fog and rain and sea and mist and wind and screaming and whistling and the ropes slapping against the sodden wood and men stumbling and men crying and tumbling and trying to stop themselves from being thrown from the very boards they love and live on. A kaleidoscope of surviving, of fighting against what will always be greater than men or women.

Fien grabs a rope that dangles next to her, at the third or fourth attempt. She wraps it around her right arm, and feels, immediately, the burn it inflicts on her as it drags her this way and that. The wheel, spinning out of control, smashes into her knee, and she hears the crack and feels the insurgent pain, understands there's nothing she can do about it, understands that now's the time to catch the wheel again, to right the ship, to turn it back the right way so that up is up, uncomprehending of how they're still alive, of how they've managed not to lose any of the men striving as hard as she to live through this rain-sodden hell of a homecoming.

She puts her hands into the spinning wheel, wills her knuckles not to break, catches it, wrestles with it, her fingers burning, her skin stripping away, the wood become harsh and bitter with the rain and the wind, braces her legs, even with the stricken knee, until she has a hold, and watches the deck straighten and bear straight, and the dark clouds shoot past her eyes, hardly any higher than her flowing hair, until they're in calm again. She wipes her face with her soaked shirt. She doesn't see or feel that final wave that sweeps her overboard and into the dark waters of England.

Chapter 25

Falling, falling. Her eyes are open, and she can't see. Her eyes are closed, and she can see. The cold water such a relief after the hot journey, she wants to bathe in it forever. An end to pain, an end to suffering. Down, down, down, to the welcoming bed of the sea. Swim back to Lil, swim back to her mother's womb, be immersed again in the water she can breathe. Back to father and mother, to see them again, to be with them again, to feel safe, to never be afraid again, to never have to fight again.

Bubbles drift from her mouth as she speaks to them all; to her mother, her father, to Lil, as holds her hands out to them, asks them to take her and guide her, to lead her down into the lightless depths of another life. It's all she wants. It's all she needs. Her hair, jellyfish tentacles, Man O'War spikes, floats upwards from her scalp, white in green, alive on its own for once, while she drifts further away from the surface, from her ship, from life.

And then she wakes, red hot blades in her mouth and throat, a panic for life, and tries to claw her way up out of the water. No breath, no breath. Silt shoots up past her face, past her eyes, eyes straining at their sockets, no sense of direction, green, all green, and dark, and no light above and none below.

Ben's the first to leap over the side, bootless, shirtless, head first into the quieting storm water. He hits the surface, cuts through it with his hands, pushes himself deeper and deeper. He looks around, peers through the fronds of whatever lives there, and can't see her. He pushes on, afraid of the sea, afraid for her, and his lungs empty in tiny bubbles. One more effort, and he's done, turns for the surface, giving up, giving in, salt tears in salt water, doubts he's able to save himself, leaps up hard. And then he sees it, the flash of the yellow-white mane, the dangling, trailing arms and legs, the gossamer strands of water clinging to cloth and flesh, the hard stomach outlined, and the stiff nipples of cold and death.

Vision fading, he stretches stretches for her, his senses bursting, his arm breaking, touches her finger tips, wrinkled and drawn already after these few seconds in the water, the shock wave of that final storm surge still roaring above, and grabs her hand. He pulls her to him, puts his arm round her waist, and drags the two of them up, up, up. His eyes close just as light appears above him.

'There they are,' Ishtar screams, pointing at vague shapes in the water.

Harry throws himself in, along with two of the others. Ishtar's still screaming, but they can't understand what she's saying. They duck underneath the nervous water towards the shapes, find them more by feel than vision, grasp at their limp limbs, pull them upwards hard, all thoughts of gentleness now gone. The ladder drops down the side of the ship, and Fien and Ben are manhandled onto the deck, the same place where Lil fell, the same spread-eagled figure, both of them. Just no blood.

Harry pushes down on Fien's chest, crossing himself before he does, and Franz does the same for Ben. Up, down, push, pump, listen, hope. Nothing. Go again. Push, pump, listen. Harry ignores Fien's shape.

Ishtar, quick as silver, darts to Fien, longest under the water, puts her fingers into Fien's mouth, pulls out her tongue and a palm full of seaweed, pushes her own mouth over Fien's, pushes her breath into Fien's throat. Next to her, Ben coughs, vomits the North Sea onto The Odyssey's planks, turns over, and stares at Ishtar.

'Please,' he mouthes. 'Please.' He can't move.

Exhaustion grips him, and he faints.

Ishtar, in time with Harry's busy hands, keeps breathing into Fien, losing any hope, lungs exploding, eyes tearing with the effort.

Fien's eyes flutter. Her mouth quivers, her lips pull back and show her teeth. Her hair is spread out on the boards, a soaked halo. Water begins to leak from her mouth, quicker and quicker, more and more, until a final rush tinged with red cascades over Ishtar's hands.

'Breathe,' Ishtar screams. 'Breathe, damn you.'

A cough, a hoarse, base howl, scrapes up Fien's throat and out of her mouth. Her eyes open and close, her arms and legs thrash around the deck, stamping on the wood, and clawing at the splinters. Harry tries to calm her, to bring her back to consciousness, his huge hands, calm and slow, holding her down, finally.

Peace.

Fien and Ben lie, face-to-face, on the drenched deck. No movement except for the slow rise and fall of their chests. They open their eyes at the same time, sigh at the same time. 'Thank you.' At the same time.

'Thank fuck for that.' Harry, still on his knees, lets himself topple forwards, face onto the boards, takes an age to turn and sit up, pulls his knees up to his chest. 'Can we get on with it now, please?'

Ishtar laughs, claps her hands, runs rings round the two rescued ones and Harry, yells his curse out loud for all to hear, without knowing what a curse it is. She holds her hand out to Fien, grabs her, pulls her up, ignoring her red face and coughing and shivers. 'Get on with it. Get on with it.'

Fien struggles to stand up, tries to speak, but no words will come out of that throat burned by the salt water. She just signals for the sails to go up again, for the ship to move forwards, out of this narrow alley of water, and out into the North Sea. She doesn't notice she's half undressed, stumbles up onto the quarterdeck and takes the wheel again.

Ben struggles to his feet, totters up the steps, and takes his place behind Fien. Gently, unnoticed by anyone except Fien, he pulls her shirt back around her to cover her. Then he retreats, almost falls down the stairs, disappears into Fien's cabin and re-emerges, seconds later, with a blanket he drapes around her shoulders. Only then does he disappear in the direction of his quarters.

Harry, slowly, deliberately, scratching his baldness, goes up to Fien. 'You shouldn't be doing this.'

'Who else will?' Her voice is till nothing but a scratch.

'Plenty of us who will, who haven't just returned from the dead.' He puts his hand on the wheel.

'This is my ship.' Her fingers cramp.

'I know. Go rest.'

'I can't.' She spits blood.

'You can. You need warmth and some good red wine to ease that throat of yours. I'll come and get you if we need you.'

'Promise?' Her legs begin to sag beneath her, her knee shooting fireworks of pain up her left leg.

'Get dry. Sleep. Wait for Ben to wake before you thank him for saving you.'

'I spoke to my father.'

'What did he say?'

'I can't remember.' She wipes her face, walks and talks like a drunk.

'You were drowning.'

'It felt nice … for a while.'

'Death is always a temptation.'

'You know?'

'I've been there,' Harry says. 'Go. You're shivering. Take the girl with you. She knows how to make something warm for you to drink.'

'I thought she'd go with Ben.'

'He's only her brother,' Harry says. 'She wants you to be her mother.'

Fien leaves wet, flat footprints on the planks. She totters into her cabin and collapses onto the bed that was Lil's. Only then does she start crying. It hurts more in her heart than it does in her throat.

Gone midnight. The moonlight shines hard into the window. Fien wakes, unfamiliar hands in her still damp hair. She opens her mouth to speak, changes her mind, coils around the caresses like a lonely cat bereft of affection. Her limbs ache, her knee jars, her lungs strain. She could sleep for a million years. Ishtar snores on the other side of the room.

'How did you get in here?' she says.

'I walked.'

'Someone must have seen you.'

'I saw no-one.'

'That's a child's game,' she says. 'Pretending others can't see you because you can't see them.'

'We are children.'

'So what are you doing here?'

'I didn't want to be without you,' Ben says.

'We said.'

'I want nothing but to be with you,' he says into her hair. 'I thought I'd lost you.'

'I thought I'd lost myself.'

'Tell me how it was.'

She takes a deep breath, her mouth dry. 'I saw them so clearly. Lil, my father, my mother. And I never knew her. I've only seen the pictures on the wall my father had,'

'That's enough for hallucination when you're drowning.'

'But it was real. They were calling me to them.'

'I saw nothing like that. Just the dark. And the fear of losing you. I actually saw that fear.' He runs the thick strands of her hair through his fingers.

'And what did it look like?'

'It was like I was looking into space without seeing anything. Just a void. That's what.'

'Nothing frightening? No unbelievable creatures, no monsters?'

'No monsters. That's what was awful; not seeing anything, not being able to fight against something that was real. I might have been able to cope with that.'

'But you saved me anyway.'

'Your hair saved you.'

'Why?'

'It's the last thing, the only thing, I saw. You were an angel under water.'

She smiles, moves into his hands, feels so safe to be with him, without any questions, not like the men Lil told her about, those who take a debt before it's made. 'Keep talking. Tell me more. I like it.' She looks at his gaunt face in the silver light.

'There isn't much more to say.'

'Keep talking anyway.'

'I thought I saw things grow down there that I'd never seen before. And I felt I was dying until I found you.'

'And I brought you back to life?'

'No,' he says. 'You dragged me deeper into something that's not this life. Like they must have dragged you into something that's more death than life.'

'I can't believe they're dead,' she says. 'They were talking to me, down there, like not a day had passed since I'd last seen them. I could have touched them if you hadn't dragged me away from them.'

'Are you sorry?'

She says nothing.

'Are you angry that I did?'

'Part of me is,' she says, and turns towards him, her hands looking for his hair, in turn. 'A lot of me isn't.'

'You said you'd wait.'

'I am waiting.'

'Why is a lot of you not angry?'

'Because you, and Harry, you've got me wanting to find that damn clock. I can't even remember it that clearly, except that it's green and delicate and small, and that it must be warm, because he always held his hands around it.'

'No other reason?' His mouth finds her mouth, his hands find her waist, naked under the nightshirt.

'No other reason,' she murmurs as she pulls herself away from him reluctantly, with difficulty. 'Because I want to be with you,' she says before her mouth looks for his again.

'Because you love me,' he says, his mouth full of her.

'Because *you* love *me*,' she says, and then her tongue is on his. 'I couldn't disappoint you.'

'You could never disappoint me.'

'I don't want a baby, not now.' She finds his hardness.

'I know. Neither do I.'

'So what will you do with this?'

'Carry it back to my bed.'

'And I with this?' She leads one of his hands to the damp hair between her legs.

'You tell me.'

'I ...' Her voice falters. 'I don't know. I don't want to be the little woman.'

'You won't be.'

'I want to be someone.'

'You are.'

'You have to be patient.'

'I will.' He moves against her hand.

She tugs on him.

180

'Careful,' he says. 'Oh.'

She wipes her hand on the top of the sheet covering them. 'That was quick.'

'That was the first time, not with my own hand.'

She smiles into the twilight. 'Good.'

'And you?'

'There are ways.'

'I thought you were innocent.'

'Innocent doesn't mean unknowing.'

'Are you going to stay with me?'

'With all of you.'

'I need to know. Will you love me forever?'

'Forever's a long time.' Her hand is still wet.

'I know.'

'You want a promise, don't you?'

'I give you mine,' he says.

'If I don't get killed, yes, you have my promise.'

'You won't get killed.'

'Lindsey's evil, and he has the king's protection.'

'You're good, and you have mine.'

'You should go.'

'I don't want to.'

'Harry'll kill us,' she says.

'No, he won't. He'll laugh and tell us off.'

'That's bad enough. I'm meant to be the Commandant now.'

'That means you can do what you want.'

'It means I have to be awake and fair and objective.'

'It means the ship is yours, and everything in it,' he says.

'And that doesn't just mean the jewels. It means the crew, too. They're my responsibility.' She pushes him out from under the sheet. 'There's a lot of this stuff.'

'It wanted to be inside you.'

'Too soon for that,' she says.

'I know,' Ben says, bends over her and kisses her

forehead. 'I didn't even expect that.'

'We'll be at battle in a few days,' she says. 'Will you follow me?'

'Always,' he says, and bows into the moonlight, his fine features sharp shadows. 'For you, anything.'

Chapter 26

The king's beard is in disarray. 'Every time you go away, you come back with less. It's not good enough, just not good enough. I have an army to raise.'

'Times are difficult, your Highness. There is less and less to be got, not just in Europe, but further afield, too.'

'There is no end of jewels and gold in this world, Lindsey, and I will have them all.'

Lindsey bows again. 'I do my very best for you and for this country of ours.'

'We have rebels massing in the North, and your very best for this country and for me are a few paltry boxes of diamonds and gold chains. Is that really what you call your very best?' He walks round the small, wood-panelled room in Whitehall with tiny, busy steps, his feet scraping on the floor. 'What are you keeping from me? Eh?' He stamps his feet where he stops. 'What of all the pirates you could catch and lighten of their stolen burdens? What about our power at sea?'

'With all respect, Sire, you send me on secret missions with one ship, not with the King's fleet.'

'Because then I would be no better than a pirate, and the world would know about it.' His face is red. 'And I don't want the world to know about it. I don't want them to think Charles the First is a king who can't control those who should serve him, *and* who has difficulties with his purse.'

'I can go to sea again, your Highness, immediately if it pleases you.'

'It doesn't please me, Lindsey, and you know it doesn't. I don't know what game you're playing.'

'I'm not playing a game. I'm trying to serve you as best I can.'

'I need more money. Parliament refuses to give me a

183

penny more, and I can't go to war against them and their northern allies without a decent army.'

Lindsey only just manages to stop himself from shrugging. 'Is there no time for me to go to the Low Countries again?'

'And start a war with them?' Spittle flies from the king's mouth. 'To do so twice in four short months is madness.'

'Then I don't know what else to suggest.'

'When I sent you out in January, I wasn't expecting you to be gone for almost half a year.'

'I had to go far to seize what I could.' Lindsey bows again, glad he's the only one in this room with the king, that there's no-one else who might guess by his face and gestures that he's lying.

The king sits down, and crosses his legs impatiently. 'You've let me down.'

'I know I have, and I apologise humbly.'

'But what will you do about it?'

'You know I'll fight if you need me to.'

'If I need you to?' The king jumps up and starts his pacing again. 'If I need you to? Should I have to tell you when to fight? You will fight. You always have fought. Why should now be any different?'

'You misunderstand me, your Highness.' Lindsey curses himself. 'What I meant was that I'm always there to fight for you.'

Charles nods, looks out of the window absent-mindedly. 'When do you think the war will come?'

'When you decide the time is right, my Lord.'

'Ha. Do any of you so-called loyal advisers ever tell me the truth? I'm not sure I've been advised wisely in the past years.'

You could always make your own decisions, you pompous idiot. Lindsey smiles at the king. 'None of us could ever presume to make decisions for you, your Highness.

You are anointed by God, as you yourself have so eloquently put it, and I, for one, will not argue with the will of God.'

The king snorts. 'If any of you believed that, you'd do more for me.'

Lindsey takes a couple of steps towards the king. 'I would die for you, and you know that. I am your most loyal servant, and always will be.'

'Is that why you advised me to become the first king to walk into the House of Commons with an armed guard to try to arrest the worst troublemakers in January? Troublemakers who'd disappeared by the time I got there?'

'It was what I believed to be the best thing for you to do, for the king, God's instrument on earth, to personally arrest those who were speaking out against God's own will. The devil only knows how those heathens found out in time that you were coming for them.'

'The devil's own work, then, eh?' Charles pats his beard down with a small hand. 'We'll show them the devil's work, won't we, my friend, when the time comes?'

'We will, your Highness, we will.'

'Well, go then, and see if you can find me some more money on these shores. Summer's here, so the peasants will be feeling better about themselves and might feel inclined to part with some more tax money.' He waves his hand at Lindsey. The audience is over.

Outside, in the cool shade, Lindsey draws a deep breath, and shrugs the tension out of his shoulders, before he walks back into the sun. 'Money for an army, the King says. There'd be plenty of money if that fool didn't waste most of it on his damn expensive wife and her masques, and on all the food and wine they guzzle.'

185

He grimaces, and heads for the stables to collect his horse. An hour later, he's back on his ship in the docks, and flings himself down the stairs to the prison where he's holding Brants.

'Come on, man,' he shouts, torch in one hand. 'We need to have a talk. A very serious talk.'

Brants is sitting in one corner of the cage. He ignores Lindsey, stares instead at the ground, one of his hands, as usual in his shirt, caressing the tiny green watch.

Lindsey lets himself into the cage, locks the door behind him, one hand on his sword. He pushes the torch into its holder on the bars, crosses the cell.

'Ah, the strong keeping the weak weak,' Brants says. 'Welcome to my stateroom.' He doesn't get up.

Lindsey, hands on hips, stands in front of the sitting man. 'Don't you want to get out of here?'

'What for? It's such a pleasant life down here. No sun to trouble me, no moon to mock me, good plain food. What more would a man of my station desire?'

'I'll give you your freedom for the watch.'

'I just told you I don't want my freedom.'

'You'd end your days here?'

'There is no end to my days, remember,' Brants says.

'Unless I kill you anyway.'

Brants shrugs. 'And deprive yourself of what you think is the greatest treasure? Really?'

'You must have family,' Lindsey says, decides to try another approach and sits down next to the prisoner, but not too close. 'Brothers, sisters, illegitimate children. Someone to be with in your old age.'

Brants shakes his head. 'I wouldn't bother getting your breeches dirty, Lindsey. Even if I did have any family, I wouldn't give you the watch of my own free will.'

'I wonder why that is,' Lindsey says. 'I should have thought of this before, but you can't be saving it for yourself, if all you've got to look forward to is this life of squalor, albeit as my guest.'

'You would still die before me, and that's worth all the squalor on earth.'

'You're not bitter, are you?' Lindsey says.

'I'm just waiting for my next beating. My bruises from the last one must almost be healed.'

'I'm bored with beating you shitless every few weeks.'

'Then why do it?'

Lindsey shrugs. 'It whiles away a few more minutes of my sad existence, and keeps my fists in trim.'

Silence.

'Which does bring me back to my question. Who exactly are you saving that clock for if not for yourself?'

'Someone better than you?'

'Is there such a person?' Lindsey laughs.

'Would your king not welcome it as a gift? And all that goes with it? A window into the future, and the ability to make things that haven't been invented yet?'

'I've done that. That was your first gift to me.'

'My only gift to you. ... You haven't even told the king about me, have you?'

'He's too busy to be preoccupied with such inconsequential matters.'

'Of course,' Brants says. 'Matters such as saving his kingdom.'

'What would you know about that?'

'You treat me like a fool because you're a fool. Everyone knows England's on the brink of civil war, that the king is losing control over his subjects. And you would deny him the ability to regain that control?'

'I'm the king's most loyal supporter.'

'And yet you withhold from him the means of winning the war, of stopping it before it's even started? And how much exactly of the gold you've plundered did you give him? Less than a third, I should think.'

'How would you know that?'

'That's the difference between you and me,' Piet says, shifting, and looking at Lindsey for the first time. His pain is obvious. 'You're just a soldier who sails. I know ships. I have spent most of my life on them.'

'You're a trader. Nothing more, nothing less.'

'You just use ships as transport, as a means of getting from one place to another. You've not taken the trouble to understand how they work, how they feel, how they shift under their cargo. I know, I've had to know. And I don't forget what I've learned. ... And this morning the ship lifted a little, but not much. That's how I know you're cheating the king you say you hold so dear.'

Lindsey gets up. 'I don't think there's much more to talk about here.'

'You're right, as always,' Piet says. 'Enjoy your day.'

'I will,' Lindsey says, and aims a kick at his prisoner's left arm. It connects with a crack. 'Of that you can be sure.'

He storms up the flights of steps until he's rid of the rank smell of captivity and torture, until he's back out onto the deck again, and into the sunshine that's followed yesterday's storm. He leaves the ship, grabs his horse, and sets off for the Dutch ambassador's residence. As he gallops through the London streets, he curses aloud. 'You're a fool, Robert, a fool. He's hiding something, and you'd better find out what it is now.'

'The Earl of Lindsey,' the servant announces, stiff under the high door frame.

'To what do I owe the pleasure?' the ambassador says, bent over his desk signing papers.

'I was hoping you might help me find someone I'd like to do some trade with.'

'So your king's not asked you to come to ask me for

another loan?'

'The king doesn't know I'm here,' Lindsey says, biting back his irritation that the ambassador hasn't got up to greet him.

'Sit, sit,' the ambassador says, gesturing with his quill. 'So many matters of state to deal with, even for a mere ambassador.

'You're very gracious to give me some of your time then, Sire.'

The ambassador leans back in his chair, and savours its creaking comfort. He puts his fingertips together, and looks at Lindsey over them. 'So who is it you're looking for?'

'A trader,' Lindsey says. 'Someone who might be able to help me with finding some final pieces for my collection at home.'

'You have time to play with the arts while your king is trying to fight off rebellion? That's very interesting indeed.'

'I'm trying to get the collection together so I can sell it to support the king's travails against the traitors.'

'How very noble of you.' The ambassador inclines his head slightly.

'Thank you.'

'And the name of this trader? I may not know him.'

'Piet Brants,' Lindsey says. 'I've heard he's quite well known.'

'I think I'm going to have to disappoint you in more ways than one, sir. And I'm surprised you haven't heard the news of Brants if you're looking for him.'

'What news might that be?'

'Old news, as a matter of fact,' the ambassador says. 'He appears to have been killed when his house caught fire in January. He must have been careless with his fire in the awful cold. The house burned so hard, for days, that when it could finally be searched there was no trace of his body.'

'That's truly dreadful,' Lindsey says.

'Yes, indeed. A sad life, really. His wife died eighteen years ago when she gave birth to their only daughter.'

'A daughter?' Lindsey works to suppress his dismay.

'Yes,' the ambassador says. 'She travelled everywhere with him, from when she was a baby. She'd become very beautiful, by all accounts, and was often mistaken for his wife. Alas, no trace of her was found either.'

Chapter 27

The sea is still, a plate of glass, almost blue. The ship glides slowly but purposefully towards the thin sliver of land Fien can see from the quarterdeck. The slight breeze is behind them. The name on the side is no longer *The Odyssey*. For anyone looking, this is *The Eagle*.

'Are you sure we can land there?' Fien says to Harry. 'It looks very small.'

'Trust me,' he says. 'I've been here before. They build good ships.'

'That's not what I'm worried about. I don't want anyone to recognise this as Lil's ship. And I want to get to London quickly.'

'They'll have horses. And we've got cash.'

'I don't want to advertise that,' Fien says.

Harry looks her up and down. 'They'll think you're some Dutch mercenary down on your luck, by the look of you. And you're still limping.'

'I hope you're right.'

'They'll look at your money and not ask questions,' he says. 'That's all that matters.'

'You'll stay here with the ship and the crew as agreed?' she says.

'Your word is my command.'

'And you'll not get drunk and forget?'

'Would I, would we?'

'No, I suppose you wouldn't.'

'I'll leave the wenching till you get back,' Harry says. 'And the looking for a wife.'

'You're giving all this up?'

'Will there be any point in it after you've got the clock back?'

'Maybe I'll decide to settle down and let you have the ship.'

'Of course you will, girl. Now you've just got the

appetite for it. ... Anyway, this is all empty talk. Too early to be thinking of all that. Get Lindsey first and avenge your father.'

'If I'm ready.'

'You're as ready as you'll ever be.'

Ben, with the crew as always, looks across the narrowing expanse of water. At the highest point of the town, he can see a church tower, the land curving gracefully from there down to the port, where a multitude of ships of all sizes are moored, and from where a steady stream of boats are leaving and arriving. 'Will there be room for us?' he calls up to Fien.

'We'll put down the boat first, and row over there when we're close enough. There must be a harbour master who can tell us if we're welcome.'

'And if not?'

'We'll let the boys row us across, and we'll get some horses and the ship can stay anchored out here till we get back.'

'That sounds like a plan.'

'It's not like you couldn't have thought of it,' Fien says as comes down from the quarterdeck.

'Maybe I had,' he says.

'Then why ask?'

'You're the Commandant.'

'This ship's only really ever had one Commandant,' she says. 'I'm just borrowing her.'

'Can I come?' Ishtar says. 'Please? I know a lot about horses.'

Fien shakes her head. 'It's too dangerous,' she say. 'When we've got the clock back, then you can help us. We'll need a lot of horses if we settle here.'

Ishtar growls, disappears away into the cabin, slamming the door.

'She's not happy,' Ben says.

'Harry'll look after her. I don't want her to come to

any harm. She's been through enough already.'

'So have you.'

'I'm an adult now,' Fien says. 'She isn't.'

A couple of hours later, they're close enough to drop anchor and put down the boat. Two of the men row Fien and Ben across to a stretch of sand to one side of the port.

'Wait here, lads,' Fien says. 'We'll have a look see and report back.'

The men nod, sit down next to the boat, and light their pipes.

'I wish England were always this warm,' Ben says as they follow the dust track northwards towards the port.

'You mean it's not?'

'You know it isn't.'

'We didn't come to England a lot. Only in the summer.'

'So your father knew the English weather, I should think.'

'I suppose so,' Fien says.

'It would have been his reason for not coming here at any other time.'

Fien, her hair up, one of Harry's caps on top of it, nods at a man walking the other way. 'I hope he's not scouting out the boys,' she mutters.

'Probably off to catch something in those marshes back there,' Ben says. 'Must be plenty of ducks out there.'

The town is busy for somewhere that looked so small from the sea. Fien and Ben find their way to the port, hear the banging of hammers before they catch sight of it behind rows and rows of small cottages, all in a straight line along the road that seems to have developed from the track they were walking. And behind the houses now, and high above them, they see the masts of all the ships.

The two push their way through the bustle of people, find their way out onto the docks. There doesn't seem to be room for any more ships, from what they can see. They watch, for a few moments, the loading and unloading of the ships, listen to the strident voices, commands and counter-commands. There's a small man at the still centre of the chaos who seems to be directing everything else. Fien walks up to him, nods at him. She can see her ship out on the sea, behind him.

'Are you in charge?' she says.

'No-one's in charge, really,' he says with a smile. 'Who's asking?' He holds out a leathery hand. 'I'm Jim.'

'Both of us,' she says, shaking his hand. 'We've got a ship out there and wondered if there was room to tie up for a week or so.'

'What cargo?' he says.

'No cargo,' Fien says.

'That's unusual.' He scratches his head. 'Best thing you can do is put in half a mile north, by the shipyard. Be out of the way there. Lots of traffic here nowadays, what with the war coming.'

'A war?' Ben says.

'Where you been?' Jim says. 'Civil war, that's what. The king's gone been an idiot, and Parliament's not having none of it.'

Ben shrugs. 'We'll be keeping well away from that then.'

'You'll have to choose a side sooner or later if you're staying,' Jim says.

'Have you chosen?'

'I'm a Suffolk boy,' Jim says. 'And ain't no king ever been on our side.'

'Then we're with you, Jim,' Fien says. 'And we'll be no trouble either.' She puts a small silver coin in his hand. 'And here's something for your trouble.' She turns to go. 'Oh, and the ship's *The Eagle*.'

'Just make sure you get her in there in the next hour or so,' he calls after them. 'Just so's I don't give the space to anyone else.'

Fien turns and waves. 'I'll come look for you later and we can have a drink.'

'Now that sounds good,' Jim says and starts shouting at those around him again.

'That was easy,' Ben says.

'Did you expect it not to be?'

'You never know.'

'It's like Harry said. Money's a universal language, even just a tiny coin.'

'What if this war starts while we're in London?'

'Then at least we know that the ship and all the others are fairly safe. And don't forget they can look after themselves. They wouldn't have been sailing with Lil if they couldn't.'

'I know,' Ben says. 'I know.'

Anchor up, Fien steers her ship northwards. It takes less time than she'd thought. They make her fast against the oak bulwarks to one side of the shipyard, where two new ships are rising from the ground up.

'Nice work,' she says when she's jumped onto land. She walks across to the yard, watches the carpenters' efforts with admiration.

'Control yourself,' Ben says.

'What do you mean?'

'All those half-naked men, sweat pouring down them.'

She elbows Ben in the ribs. 'Stop it.' She giggles. 'Although, now you mention it.' She's out of reaching distance by the time he tries to elbow her back. 'I don't mean it. You know that.'

'I know nothing.'

'Just be serious for a minute,' she says. 'None of us know anything, really, do we?'

'It was a joke,' he says. 'I know you love me.'

'And don't forget I'm supposed to be a man.'

'I won't forget. ... What do we do now?'

'We eat, find somewhere that'll sell us some horses, find some decent horses, have a drink with Jim, and then we get an early night and off to London tomorrow.'

'You don't want to go today then?'

'I don't see the point in rushing.'

'The war?'

'That'll come if we go tonight or tomorrow.'

'True,' Ben says. 'Sad, though.'

'Inevitable.'

'Maybe we'll get a chance at the king.'

'What do you mean?'

'He's caused all this, hasn't he?' Ben says. 'He may as well have killed your father and Lil himself.'

'We'd never get anywhere near him.'

'You never know.'

'Let's get the clock first, then we'll see.' She looks at him. 'You do realise you're talking treason, don't you?'

'And what we were doing at sea, what was that?'

Fien laughs. 'You're right, you're right. I'm thinking too much.'

'I've had a thought,' he says.

'And?'

'Let Ishtar come choose the horses with us. It's not dangerous here, is it?'

'I suppose not,' Fien says. 'But let's not give her the idea that she can come to London with us.'

'No, no. That's not what I'd intended anyway,' Ben says, his hands up. 'She's better off here when we're gone.'

'And Harry could do with the distraction.'

'Yes, to keep him from his women until we get back.'

'Although he'll complain about nursemaiding again,'

Fien says.

'He won't.'

They clamber back on board. Fien ducks into the cabin, where Ishtar is still sitting at the chart table, playing with one of her daggers. She doesn't even look up when she hears Fien come in.

Fien runs her hands through the girl's thick black hair. 'Come with us to choose the horses,' she says.

'I thought you didn't want me to.'

'I didn't say that. I said that I thought it was too dangerous for you to come to London with us. And now we know it's safe here, I think you should help us with the horses.'

'And if I don't want to?' Ishtar's mouth curls.

'Then we'll choose some without you, and you'll keep being angry until we've been to London and back. And that wouldn't be a good thing.'

Ishtar jumps up, gives Fien a hug. 'Are we going now?'

'Yes, we're going now.'

'I'll bring the knives.'

'If you must.'

'You've got yours, haven't you?'

'Always.'

'Then I shall have mine, always.'

They make an odd group, the boy become man, the girl become woman and dressing as a man, and the dark-skinned, wild-haired, brown-eyes girl from halfway across the world, as they walk past the shipyard into the town. But no-one looks at them, no-one thinks they look strange, used as these people from the remotest part of Suffolk are to sailors from all around the globe. They live next to the sea, so they accept everything its water washes ashore, the living, the dead, the immediately useful, and that which might become useful one day. There's no waste here, and no questioning either.

It doesn't take them long to find someone who sells horses. A large hall, wattle and daub, beams and lime wash, is only a short walk away from the shipyard, and around it is what looks and feels like a market place, and around that a circle of houses, loosely dotted here and there. The market's busy and noisy, not on the same scale as Gombroon, but hot and humid all the same. And one part of the market is given over to sellers of horses. Ishtar's face lights up as soon as she sees the creatures, ranging from the sturdy, wide-shouldered beasts that would be of use on farms, to the slender, delicate, prancing thoroughbreds that would make good racers.

'Oh, look,' she says. 'How wonderful they are. And in such good shape. They obviously know how to treat their horses here.' She walks up to the nearest, a simpering, nervous grey mare, strokes her neck, and whispers words Ben and Fien can't decipher. The horse calms down at once.

'You buying?' A tall, broad man, at least a head taller than Ben, comes across to them.

'Yes,' Ishtar says.

'You calmed her down quick.'

'She just doesn't like the noise,' Ishtar says. 'She's beautiful.'

'Aye, she is a beauty, at that,' the man says. 'How many you looking for?'

Fien looks at Ben, then at Ishtar. 'Two, I think.'

'Three,' Ishtar says. 'One for me to keep here.'

'Ah, alright,' Fien says. 'And we'll let her choose.'

'How's a girl that little know anything about horses?' the man says.

'What's your name?' Ishtar says, reaches out to him with her small hand.

'They call me Nathan,' he says. 'Old Nathan.'

'The horseman.'

'Man and boy.'

'You're a good man,' Ishtar says. 'These are good horses. Do you want to come with me while I look at them?'

'If it's all the same to you.' Nathan looks at Fien and Ben. 'You comin', too?'

They nod.

A brief half an hour later, not only has Ishtar found three excellent horses, the grey mare one of them, and all the saddles and bridles and reins they need, but has managed to get a good price for them, too, one that leaves Nathan happy, and rather bewitched by a tiny foreign girl, and Fien even happier, her real wealth undiscovered.

As they lead the horses back to the ship, Ben and Fien hang back and watch Ishtar lead her grey ahead of them. The girl is on her tiptoes, prancing like a thoroughbred herself, and leaning against her horse, making a bond.

'A lifelong friendship, do you think?' Ben says.

'Who knows?' Fien pats the black horse Ishtar chose for her. 'Although it feels like that to me with this one already. I just need to think of a name.'

'Lil?' Ben says.

'And you wouldn't mind?'

'How could I?'

'And yours?'

'Oh, I think I'll call this old lump Harry.'

'He'll be grateful for that,' Fien says.

'The horse or the man?'

'Both.'

When they get back to the ship, Harry's on the quayside, arms on his hips. 'You want them on this ship?' he says. 'How the hell are we going to look after them?'

'Only for tonight,' Fien says.

'And what about hers?' Harry says. 'She'll be wanting it to stay indoors with her at this rate.'

'Keep it on the deck by the main mast,' Fien says. 'That'll keep her happy.'

'If we must.'

'It could be a wonderful watch horse, Harry,' Ben says. 'It'll neigh when the King's army arrives.'

'We'll be well bloody gone before then,' Harry says. 'And if that does happen, you'll just have to find your way up to Montrose on your own.'

'Where's that?' Fien says. 'I've never heard of it.'

'Scotland,' Ben says. 'Lil loved it up there. Proper mountains, she said. And nicer people than the English.'

'Aye,' Harry says. 'Always will be. Proper pagans, we Celts.'

The next morning, early, just after first light, Ben and Fien saddle up and push their horses gently westwards, to find the road to Ipswich, and then to London. They turn as they reach the crest of the hill, next to the church, look down at *The Odyssey* and wave to the two tiny figures and the grey horse watching them as they go.

'I hope we see them again,' Fien says, turns forwards, and pushes her horse into a gallop.

Chapter 28

'Where did you learn to ride so well?' Ben says.

They've covered 30 miles in six hours. He's covered in sweat, and his back is sore.

'The Persians,' she says. 'My father and I spent over a year out there when I was about ten.'

'Good memories?'

She nods. 'Of course, I don't remember everything I did, but I do remember how to ride, and how to look at horses.'

'So we didn't need Ishtar to help us?'

'There wasn't any point in telling her that. I wanted her to be part of this.'

They trot to the nearest group of trees, walk their horses into the shade, and dismount.

'That was very thoughtful of you,' Ben says.

'You'd have done the same.'

'I'm not sure I'd have had the presence of mind to do that.'

'No matter.' She sits down on a clump grass. 'How much further should we go today?' She gets a map out of her pocket. 'We're not even a quarter of the way there.'

'Let's rest up here for an hour or so,' he says. 'And then we can do another three hours. 'That'll take us close to fifty miles for the day.'

'We need to look after the horses, too.'

'Don't you think they'll cope?'

'I don't want them to be too tired in case we need to get away quickly.'

'Then let's make sure we take four days to get down there.'

'And then what?' Fien says.

'We go to the docks and see if we can find Lindsey's ship.'

'That simple.'

'That simple.' He gets up. 'Now let's see what we've got to eat and drink.'

'Not much,' she says. 'I told Harry we'd need to travel light.'

Ben unwraps some bread and cheese, passes it to her. 'And you really don't know where your father got the clock from?'

She shakes her head, wipes a tear away. 'I never asked him, and he never told me. I just thought it was something beautiful, something to remind him of my mother, because all he ever said was that he'd got it for her.'

'Strange.'

'It is now,' she says. 'It didn't seem so strange when he was still alive. As children we question the smallest things, but not the big ones. It was just the way it was. I didn't even think about it much. Getting cross with him for not letting me do the things I wanted to seemed much more important.'

Ben leans against a tree. 'And we were still children, you and I, not so long ago.'

She looks at him, long and hard, bites back what she feels rising inside, and nods. 'We were, and I'm still wondering if I've grown up too quickly, in all sorts of ways.'

He reaches out to her. 'Hopefully we have time, lots of time, to grow up in a way we understand.'

'If there's anything to understand.' She jumps up, puts the remainder of their meal into the bag, and walks to her horse. 'We need to move on, I think.'

'You're right.' He stands next to her, puts his hand on her shoulder. 'I'm sure I love you.'

'And I you. I just don't want to do anything about it, not right now, not until I know we're all safe.' She turns and kisses him, a brief butterfly wing's flutter of heat.

'Come on.'

That evening, in an inn just south of Colchester, two rooms rented for the night, careful to have the coins in hand before having gone in, they sit in a corner, beer in front of them, stomachs full of roast pork.

'An early start?' she says.

He nods. 'Not much sign of a rebellion here.'

She looks round. 'No. Maybe they're just waiting to see what the king decides to do.'

'If he's still in London,' Ben says.

'And if he isn't Lindsey won't be either. He's bound to go where the king goes.'

'If it's even got to that stage yet. Perhaps the king will have told him to get more money together before he starts a war.'

'I suppose we'll find out when we get there,' she says, takes a sip of her beer. For a moment she says nothing more. 'Has Harry spoken to you about Lil?'

He shakes his head. 'Not really. Too much other stuff to think about. And I suppose neither of us wanted to open up the other's wounds.'

'Do you want to know?'

'I'm not sure,' he says.

'She did tell me quite a lot.'

'I'm sure she did.'

'But not about her and Harry.'

'I'm sure she didn't.'

'Just tell me if you want to talk about it,' she says.

'I will.' He gets two more tankards of ale.

'Of course I won't say anything if you don't want me to.'

'I understand.'

'Is anything wrong?'

He tries a smile. 'Not really. I just find it odd that you know more about your father and my mother than I do.'

'Sorry.'

'No, no. Don't be. It wasn't meant horribly. Life's just so unfair.'

'It is. I sometimes wonder what the point is.'

'Only sometimes?'

'All the time, then,' she says.

'And yet you're going after Lindsey.'

'If I can't get revenge then there's certainly no point to life.'

'It's sad, isn't it, that there's always evil around the corner? That good people always have to make themselves bad because that's just about the only way to try to make things good again.'

She suppresses a laugh. 'Sorry. It just sounds so complicated when it should all be so simple.'

'Why does evil even exist?'

'It's human nature,' she says. 'People will always want influence over other people's lives. They'll always want to deprive others of what they don't want them to have. People will always want to be rich easily, and trying to do that makes them bad. After all, what would you rather be – a farmer who has to work all the hours there are, or an earl who has pockets full of money and doesn't have to work?'

'I'd rather work hard and be good.'

'That's easy to say until you get the choice.'

'I suppose so.'

'Why do you think Lindsey wanted the clock so badly? Because he thinks it will bring him something for nothing. Because he thinks it'll make him even richer than the king, than any king. I bet he hasn't given it to his king.'

'It didn't make you father rich, did it?'

'No.' She shakes her head. 'But he didn't want it for that. He wanted it for my mother, and then she must have given it back to him otherwise she'd still be alive. And then he only wanted it to remind him of her, not for some other reason. Certainly not for power.' She looks around. 'In the last few years we've hardly even travelled. We just sat in that house full of books reading. It's almost as if he was waiting for Lindsey to come, especially with the way he'd prepared for me to escape.'

'I wonder why he didn't give you the clock sooner then.'

'Well, he wasn't going to know exactly when Lindsey was going to make his move, did he? And then, when Lindsey did, there was no time.'

'I wish I knew more about the clock,' Ben says.

'So do I. If we ever get our hands on it, we'll know.'

'Then let's make sure we do.'

In her dark room that night, Fien can't sleep, even though she's tired to her bones. She misses the motion of the sea, the constant sounds of the ship, the creaking, groaning, whispering, like the ship was alive and talking to her. She gets out of bed, pads over to the window, used to finding her way around in absolute blackness. Standing to one side of the window, caution now as innate as breathing, she watches the emptiness of the track that passes by, feels rather than sees the tops of the trees swaying in the almost non-existent summer breeze.

The gloaming lifts, briefly, the heat glowering through the night. Fien starts, think she sees a twitch at the base of one of the trees, a shape that shouldn't be there. She blinks, squeezes her fingers along the bridge of her nose, looks again. Nothing. She stands and waits. This is a dangerous country. She can sense it. She crouches down by the window, keeps her eyes on where she thought she saw the shape. Her knees start to hurt as she waits. Still nothing. Just as she's about to turn away, convinced she's imagining things, she sees it again. A glint of something, just a tremble of light, a reflection, not a complete movement. She grinds her teeth. A remnant of the taste of pork and beer lingers.

Fien moves slowly backwards, never taking her eye off the void in the trees where the sparkle was. She reaches behind her, her fingertips reaching for her knives, manages to drag the belt towards her with a subdued grunt, an effort of searching by touch rather than sight. She ties the belt around her, over one naked shoulder, and its weight resting on her bare hip, the air shifting with her movement, shaping to the contours of her body. She wishes now she'd kept at least some clothes on her, rather than giving in to the humid heat that is England, rather than falling into trap of assuming her modesty was the least of her worries.

The door creaks. Fien drops to the floor. A narrow shaft of light crosses the boards, and a dark shape crosses into the room.

'Where are you?' Ben's voice, a whisper.

'Close the door.' Fien, urgent.

'There's something out there.' Ben pushes the door closed and the light disappears.

'You saw it, too?'

'Why else would I be here?'

'You may have been thinking wicked things.'

'This isn't the time for jokes.' His voice is gruff, his response taut.

'Should we go down and see what it is?'

'I'm not sure that's a good idea. Best to stay here together and see if it's an enemy.'

'Take it in turns to sleep?'

'Yes,' he says. 'You first.'

'You can't see me, can you?'

'No, not really. Why?'

'No reason,' she says and blushes in the dark.

'Oh,' he says. 'Sorry.'

'Keep watching the window.' She searches the floor for her clothes, drags them over her quickly.

'You didn't have to.'

'I did.'

'I'll wake you in three hours,' he says.

'Sure you can stay wake that long?'

'I don't feel tired. I couldn't sleep.'

'I couldn't sleep, but I'm exhausted.'

'Then sleep, now.'

She gets onto the bed, doesn't cover herself. It's too hot now, with her clothes on, and her knife belt already sliding across the sheen of sweat on her back.

'Make sure you do wake me.'

His voice comes from low by the window. He must be sitting on the floor. 'I will. Get some rest.'

When Ben shakes her awake, she feels like she hasn't slept at all. 'Three hours,' she mumbles. 'You said three hours.'

'It's been more like four.'

'Sorry.'

'I am tired now.'

'Did you see anything more?'

'Just indistinct lights,' he says. 'If it was an enemy, it would have attacked by now.'

'You don't know that.'

'I can guess that.' He sits down on the bed next to her.

Their hands find each other. Their lips find each other.

'We must be careful,' she says, when they finally separate.

'I know,' he says, and swallows hard.

'Sleep now.' She strokes his hair. 'I'll wake you when

the light starts rising.'

'That'll be enough to wake me anyway.'

'I wouldn't bet on it.'

He stretches out on the bed, grabs the pillow. 'It smells of you.'

'Stop trying to romance me.'

'I wasn't. I was just telling the truth.'

'London,' she says. 'London. Then we'll have time.'

'I hope.'

'So do I.'

'Really?' he says. 'Can I be sure?'

'Stop asking questions all the time,' she hisses. 'Now close your eyes and sleep.'

'I'll only see what I saw before.'

'So you lied about not being able to see me,' Fien says.

'It was only a small lie.'

Chapter 29

When light does come, early summer light, Fien feels like she's been crouching by the window forever. In the three hours she's kept watch, she's seen nothing, no repeat of the movement she thought she'd seen, no indication of danger, nothing. The trees are in clear view now, and there's nothing beneath them except for the lush green grass of the English summer, and beyond them the road stretching south.

She sits down on the bed heavily. Ben groans, but doesn't wake. She reaches out a thin hand, runs her fingers down his back. 'Time to go,' she says, not too loudly, in the hope of garnering a few more moments of being able to touch him. He snorts, and a drop of fluid dribbles from his mouth.

'Bloody hell.' He sits up with a start. 'Are you trying to get me to kill you?'

'I could have killed you a dozen times over,' she says.

'But you didn't.'

'Enough. We need to go, if you didn't hear me the first time. It's light enough to go.'

'Then let's go.'

She packs what she has into her saddle bag, and follows him to his room, where he just picks up his bag. 'You didn't even bother getting undressed, did you?' she says.

'Last night, when I came up here, I felt like we were being followed, so I didn't even think of going to sleep.'

'You just sat by your window and watched?'

He nods. 'Until I came to your room, yes.'

'Tonight, when we stop, we should stay in the same room,' she says. 'It'll be safer that way.'

'In one sense.'

'I wish we were in London already. Then we'd know

what we're really up against. We can't tell here in the country. It's still the middle of nowhere.'

'Who knows what we might see today?'

They're at the bottom of the stairs by now. There's no-one else about. The house is still silent.

'If we'd not paid last night, we could have got away without paying at all,' she says.

'I'm not so sure about that.' A voice rises from one of the benches in the drinking room. A lazy head appears over the top of it. 'I always sleep here when we've got strangers in.'

'Even though we settled up?'

'Never can be too sure,' the landlord says. 'Can't have people nicking off with my ale.'

Fien laughs. 'I don't think it would be of any use to us or the horses.'

'I'll go back to sleep then,' he says. 'Safe journeys.' His head disappears again, and he's snoring before they reach the front door.

'Carefully,' Ben says. He doesn't turn for the stables, but moves slowly the other way, holding one of his hands out behind him to slow down Fien.

'Wh ...' And then she sees where he's taking her.

They move together now, on the balls of their feet, to the side of the inn where their rooms are on the first floor, towards the trees from where they saw the flicker of light in the night.

There's nothing there, just an emptiness of grass under the branches. Ben stops her from going any further. 'Look,' he says. 'There was someone here.' He points at a trampled area of the green, the grass blades compressed into the baking dust. He squats down, runs his hands over the broken stems. 'One person and a horse.'

'Lindsey?'

He shakes his head. 'I don't think it was a very tall

person.'

'And you learned all this from being on board a ship all your life.'

'Lil didn't make me stay on the ship all the time. She said it was important that I learned to read the land, too, so she taught me how to decipher tracks left by others. She said it might come in useful some day.'

'And yet she didn't teach you to read or write.'

'She didn't have the patience. You know that.'

Fien smiles at the memory of the red-haired woman who took her in, and who, if anything, encouraged her to be patient rather than following in her saviour's more impetuous footsteps. 'So it could have been one of Lindsey's men,' she says.

'It could've been,' he says, getting up again. 'But how would he know we're here? And if he does know there's either a traitor in the crew, or he had someone ready and waiting for us at Aldeburgh. And if he had someone at Aldeburgh, he'd have had to have had someone at every port.'

'I can't see any of the crew being disloyal,' Fien says. 'They're going to be very rich when we divide up all the loot.'

Ben nods. 'I don't think so, either. But then I don't think Lindsey would've been able to find men to put one in every port round the coast. For all he knows, we've gone to Europe, or sailed round the west coast.'

'Someone just following us because we don't look as poor as anyone else?'

'I suppose we'll just have to wait and see. We've got to be on our guard from here in.'

'As if we weren't already.'

'More on our guard then,' he says.

The sun is warming the air already, and the inn's cockerel crows. 'Let's be getting on,' Fien says. 'Or we'll just have more questions to answer.'

Five minutes later they head out of the village and southwards again, a cloud of dust marking their trail.

By early afternoon, they're nearing Chelmsford. They see it from a distance, like a fort, and pull up their horses.

'Would it be wiser to go round it?' Fien says, her lips dry.

'Probably,' Ben says. 'But we need to water the horses and ourselves.'

'There must be some brooks and inns one side or another of the place. We'll find them, sure enough.'

'If you're entirely sure.'

'We'll go round the east side,' she says. 'I really don't want to risk bumping into people who might already be fighting with each other. Colchester was bad enough with all the crowds talking of how the cavaliers were the ones at fault for poor trade, and how they reckoned the local earl was going to send men to London to help the king and they were going to stop him.' She sits up in the saddle. 'Come on, to the left we go.'

After just a few miles, they find a small stream, and a little valley of coppiced trees, where they jump from the horses and let them roam, to feed on grass and fill their stomachs with the cool water.

'Two-day-old bread and cheese,' Ben says as he pulls the battered package out of his saddlebag.

'Better than nothing,' Fien says. 'And anyway, we stuffed ourselves with that pork last night.'

'I'm glad we did. That was a fair half day's ride so far.'

'You're managing to keep up with me now,' she says.

'I was just letting you think you were better in the saddle than me.'

'Of course. ... Is that sense of superiority something that men are born with?'

'Must be,' Ben says through his mouthful of cheese.

Fien shakes her head. 'There's no hope for the world.'

'Oh, there will be once you're ruling it all.'

'That's not going to happen, and you know it.'

'You rule mine already.'

'Fool.' She rolls over onto her stomach, her knife in her hand quicker than sight can trace, makes a sign to him to get down and be quiet. She nods her head north-westwards, touches her ear. 'Did you hear that?' she mouthes at him.

He shakes his head and crawls over to her so he can hear what she's saying.

She laughs a quiet laugh when he gets to her.

'What?'

'All this shit about Lil teaching you to read tracks and things, and you can't hear an army of horses five miles off.'

'How can you laugh at that?'

'Get your sword ready,' she says. 'I've a feeling you might need it.'

'What about our horses?'

She shrugs. 'We'll have to wait and see.'

Just then they hear a little whinny behind them. They both turn, as one, and there are their horses, and one more. A grey one. And Ishtar, holding the reins for all three.

'What the hell?' Fien says.

Ishtar, as if she has all the time in the world, ties the reins around the tree nearest her, drops into the grass in between Fien and Ben. 'You're not happy to see me?'

'It's dangerous,' Fien says between gritted teeth. 'You'll get yourself, and us, killed.'

'You need me against that army,' Ishtar says.

'How many?' Ben says.

'Twenty. Riding fast.'

'We got the riding fast part already,' Fien says. 'They'll be here in the next few minutes.'

213

Ishtar grins, and weighs one of her knives in her hand. 'A proper fight.'

'Maybe not,' Ben says. 'They might be riding against the king.'

Ishtar shakes her head. 'They were all shouting *For Charles* when I saw them.'

'Damn it,' Fien says. 'We came this way to avoid this sort of thing. They must have got away from the crowds in Colchester.'

'They'll be everywhere then,' Ben says. 'Is this part of the world really that backward, to support a king's absolute power?'

'People everywhere are fools, especially the nobility,' Fien says. 'They don't read enough.'

'Maybe they'll just ride past us without noticing,' Ben says. 'And if they don't, we can always say we support the king.'

'Then they'll get us to ride with them,' Fien says.

'Good disguise?' Ishtar says. 'No-one knows who we are.'

'Yet,' Fien says. 'And they'd be able to tell if we were lying.'

'Let's wait and see,' Ben says. 'There's no point starting to fight them if we don't have to. Not very good odds, three against twenty.'

'I don't know,' Fien says. 'It's not something Lil would turn her nose up at.'

'She was mad.'

'Any minute now,' Ishtar says.

And then the storm breaks, in the distance. The rumbling of hooves turns into a thunder, the ground begins to tremble, the trees to shake. The three horses crowd into each other, shake their heads hard, as if trying to rid themselves of their tethers. Fien, Ben, and Ishtar stay lying in the grass.

Men roar, pulling their horses to a stop. They've not

ridden past, and surround Ben, Fien, and Ishtar. One of the men dismounts, the white feather in his hat brown from the dust. 'What have we here?' he says. 'Three little commoners?'

Fien stands first. 'Three friends,' she says.

'Friends of whom?' the man says, removes his hat and bows.

'Each other,' Fien says.

'And will the young man not tell me who he and his friends are?' He puts his hat on again, and walks to within touching distance. 'I, for the sake of completeness, am Sir John Lucas, but you may call me Sir John.'

'I'm Finn,' she says. 'And this is Ben and his sister Beth.'

'They look a tad foreign,' Sir Lucas says. 'They're not here to invade this great island are they?'

Fien smiles, and finds it hard to do so. 'I think that would be a rather small expeditionary force for any invaders to send.'

'And yet they still look foreign and don't say a word.'

'They're my servants,' Fien says, quickly. 'They'll only speak if I tell them to. Their English, too, is rather poor.' She gabbles in Persian to Ben and Fien *Behave like servants.*

'Ah, a linguist,' Sir John says. 'How splendid. I'm sure the king would very much like your services.'

'I'm afraid I'd have to decline,' Fien says. 'However much I'd like to meet His Majesty, I'm needed further north.'

'Not by the Parliamentarians?' Sir John says. 'Because if that were so, I'd have to slit your throats.'

Fien lightly nods. 'We'll let you go in peace if you let us go in peace.'

'That's impossible, I'm afraid, my dear young man. I can't risk more rebellion than I already have on my hands.'

'You'll never make London alive,' Fien says. *Get ready to fight* to the other two.

'Nor you the North.' Sir John salutes with his hat and walks back to his horse.

'You'll regret this,' Fien says quietly, and starts backing away towards the bigger trees.

Sir John grins. 'No,' he says. 'I think you will.' He pulls his sword. 'Get them,' he shouts.

Six of his men are dead before they've even moved, knives embedded in their throats, blood flooding from their gaping mouths. Another four crash to the ground a few steps forwards. Nine men and Sir John remain. The air is full of screaming, from the dying and the living. Ben pulls his sword, waits for the rush of men. Fien, too, has her sword in hand, two knives left in her invisible belt under her shirt. Ishtar leans against one of the trees, her two knives back in her hands, the blades dripping bright red blood onto the grass. She grins, and looses her daggers again. Two more men drop, their throats ripped apart by the spinning knives.

Sir John holds back. He's lost most of his men already.

Fien smiles at him, her sword cutting down yet another man, and the knife in her left hand shredding the face of another. She ducks under the sword of a third attacker, loses her hat, and her hair tumbles down to her shoulders, a bright flash in the shadows. 'Not coming to help your men against a woman, Sir John?' she shouts above the ringing swords as she parries another blow, and jabs her sword into her opponent's shoulder and twists it. She whirls, and her hair whirls with her, as she swipes at another one of Sir John's men attacking Ben. She sways out of the way of yet another sword, ignores the shallow cut it opens on her left cheek.

Ben hacks away at a bear of a man, whose chest seems to be made of iron. The bear shows a gap-toothed grin when the tip of Fien's sword crashes out through his sternum. 'Thanks,' Ben calls. He roars and throws his sword at Fien who ducks. Strands of her hair go flying with the sword which implants itself in the chest of one of the last of Sir John's men.

Sir John spurs his horse into action at last. He's lost seventeen men in less than a minute. He rides straight at Fien, thinking she has no weapons left. He raises his sword. Ishtar is still leaning against her tree, arms crossed. She shrugs. Sir John roars, his face set. Fien stands there, lets him come as close as possible. She jumps to one side when his sword comes crashing down, rolls until she's on her feet again, slices at his left boot with her left hand, severs his Achilles tendon with one deft swipe, dives between his horse's legs and does the same to his right leg before he's even managed to scream with pain. The sword drops from his hand. Only his stirrups hold him in place now. His ankles are useless.

Ben clubs one of the last two men in the face with the hilt of his sword, topples him, rams the blade through him, and slumps onto the slippery grass, exhausted.

Ishtar giggles as the last remaining man charges towards her. She doesn't move, doesn't flinch, as he throws himself at her. A flash of steel, and he, too, is down, the grass a sea of blood and death.

Fien takes the reins of Sir John's horse. 'Who's regretting this now?' she says.

He says nothing, using all his strength to stay in the saddle.

'I'll have to ask you to get down,' Fien says.

'Can't,' he says through clenched teeth. 'You Parliamentarians are demons.'

'I don't fight for any sides,' she says, and smiles up at

him. 'I fight for myself alone, and for my friends. Your men would still be alive if you'd just ridden by in peace. We meant you no harm, but you threatened us. We didn't challenge you, but you attacked us.'

His blood is dripping down his horse's sides. 'You'll pay for this.'

'One day, perhaps,' she says. 'But not now, not here. Perhaps you should try to ride home, after all.'

'You're not going to kill me?'

'The odds are against you now,' she says. 'Even with your horse.' She retrieves her sword from one of the dead men. 'But if you try to follow me again, I will kill you. If you try to get to London, I'll know, and you'll die.'

'Bitch.'

'Words,' she says. 'Nothing more. That's all.' She slaps the rump of his horse with the flat edge of her sword, and it goes running off, northwards, with its unwieldy and struggling cargo.

'We'd better clear up,' Fien says, wiping the blood from her face. 'Retrieve what's ours and bury these poor bastards.'

'Waste time on them?' Ben says. 'They wouldn't have done the same for us. They'd have put our heads on stakes.'

'No matter,' she says. 'I want us to try.'

The three of them gather all the weapons into a pile, manage to scrape shallow graves for the dead, cut branches from the trees, and cover the graves with them. Then they bathe in the stream, each one alone.

By late evening, the sun only a smudge of red in the distant sky, they find a deserted inn a fair way south of Chelmsford. Even Ishtar tries the beer. Tomorrow they'll reach London.

Chapter 30

Lindsey digs his spurs into the horse's flanks. Dust scatters. People on both sides of the narrow alley jump out of the way. His rage drives him onwards. He doesn't see where he's going, just follows his instincts until he sees the water in front of him. He jumps from the bleeding horse before it's pulled up, legs juddering on the uneven ground. He throws down his gloves. 'Shoot the bloody thing. I need a faster one,' he shouts to the men who pull the sweating thing to a halt, mouth foaming, bridle half-ripped, eyes wide open. He stomps across the gang plank onto the ship, runs into his cabin, rips off his hat, throws himself into a chair, and opens the decanter of red wine.

'Bring me some dinner for two,' he says to his servant. 'And bring him up here.' He lobs the cage keys to the servant. 'Now.'

Glass in hand, he gets up and stalks around the cabin until the food arrives. His servants know his temper, don't keep him waiting. Cured ham, fresh bread, and any amount of fresh vegetables, taken free, or at any price, from the gardens of London. He pours himself another glass and stokes even higher the flames within. When he hears footsteps outside, he breathes deeply, sinks into the chair again.

Piet is brought into the cabin, feet manacled, his face still swollen, his arm bent and crooked, but standing up straight, an unquenchable light in his eyes.

'Come, eat with me,' Lindsey says, and curses the time the lies will take to tell. He points at the chair the other side of the table.

Piet sits down slowly, painfully. He says nothing, just leans back and waits.

'Help yourself,' Lindsey says.

'You first,' Piet says.

'As if I'd poison you.'

'That's not the point. Why this sudden change in hospitality?'

'I have some new information.'

'Oh?' Piet's legs cramp.

'Yes,' Lindsey says. 'I've been to see the Dutch ambassador.'

'Is he well?' Piet smiles through the blood and the bruises. 'Does he know you're holding a Dutch citizen prisoner on English soil?'

'I didn't trouble him with meaningless details. But he told me many things I needed to know.'

Piet folds his arms, and manages to do so without grimacing. 'Good for you. And this has brought fresh food to your table?'

'It has made me, how shall I say, more generous.'

'Then help yourself to your own generosity.'

Lindsey takes a bread roll, rips it savagely apart and presses some ham into it. He takes a bite, the picks up a small tomato and bites it in half, its juice running, like blood, down his chin. He doesn't bother wiping it off. 'He told me a lot about your home life.'

'Is that so?' Piet still doesn't touch the food.

'It's not poisoned.'

'But you are. By greed.'

'Oh, spare me the sermon, Brants. You're a trader.'

'A fair one.'

'Then how did you get the clock?'

'My wife gave it to me.'

'She gave her life for you?' Lindsey is incredulous, rips another mouthful of ham and bread into his mouth. 'She must have been mad.'

'That's what I think, too.'

'Your daughter must be a pretty young thing.' Lindsey's mouth is open, spittle running from it to join the remains of the tomato.

'She was a fine woman the last time I saw her.'

'Why the hell didn't you tell me about her?' Lindsey hurls the remainder of his meal, along with his plate, at the wall.

Piet, unmoving and unmoved, smiles. 'You didn't ask me.'

'Where was she that night?'

'Under your feet, my lord, right under your feet. She must have heard every single word you said.'

'And what does she look like?'

'Like her mother.' Piet rips one tiny sliver of ham from the slice he puts on his plate.

'And what, pray, was her mother like?'

'If you'd have taken time to look at the picture on the wall of my study you'd know.'

Lindsey closes his eyes, a volcano close to erupting. *Picture, picture.* 'Tall, blonde, almost white, hair. Straight hair, straight face.' He forgets himself. 'Dear God. I had her in my sights when I got that damn pirate woman.'

Piet's face goes white. 'What?'

'Ah, that's one thing you didn't know, then,' Lindsey spits. 'That she must have found her way onto Red Lil's ship, that she must have gone with her to Gombroon.'

'That's too much of a coincidence.'

'It's no coincidence. She must have told Lil about me, and guessed where I'd be headed with the loot from your house. And even if she didn't, Gombroon's where everyone trades now anyway, as you well know.'

Piet slumps forwards. 'That's where she is.'

'She won't be there any more. That's why we scorched the island. But fuck knows where she is now.'

'The clock nearly helped you kill her.' Piet takes his hand out of his shirt. 'I should break it into tiny pieces.'

Lindsey stifles a laugh. 'Too late now, you fool.' He smashes his fist into the table. 'But I've been a fool,

221

too. I should've known then who she was. Such an easy target she was, too. What was I doing, thinking you were all on your own?'

'She'll be thinking I'm dead.' Piet's voice is flat, resigned.

'I hope so.'

'She'll be …'

'… looking for me.' Lindsey laughs. 'Oh, yes. She'll be running straight for me, and I'll be ready.' He reaches across to Piet before he can react and rips the clock from around his neck. 'There. It's mine now.'

'It won't save you from death,' Piet coughs. 'It'll be no use to you at all.'

'We'll see about that. Now piss off back to your cell.'

Piet is too weak to resist the two men who grab him and drag him out of the door. He slumps against them, defeated.

Once the door has closed, Lyndsey puts the clock on the table. Carefully. He leans back, chews on another piece of bread and ham, rubs his face. 'I should have done this straightaway,' he says to himself. Still, he doesn't touch it. After a few minutes, he leans forwards, touches it with his finger tips. It's cold to his touch, not warm like Brants always claims it is. He raises an eyebrow. Probably nothing. Just because Brants hasn't had it under his shirt for a quarter of an hour.

Lindsey opens it gently, slowly, as if it were about to explode. He expects light to jump from it, like it did when Brants allowed it to show him how to make the gun, when plans and pictures of the new weapon spiralled around the room. Nothing happens. 'What the hell?' He picks it up, open as it is, looks at its base, swivels it this way and that, turns it through every conceivable angle. Nothing. He shakes it, not violently, but the way you would rock a baby to sleep. Still nothing. He puts it down again, and scratches his head. Nothing's different, is it?

'Ah.' he smiles. 'That must be the trick.' He takes the leather strap and the watch, ties it around his neck, drops the clock into his shirt, leans back so that the cool stone rests against his chest. He puts his hands behind his head, closes his eyes, and waits. 'Patience, my boy. Patience, that's the key.' He keeps his eyes closed, thinks of all the things he wants to do, just like he was thinking of the perfect weapon with which to ambush the pirate woman, the thief of his wealth, on that first day after he'd broken into Brants' home. And then he'd had two months in which to have the gun made. They'd even only had to test it once, and it shot true the very first time. A shame he'd lost a crewman with that test, but to blow a man's head off from a distance of over one mile was truly something wondrous. He'd enjoyed having a weapon in his hand that almost took aim itself, that almost completed the kill itself. All he'd had to do was pull the trigger.

He's pulled from his waking slumber by an uncomfortable prickling on his chest. He thinks nothing of it, puts his hands into his shirt to take out the clock, to open it. It is suddenly hot, not just warm, and his fingers sizzle at its touch. His chest is now bright red, hot and peeling. 'Get off me,' he screams. 'Get away.' The heat smells of singed flesh, and the pain becomes unbearable. He leans forwards again, so the clock isn't touching his skin. It burns black holes into his shirt. 'What the hell?' He fumbles with the knot he tied, and can't fathom it, although he knows his knots better than most men. His fingers are bleeding now, and his shirt smoking. He tries to pull the leather strap up over his head, but it won't fit. It seems to be tightening, like a noose, with every second, with every breath he takes. He bolts, a man possessed, out through the door, and down the stairs to Piet's cell. The pain almost makes him faint.

'Take it off me,' he shouts through the bars at the man cowering in the corner. 'Get it off me. It's killing me. It's killing me.'

Piet slowly raises his head. 'Perhaps I should just let it.'

'I'll let you go,' Lindsey says. 'I promise.' He falls to his knees, too weak to reach for the key with which to unlock the cage door. He pushes his head against the bars, pleads. 'Please. I'll let you go now.'

Piet stands up, walks across the cell with a measured step. 'I told you it would be of no use to you.'

'You didn't tell me it would kill me.'

Piet kneels down next to the bars. 'Because I didn't know it could do this. I've never even heard of it doing that.'

Lindsey's head is heavy, and the burning on his chest grows worse. 'Just take it back, take it back.'

'It must have thought I wanted that gun,' Piet says. 'Because it was still round my neck when you touched it, when you opened it, because you were too afraid to take it from me then.'

'Stop talking, man, and take what's yours.' Lyndsey's groans are interspersed with suppressed squeals of pain.

Piet fumbles with the knots, his broken fingers slow to obey him. 'It seems you've injured the very hands that would save you,' he says.

'You wouldn't let me die, would you?' Lyndsey says. 'You can have all your things back.'

'Those you haven't given the king, you mean.'

'Everything I have.'

'Oh, how the mighty fall.'

'Just do it,' Lyndsey says through clenched teeth, the strap cutting into his straining neck.

'And if I don't?'

'We'll both be dead, because my men will never let you get away.'

'If you say so.' Piet finally manages to loosen one of the knots, and drags the clock through the bars, and lets it down gently onto the floor. It doesn't even mark the boards. He picks it up. 'I don't know what you're talking about,' he says. 'It's just its normal temperature.'

Lindsey, half-blind, half-dead, and senseless, reaches down to his belt with an instinctive, hidden gesture, rips out his dagger, and plunges it between the bars and into Piet's chest. 'Never trust a dying man,' he says, and collapses onto the floor.

Chapter 31

Mid-afternoon, Fien, Ben and Ishtar see London in the distance, a mass of ramshackle thatched houses, and, around them, the stone and brick of mansions and towers. At the gates, people come and go, more leaving than entering. The tension is palpable.

'This doesn't feel good,' Ben says.

'No.' Fien pulls her horse to a halt, dismounts. 'Make sure you have your hand on your sword,' she says, standing next to him. 'Lindsey could be anywhere.'

'We need to find the docks.'

'It's as good a place to start as any.' She makes sure her hat is firmly over her hair, that the buttons of her loose shirt are done up, feels the weight of her knives under her shirt and feels, for a short moment comforted by their presence. 'Let's find the bastard.'

They keep Ishtar between them, don't want her obvious foreignness to grab anyone's intention. She's not bothered, though, and saunters along the dirty roads without a care. She holds her horse close, whispers in her ear almost constantly, as if describing the city. She strokes her flank incessantly. No-one seems to notice her dark hair or dark skin.

Progress is slow. They have to fight against the oncoming flood of people leaving the city. They have to squeeze past groups of people standing in the alleys. Snatches of conversation drift their way.

'They say the king's gone already …'

'Parliament's not going to stand for this …'

'What if there is war? It'll destroy our trade …'

'It's not the king, it's the others …'

'We'll be ripe for the plucking if this war happens. The French or the Spanish will just come and take us …'

They keep walking, sure to blend into the crowds,

sure not to look too interested in what's said and who says it. The stench of the city is awful, but, however much they long to pull something up over the mouths and noses, they can't. It will make them look out of place, like the foreigners they are. And the last thing they want to do is to attract attention.

The road slopes ever so slightly, and they keep following it down. It has to lead to the river or the sea, they reason. They push steadily forwards until they see, no more than a mile away, the white walls of some tall tower, an immense fortress.

'In the middle of a city?' Ben says.

'We never came here, for some odd reason,' she says.

'Is there any chance Lindsey and your father knew each other? Perhaps that's why he never came here, because he didn't want to bump into Lindsey, because he didn't want him to know he had a daughter.'

'You're asking too much,' she says, her mouth close to his ear. 'I can't guess. I don't want to guess. I don't want to suddenly find out that what I'm fearing is true, that my father was one of the bad people we're trying to defeat.'

'You're father wasn't a bad man,' Ishtar says. 'He was kind, and gentle, and wise.'

'How would you know?' Fien regrets the sharpness of her words as soon as they come out of her mouth.

'You wouldn't be as you are if he hadn't be,' Ishtar says. 'Judge a man by his daughters, not by his sons, is what we say where I'm from.'

'And a mother?' Ben says.

'By her sons, of course,' Ishtar says. 'Obvious, no?'

'Naturally,' Ben says. 'How stupid of me.'

Ishtar laughs. 'And now you think I'm judging your mother badly, because you think so little of yourself.'

'I didn't say that.' Ben furrows his brow and slows down.

Fien touches his elbow. 'Come on.'

'I miss her.'

'So do I,' Fien says. 'I wish she was here with us.'

'At least Harry won't be judged by me,' Ben says.

'What do you mean?'

'I knew about them, a long time ago,' he says. 'I just never guessed he was my father.'

Fien coughs. 'He's not,' she says, afraid of not telling the truth.

'What?' Ben stops walking. 'Who then?'

'Oh dear,' Fien says. 'I never thought to tell you in that hell of days we lived through after she died.'

'Tell me what?'

'She killed your father the night before she died, when we saved Ishtar.'

'Why didn't you tell me straightaway?'

'Is that really something you'd have wanted t think about when we were burying her?'

'Don't you think a man has a right to know his parentage?' He pulls hard at the reins of his horse. 'Didn't you think I had the right to know where I come from?'

'I … I suppose I didn't have the courage. I was hurting, too.'

'Hurt, hurt. You know nothing about hurt.'

'I lost my parents, too.'

'And one of them killed the other?' Ben says.

'No,' Fien says drily. 'I killed one of them, because she refused to save herself from the wounds I inflicted on her.'

'Stop arguing, you two,' Ishtar says, gently. 'This won't bring them back. And it won't help us either. People are staring.'

Ben shakes his head, and starts walking again. 'Craziness,' he says. 'Tell me about it.' He looks across to her, over the back of Ishtar's horse, over the top of

Ishtar's head. 'I promise I won't shout or argue again.'

'Does it matter anymore?' Fien says.

'To me, it does, because I don't understand it.'

So she tells him, slowly, falteringly, tells him of love and betrayal, youth and misjudgement, recognition, regret, and self-abasement, and the flight from hate. She tells him about that night, that last night with Lil, about the trade in slave women, neutered, bereft, torn from their communities, about the look on Sachin's face of arrogance and the lack of pity, of his willingness to put women to death, to corrupt them, to tear from them incompleteness from completeness. And she whispers to him that his father was never his father, that his parentage matters nothing, that Lil was protecting him, that all she wanted was his safety, that all she thought about, that freckled woman who was so strong until a bullet from the future broke her, was what path her son might tread, that he should never become what that so-called prince became. And her steps are light and careful, and her words gentle and kind and without gore and without hate, just a retelling of events without the embroidery of emotion. It exhausts her. And then they reach the walls around the big white tower, and there are no more words.

'Don't stop walking, don't stop,' Ishtar hisses.

The Tower is surrounded by guards, on horse and on foot. A banner flies from the pole at its highest point.

'The king's in there?' Ben whispers.

'Must be,' Fien says, and forces herself to keep walking. She's suddenly tired, oh so tired.

'Or maybe it's just for show,' Ben says.

The three don't change their gait, don't slouch or try to hide their faces. They just keep walking, backs straight, horses on a tight rein, looking straight ahead, ignoring the danger, the opportunity, the temptation.

'Remember,' Fien says when she thinks they're out of

hearing distance of the soldiers. 'Remember it's Lindsey we're after, not the king. He can do what he wants for all I'm concerned.'

'Even though his greed killed your father?' Ben says.

'Lindsey would have gone hunting for riches without the king,' she says. 'The king just gave him an excuse, something for him to hide his real reasons behind.' She shrugs. 'But he's going to be made to pay for it. And I'll take what's rightfully mine.'

They crest an undulation in the hill, and, all at once, can see all the way down to the river, where a fleet of ships floats, anchored against the current, water brushing against the swaying hulls, forming white-crested bow waves against stationary wood. And tallest amongst them all, a collection of black masts, black furled sails, and blackened oak boards, evil even at this distance.

'He doesn't believe in hiding himself, does he?' Ben says.

'No,' is all Fien says.

'I guess we need to keep ourselves out of sight from here in. He may still have the gun,' Ben says. 'And he must have seen us clearly if he was able to hit Lil at that vast distance.'

'Probably,' Lil says, but makes no attempt at hiding herself. 'On the other hand, he might not be looking. And he certainly won't be expecting us, not together, with our hands still sore from killing nineteen of the king's men.'

'So what do we do?' Ben says, his hand on the hilt of his sword, his hair tangled and knotted, his eyes strained and alert.

'We keep walking,' Fien says. 'And hope he can't see us. And we don't stop until we're on board the ship and we've killed him.'

'What if he's not there?' Fien says. 'What then?'

'He'll have to come back at some point,' Fien says. 'He has to. And then we'll get him.'

'What about the crew?'

'We'll work out a plan when we get there,' Fien says. 'But no sooner. There's no point. We know nothing about the ship or her crew.'

'Maybe we should just steal the ship along with everything on it,' Ishtar says, and grins.

'That may not be such a bad idea,' Finn says, and puts one foot in front of the other, strides widened by the irresistible drag of gravity and revenge.

Chapter 32

Lindsey stumbles up the steps, bloody dagger in hand, out onto the deck. His men are alarmed at his appearance, at the black holes in his shirt, at his red face, at his hands, clawing all over his body. He drags himself to the side of the ship and, without stopping, hurtles himself into the water. One of his men jumps in after him, lands next to the whirlpool of Lindsey's struggles in the water. He tries to grab hold of his master, but gets pushed away again and again.

'Leave me, leave me. I have to stop this burning. So hot.'

Some of the men watch from above, bemused, bewildered, frightened. They've never seen him like this. It's as if he's gone mad, as if his senses have left him. He's even foaming at the mouth.

Lindsey's still scrabbling around in the water, the stinking, fetid water of St Katherine's by the Tower. He dives under the water again and again, surfacing only to splutter and cough before he dives again. Only when he hears the bells chime does he stop, does he calm himself, and swim back to the quayside, where he drags himself out of the water like an old man dragging himself out of bed for an unwanted occasion. He stomps back on deck, his clothes dripping everywhere. His eyes are a pale green, sharp and furious, his face pale and drawn. He shakes himself off. 'What the hell are you looking at?' he shouts. 'Get back to work.'

In his cabin, he rips off his clothes, pours the pail of fresh water that he always has next to his bed over himself, looks down at the clock-shaped burn on his chest, makes himself touch it, winces, and pulls a fresh shirt from the cupboard next to this bed. 'It'll just have to hurt,' he mumbles. 'I've got to think.'

He throws open the stern windows. 'No bloody air.'

232

He sits at the table for a few seconds, jumps up, wanders around the room. 'At least I got rid of him.' He's gabbling. 'What for the clock now? No use to anyone, not even his daughter. Oh, I'll make myself a fine meal of her when she comes. She's bound to come. I'll rip her apart, slowly, make her wish she'd never been born.' He moves without thinking and the burn catches on his shirt. He urges himself to calm down with a wave of his arms. He can't stop pacing. 'We've got to get rid of the body,' he shouts at no-one, rushes out of the room, down the steps to the cell, ignores the roughing of the cotton on the wound, bursts into the chamber.

'I don't think you managed to kill me,' Piet says quietly, blood all over his shirt and face. 'I don't understand it.' He looks down himself, touches his wet shirt with his hands which come away covered in blood. 'It's not supposed to stop its wearer from being killed by force.'

'You're the devil,' Lindsey spits.

'Perhaps I am. I don't know what I am.' Piet puts his hand inside his shirt to where the wound should be, rips the shirt open. 'Look, it's gone. Healed in a few moments.' He laughs hysterically. 'This is madness, madness. She could have saved herself, not given herself to death. She could have been a mother.'

Lindsey's having trouble standing up straight. 'You're not real,' he says, makes the sign of the cross with his fingers. 'I'm dreaming this. It's the pain that's doing it.' He scratches his head, looking for a memory. 'Or it's that damn Thames water. Full of shit. I shouldn't have jumped, but I needed to cool myself.'

'I am real, Lindsey,' Piet calls. 'Come here and feel how real I am.'

'Never,' Lindsey says. 'Never.' He turns this way and that, can't stand still although he's almost falling over.

'The king, the king needs to know about this. He must to war now before the devils take London.' He rushes up to the main deck, skids across the gang plank, and snatches the nearest horse. He launches himself onto it, drives it, bareback, out onto the road that leads up to the Tower.

Chapter 33

Fien is nearly knocked over by the horse thundering along the path, dust thrown up by its panicked hooves. The man on the horse doesn't look down, his face manic, arms and legs working as hard as they can, blood spraying from his horse's sides, spurs dug in as far as they'll go. But she, looking up, jumping back, stumbling, recognises him, would know his face anywhere, the face of her nightmares, the face she saw through the kitchen window all those months ago, the face that killed her father. She draws her blade and slashes at the horse, but she's too late. He's already yards past her, without noticing her. She reaches inside her shirt for one of her knives.

Ben puts a hand on her arm. 'Leave it,' he says. 'You'd only hurt someone innocent.'

She shakes him away, angrily. 'You think I can't hit him from here?' she screams.

'Not at this distance, no. And do you want him to die without knowing who you are? And do you really want to risk killing someone who's not involved at all?'

People are looking at them now.

'An ale or two too many,' Ben says, and waves them away. 'Just a little misunderstanding amongst friends.'

The crowd grow disinterested as quickly as they became interested, shrug and turn away, trudging away to what ever it is that should be occupying them.

'This is our chance,' Ben says, quietly. 'We can get the ship.'

'You think he's left it without guards, do you?' Fien says, her cheeks still red with rage. 'You're a fool.'

'Not a fool,' Ben says, bowing his head as if trying to get out of the way of her sharp words. 'Just a friend trying to protect you from your enemies and from yourself.'

'You are both fools,' Ishtar says, her arms folded, and her eyes full of amusement. 'You love each other and you argue in public. You love each other and yet you've not slept with each other. You're in love, but you do nothing about it. Tomorrow could be too late.'

'There are more important things to do right now,' Fien says.

'More important than love?' Ishtar says. 'It can't be real love then.'

'It's real enough to me,' Ben says. 'But we need to get Lindsey and the clock first.'

'And what if you die trying?' Ishtar says. 'Then you'll never know what it would have been like. And that's sad.'

'What do they teach you in Persia?' Fien says. 'To throw yourself under the first man you like, no matter how young you are?'

'I was always taught to follow my instincts and not to ignore them.'

'Well, my instinct was to go after Lindsey. He killed my father, after all.'

Ishtar shrugs. 'Maybe things are different for you two?'

'You haven't, have you?' Ben says to her. 'You're only thirteen.'

Ishtar doesn't blush. Instead, she laughs. 'No, and I haven't, and I won't for some time. You must try to understand people as people not as things. And every person is different. ... But you two, you're old now, and you're free to do what you want.'

'Now's not the time,' Fien says. 'Let's go and see if we can get onto Lindsey's ship.'

The three make the final walk down to the quay, straight towards Lindsey's ship. As they get closer, they can see that it's riddled with guards, bored guards by the look of it, on all sides.

'Impossible,' Fien says. 'They'd catch us in less than a minute.'

'We can kill them all,' Ishtar says, her knives in her hands already. 'Just like we killed all Sir John's men, and they were attacking us, not hanging over rails looking bored and uninterested.'

''Where can Lindsey have gone?' Fien says. 'The king? Or somewhere else?'

'It doesn't matter,' Ben says.

'I'm trying to work out when he might be back,' Fien says.

'He could be back any moment or not for hours,' Ishtar says. 'It doesn't matter.'

'He'll have taken the clock with him,' Fien says. 'So we'll have to get on the ship and wait.'

'Or not get on the ship and wait,' Ben says.

'What I'm trying to say is that there's no point trying to capture the ship, because we want Lindsey not his ship.'

'Let's just get on the damn thing and see what's there and what not,' Ben says.

'And how do you suggest doing that without getting us killed?' Fien says.

'We could always pretend to be someone we're not and persuade the guards to let us on so we can wait for their master.'

'Ridiculous,' Fien says. 'They'll not see through that ruse at all.'

'Why can't we just kill them all?' Ishtar says, and flashes her teeth.

'You're a bloodthirsty little woman,' Fien says.

'Is that a bad thing?' Ishtar says. 'I only like killing bad people, not good people. There can't be any good people on that ship if they're helping your enemy. Let me go on there alone and kill all of them, nice and quickly and silently.'

'No,' Fien says. 'Either we all go together or none of us go. You're both my responsibility.'

Ishtar kicks at the ground with her boot, her face sullen, the smile gone.

'Come on,' Fien says. 'Try to understand me. And remember that I am the Commandant.' She smiles sadly. 'Even though I'd rather the real one was here with us. She'd know what to do.'

'She'd probably have sailed up the river all cannons blazing, and the devil take the hindmost.'

Fien shakes her head. 'No, she wouldn't. She valued all your lives too much.' She takes a deep breath. 'Right. We need to find somewhere to hide the horses, and then we'll see if we can get onto that damned boat without getting noticed.'

The Thames is a bloody red. The three leave their hiding place, where they even managed to sleep for a few short hours, each in turn, and two on guard. The sun falls rapidly below the horizon now, the red fades to black, and the current seems to stop still before reversing. The tides are huge here, but go unnoticed because they've become a part of what everyone expects.

'Bloody hell, it's huge,' Fien says as they stand near Lindsey's ship, its black walls towering above them.

'Twice the size of *The Odyssey*,' Ben says. 'At least. We'll need rope to get on board.'

Fien grunts. 'There must be another way.'

'Get in the water and swim round to the other side,' Ishtar says. 'I'll drop a rope from the ship.'

'And you'll get on how?'

Ishtar shrugs. 'I'll get on. That's all you need to know.'

'The water's not exactly healthy,' Ben says.

'If we get ill, it won't be straightaway, and it'll pass,' Fien says.

'Wait,' Ishtar says. 'Let me have another look. Stay here.' She disappears into the gloom.

Fien and Ben kick their heels, trying not to look suspicious, walk along the length of the ship and back, very slowly, doing their best not to look up at its deck, doing their best to look as if they just happen to be passing.

'You don't need to swim,' Ishtar says, appearing from nowhere. 'Right at the back of the ship, it gets so wide I can get a rope to drop down onto the land.'

'But that'll be from where the wheel is.'

Ishtar shakes her head. 'Further back, higher up.'

'I don't understand,' Fien says.

'Just be there,' Ishtar says. 'Half an hour.'

'Don't go killing anyone just for the sake of it,' Ben says.

'We mean it,' Fien says.

'I know,' Ishtar says. 'Unfortunately.' She turns. 'See you later.' She disappears again.

'We really ought to have left one of us here on the quayside to warn the others when Lindsey gets back,' Fien says.

'If he comes back tonight,' Ben says. 'Maybe he's decided to visit a whorehouse.'

'Perhaps. Although, judging by the crazy look on his face, I can't think he'd want to waste his time on that. He looked like he'd seen a ghost, and like he was in a rage.'

'Perhaps he just pulls stupid faces when he's riding hard.'

'Maybe.' Fien sighs. 'Too late for us to guard ourselves now, anyhow.'

'We'll be fine. Who cares if he comes back when we're still on there? It'll give us a better chance of finishing him off once and for all.'

'We've never had that chance before.' Fien chews Lil's

pipe. 'Come on, Ishtar.'

'I hope she's alright.'

'She's very resourceful,' Ben says.

'You can say that again. What is it with *The Odyssey* that she attracts such clever people?'

'Fate?' Ben says, sounding less than convinced.

'You might doubt it deep down, but I don't,' Fien says. She stamps at the ground impatiently. 'We're going to have to go and find her.'

'Be patient, for God's sake.'

'I am being.'

'I'd hate to see you when you're impatient then.'

Just then a rope coils its slow, invisible way down the corner of the ship, and an owl hoots.

'You first,' Fien says, tugging the rope to signal to Ishtar they've found it. There's a tug back.

'No,' Ben says. 'You first.'

'Let's not argue about this as well. Do as you're told.'

Ben starts climbing, slowly, circumspectly, trying desperately not to collide with the ship's side. Fien's eyes follow him until he disappears into the ship, somewhere.

Fien grabs the rope, wraps her legs around it, pulls herself up with her arms, pushes with her feet. God, she feels tired. *This must stop soon*, she thinks, grits her teeth. She thinks she's about to fall when two pairs of arms grab her and drag her into the ship. She falls unceremoniously onto the floor of wherever it is she's ended up. They all freeze in case the sound of her falling has attracted anyone's attention. There's no movement from elsewhere.

'Good,' Fien says, jumps up, brushes herself down, and looks around. 'It's the bloody captain's quarters, Ishtar. I thought you were going higher up than the wheel.'

'The door was open, so I came in here. It overhangs

the quay as well.'

'How did you get past the guards?' Fien says.

'I'm only little. I crawled and they weren't looking down.'

'So you kept your promise?'

Ishtar nods. Her hands are behind her back where no-one can see them, fingers crossed.

'Good.' Fien takes another look out of the window. 'I suppose we could make start in here, just in case Lindsey didn't take the clock with him.'

'He's bound to have,' Ben says. 'You wouldn't leave something that precious lying around.'

'He's left something else precious lying around, though,' Fien says, and points at something leaning in the corner, long and narrow, a warm golden glow coming from it. 'It must be the gun that killed Lil.' She walks across to the thing. It's half as tall as she is. She picks it up. 'It's not as heavy as I expected it to be.' She runs one of her hands along the barrel. She feels resistance, can only half-see what it is she's holding. She takes it towards the window. 'Oh. A collection of bullets.' In the half-light of the early night, she sees the delicate engraving on the gun, engraving matched by the same pattern, smaller and in greater detail, on the bullets. 'I'm taking this.' She feels around next to the gun. There's a box full of bullets on the floor next to it. 'And these.'

'Is that a good idea?' Ben says. 'You don't know how it works. You could end up killing yourself instead of someone else.'

'That's a risk I'm happy to take. If the aim is really true, I'll injure him with one of his bullets and then make him lie there wand watch me cut it out of him while he bleeds away.'

'And you say I'm bloodthirsty,' Ishtar says.

'I have a good reason.'

241

'And I don't?' Ishtar says, and grins. 'He's a man. Isn't that enough?'

Chapter 34

Lindsey clatters into the Whitehall courtyard, the front of his shirt covered in blood from the chafing of the shirt on the burn the clock inflicted. He jumps from the horse, runs across to the gate.

'Two visits in one day, Lord Lindsey?' the gatekeeper says.

Lindsey rushes past him without stopping, without acknowledging. He runs down long corridors, up flights of stairs, breathing hard, the vision of the resurrected Piet still in front of his eyes, wondering if he's going mad, wondering if he's just making it up for himself. *No!* he skids to a halt in front of the King's chambers. The guards step in front of the door.

'The King,' he shouts. 'I have to see the King.'

'The King is busy,' one of the guards says.

'Busy with what?'

'He's preparing for the feast that's about to start.'

'Feast, what fucking feast?' Lindsey is frothing at the mouth. 'I wish he'd stop wasting money on feasts. Let me pass. Now.'

'I can't.'

'Bloody hell, man. This is important.'

'It's close to treason, Sire,' the guard says. 'Please desist, or I'll have to arrest you.'

'You and whose fucking army?' Lindsey's voice is shrill by now.

'Let him in.' A shout through the door. The King's voice.

The guard opens the door just wide enough for Lindsey to squeeze through.

'I wasn't expecting to see you again for some time,' the King says. 'What's made you so frantic?'

'The demons are in London, Sire,' Lindsey says, out of breath.

'Are you mad?' Charles doesn't smile.

'I … I don't think so.' He really doesn't want Charles to know about the clock. 'I just think you should march for Nottingham as soon as possible and leave London for your loyal troops down here.'

'That's as good as deserting, man.' Charles begins to pace again, keeps looking at the door to another room.

'Your Highness, would I advise you against my better judgement? There is real danger here, but it's danger I can't put my finger on, and there's real physical danger to your kingdom in the North. Quell the rebellion there, as soon as possible.'

Charles looks at the door again, indecision on his face.

'What is it, Sire? Is someone listening?'

Charles throws himself into a chair. 'In a manner of speaking. Someone who everyone thinks isn't here.'

The door creaks and opens.

'Maria.' Charles holds out his hand.

Lindsey gasps, and bows deeply, hardly recognising the queen who is in plain clothes, haggard and drawn. 'My lady.' His heart is beating up into his throat. He has to control his anger. 'I thought you were in The Hague.'

'I still am, because no-one knows I'm here, except for my husband and, now, you.'

'Have you raised enough money then?' Lindsay says.

'No-one there will accept the royal jewels as security,' she says. 'Especially not the big pieces. And I wanted to be with my husband just for a short time. Is that such a dreadful thing?' She sits down next to Charles.

'It's not safe in London, my Lady,' Lindsey says.

'It's not safe anywhere,' she says. 'And it tires me that it is so.'

'You're not planning to go to the feast with His Highness, are you?' Lindsey says.

She shakes her head. 'I wish I could, but I don't think that would be a very good idea.'

244

'I don't think having a feast at all is a good idea. They cost too much f… money.'

'The people should be providing for the Crown,' Charles says. 'It's an outrage they choose to withhold the funds their ruler appointed by God needs.'

'They think you're causing them to starve,' Lindsey says.

'You're on their side now, are you?' Maria says, her face and voice sharp. 'You should have his head for treason,' she says to her husband.

'You misunderstand me, Your Majesty,' Lindsey says. 'I am merely counselling cautious politics. If a rebellion gathers momentum.'

'There shouldn't even be a question of rebellion,' the Queen says. 'The people are lucky to have us.'

'*We* know that,' Lindsey says. 'But they don't. And it would be advisable, for a little time, for the Court not to be seen to be as extravagant as people might perceive it to be.'

'I think the Queen's advice on these matters is quite enough,' Charles says without looking at Lindsey. 'Is that all?'

Lindsey bows even lower. 'I must ask Your Highness to consider marching to Nottingham to raise the Royal Standard there. I might be mistaken about London.' His head is clearing now. 'But there is imminent danger to the kingdom in the North, and if you do not strike the first blow, I'm afraid of the consequences. There may be many more who cross to the Parliamentarians' cause if you don't teach them an early lesson.'

'What do you think, my heart?' Charles says, leaning across to the Queen and taking her hand in his.

She's close to tears. 'If what he says about Parliamentarians massing in the North is true, he's right, I'm afraid. What happened to the peaceful kingdom we created?'

You fucking destroyed it with your masques and feasts and ridiculous talk of God-given majesty, Lindsey thinks, a smile fixed to his face. 'It will return once you are victorious,' he says. 'One battle, I think, and all this will be over.' He feels his heart slowing down.

'What happened to your shirt, Lindsey?' Charles says. 'Is that your blood?'

'Just a slight mishap on the ship, Sire. I didn't want to waste time changing. I am very sorry to have appeared before Your Majesties in such disarray.'

'Of mind and body,' Maria says. 'These times tax us all.'

'I am fully recovered now,' Lindsey says. 'When do we march?'

'In four days,' the King says. 'I don't want this to look like we're withdrawing from London.'

'I can send word out to all your troops in the North, to await your arrival. I don't think we need take any of our men from here with us.'

'We'll take a guard, at least,' the King says. 'Await my command. I will send word to you. Now leave us.'

'Very well, Your Majesties.' Lindsey bows and walks backwards to the door through which he came.

'And not a word about the Queen to anyone,' Charles says. 'Or I'll have your head.'

Lindsey nods, his mouth set. He'll be back with his ship in under the hour.

Charles and Maria, on their own, sit silently, not moving, their hands entwined. Finally, he lets go of her.

'You took a great risk travelling here on your own.'

'In disguise,' she says.

'Someone might have recognised you anyway. Someone might have talked, like someone must have talked when I went to the Commons to arrest Pym and the others.'

'I wanted to see you. I had to be with you.'

'You are too loyal, my heart.'

She shakes her head. 'You are too kind. To everyone.'

'I try not to be.'

'The crown is a great burden to you, isn't it?'

'Only because the people I rule don't understand me and won't let me rule them. They don't think I'm kind.'

'They don't know you,' she says.

'Not like you know me, no.'

'Do you still trust Lindsey?'

'In some things. Not in others. I don't think he gives me everything he collects on his travels.'

'Building his own purse?'

'I think so.'

'Don't let him be the only commander of the army when you stand against the Roundheads,' she says. 'He would lead you astray, I fear.'

'Are you saying he's disloyal to me? I'll have him executed on the spot.'

'No, no,' she says and puts a calming hand on her trembling king. 'I just think he is an old man who may not understand war as well as he may once have done.' She looks at him. 'And don't forget that he's an old comrade of Essex. They studied together in Holland.'

'Do you have anyone else in mind?'

'When the time comes, use the cavalry and let Prince Rupert command them and report to you alone. He understands war, although he's so young.'

'I will ponder what you say.'

'Promise me you'll do what I ask. I am worried for you, and fear I may never see you again if you allow Lindsey alone to lead your forces into battle.'

'And where shall I be in this decisive battle?' he lowers his head onto her lap.

'At the back, where you must be to be safe.' She strokes his hair under his wig.

'It's not much of a king who leads from the back.'

'It's a prudent king who directs his men from where he can see the whole field of battle.'

'I am lucky to have such a wise wife,' he says.

'And I to have such an obedient husband.'

'To think we didn't like each other much when we first were married.'

'We were young and didn't understand what we were intended to do.'

'It was a long time ago,' he says.

'And now we love each other.'

'And you have given me the heirs my kingdom needs.'

'Promise me you'll be careful.' She makes him sit up again. 'And don't wait those four days. Get yourself to Nottingham as soon as you can and form an army.'

'You agree with Lindsey on that at least.'

'I would have advised you first if he hadn't interrupted us.'

'There was no point letting him shout the place down outside the door. And no point whatsoever in getting the guards to cut him down. I need him, one way or another.'

She nods. 'It's just a shame he arrived when he did.'

'I'll cancel the feast.'

'You can't do that,' she says. 'There will be too many questions. But you can just put in an appearance. Tell the assembled that you must plan for war, although you'd prefer there to be none. Encourage them to be loyal to their anointed king, make them cheer for you so loudly that the walls of the Banqueting Hall shake and so the people outside know that England supports its king, and will always do so.'

'A victory speech before the battle. That is a good idea.'

'And then come back to me so we can share a few hours before I leave in the morning.'

'It's your turn to make a promise now, Maria.'

'And what promise would you like, my dear?'

'Promise me you'll take care on the way back, and that you'll send word as soon as you get to The Hague again.'

'I promise, my husband.'

'And tell those who will listen that their money is safe with me, that it will be used to keep this Britain great, and that this Britain will be their greatest ally for all the help they give.'

'I promise that, too.'

Charles gets up and goes down on one knee in front of her, and takes her left hand. 'With the hand connected to your heart, would you marry me again?'

'Oh, yes,' she says. 'With more fervour than the first time, with more love and admiration for you in my heart than ever.'

'Thank you,' he says, and kisses her fingers. 'I can feast now with a glad heart and a clear head. And I can give the lords and ladies the right words on which to feast in addition to the fine food and wine we have for them.'

Their lingering hands part as he makes his way to the door.

'Hurry back to me, my dear heart,' she says. 'Hurry back.'

Chapter 35

Just as Fien is about to open the drawers in Lindsey's cabin, Ben hears a commotion down on the quayside.

'I think Lindsey's back,' he says. 'We've got to go. Quick.'

'Dammit,' Fien says, exasperated. 'That didn't take him very long, whatever it was.'

'The whore will be happy to get him out of the way so quickly,' Ishtar says, sniggering.

'Or he's had an argument with the king,' Fien says.

'Whatever it is, he's back, and we need to get out of here,' ben says.

'Or we could just wait in here, and I could kill him the minute he walks in through those doors.'

'And then die yourself?' Ben says. 'Don't you value your life enough to get the clock and make yourself immortal?'

'Not if I can't be immortal with you,' she says.

'That's stupid talk. Now come on.' He grabs Ishtar. 'You first.'

Lindsey roars as he find the dead guards outside.

'You broke your promise, Ishtar,' Fien hisses, but the girl's already gone over the side.

'You next,' Ben says and pushes Fien out of the window, and jumps straight out after her, only narrowly missing Lindsey's gun she has slung over her shoulder.

Lindsey rips open the window, sees the dark shapes scaling the side of the ship, feels the rope next to him, pulls out his dagger and severs the cord. He doesn't hear any splashes in the water. He runs out of the cabin. 'Get down there and find the people who killed your mates, you useless bastards. Get down there and bring them back. There were at least two of them.' He stamps back into his cabin, ignoring the two dead men outside, throws himself into a chair and opens his decanter of red wine. The first glass is gone within seconds.

When the rope goes slack, Fien's almost down. She lets herself drop to the ground, rolls, and grabs two fistfuls of pebbles, throws them onto the water, all in one motion. She almost feels Ben falling through the air, hardly hears him hit the surface of the water disturbed by the stones she's thrown out for him. A few seconds later, she's holding her hand out to him to drag him out of the water.

'Disgusting stuff,' he spits, and hauls himself fully from the river. 'I really didn't need that.'

'Shut up and run.'

They sprint towards where they think their horses are. Ishtar's already waiting for them, on her horse.

'Where to?'

'Anywhere but here,' Fien says. 'And quickly. They're after us.'

'Can't we wait and kill them?'

'No, we can't. If you'd kept your promise, Lindsey would never have noticed anything.'

'Then you wouldn't have his gun, because I wouldn't have got in.'

By now they're galloping westwards along the course of the river, into the narrow alleys that make up the centre of London.

'Just keep riding,' Fien shouts. 'Until it's so dark we can't see anything.'

Ishtar pushes her horse hard, put her fingers between the mare's ears and mutters something in Persian. The horse speeds up even more, and the other two have difficulty keeping up with her. The alleys become narrower, darker, damper, and then black.

'Stop,' Fien calls.

Ishtar's horse rears when she pulls her up, and the

other two almost run into her back. 'Here,' Ishtar says. 'This is a good place to hide, but not so good a place to stay safe.'

'We'll be alright here for a while,' Fien says. 'We'll walk from here. There must be church or something we can shelter in.'

'You believe in God?' Ben says.

Fien shrugs. 'When I need to, and when there's sanctuary on offer.'

They walk on, until a dark shadow looms ahead of them.

'I told you,' Fien says, and pushes against the massive wooden doors. 'I'm sure they won't mind three horses sheltering with us.'

The church looks empty, just a few desolate candles flickering in front of the altar. The horses' hooves echo all around. A single dark figure rises from in front of the candles, turns towards them, face hidden by a hood. 'Welcome,' a voice says. 'Welcome to my church.'

Fien approaches carefully, a knife in one hand, her horse's reins in the other.

'Don't you trust a man of God?' the figure says. 'Especially after welcoming you into this house of God?'

'I trust no-one,' she says.

'That's sad.' He drops his hood, and she's looking into a face scarred by fire. 'I'm Giles The Priest,' he says. 'And you are safe in this church.'

Fien puts her knife away and holds out her hand. 'Thank you, Giles.' The hand she holds is as scarred as his face. She daren't ask him what's happened to him.

'I can read faces, child,' he says. 'They tried to burn me as a heretic some time ago. A long time ago, in fact.' His face creases as he smiles. 'It doesn't hurt anymore. Not physically, anyway.'

'Why would they do that?' Ishtar says, moving into

the circle of the candles' light. 'Can't they just let people live how they want?'

'Oh, this is England,' Giles says. He can't be young anymore, but the flames have licked his face clean of anything that might tell of his age. 'You have to choose sides here, you always have had to. There's never been a middle way, and maybe there never will be.'

'Yet you appear to have been put in charge of a church,' Ben says. 'So you must have chosen a side.'

'A wise young man,' Giles says, puts his hands together, as if in supplication, and looks up to the ceiling of his church. 'But I think my god doesn't mind small lies instead of big ones. I may have chosen a side for all those who choose to watch me, but I haven't chosen one in my heart. Because in my heart there are no sides. Just the poor and needy, just those seeking salvation of any kind.'

'And your congregation?' Fien says, struggling with the English word.

'They're happy to choose as middle a ground as they can, if they can. So nothing matters.' He sits down on a wooden bench, his breath heavy. 'Oh, my Lord, I am getting old. Death holds no fear for me any longer. Nothing can hurt as much as the fire did.' He waves his hands around. 'Please, tie up your horses, make them comfortable. I don't think we'll have a bigger congregation than this tonight.' He puts his hands on his chest, his breath now normal again. 'I'll lock the doors to make sure. And then I'll bring you and your beasts some sustenance. You all look as if you could do with some.' He looks at Ben, still dripping. 'And for you, young man, I'll get some dry clothes.' He pulls a huge key from the rope around his waist holding his robe closed. 'Just a moment.' He limps into the dark hole that's the nave, and they hear his irregular footsteps over the stone floor, the creak of the key in the lock.

Giles shuffles back into the light. 'All done,' he says, a gentle smile on his face. 'On second thoughts, bring the animals to the vestry door. There are some comfortable chairs in there. And I can light a fire. These English summer nights aren't as temperate as they used to be.'

They cross the church, and as he opens the door, more light shines at them.

'Please,' he says. 'Follow me. This is the hearth of my home.'

The vestry is bright compared to the rest of the church. Wood is piled in the grate, ready to be lit, The walls are covered in what look like ancient tapestries. The windows are barred and shuttered.

'First things first,' the priest says, his hood following his every movement. 'The fire.' He calls fire from the firebox in his palm, his lashless eyes delighting at the warm flame that jumps onto the wood.

'You still love fire?' Fien says.

'It's a life-giver,' he says. 'It's not its fault that evil people use it to kill the good.'

'You're a strange man,' Ishtar says. 'Full of courage.' She picks her nails with one of her knives. 'And no hate in your entire body.'

'Why waste my emotions?' he says. 'What use at all would that be?' He spreads his hands, points at the chairs, which look too luxurious to be in a church. 'Please, make yourselves comfortable. My home is your home for as long as you wish.' He turns to another closed door. 'And now some food for our weary travellers.'

'Do you trust him?' Ben whispers when Giles is gone. 'It seems odd that a man so mistreated should bear no grudges to anyone.'

'He carries pain in his heart,' Ishtar says. 'And kindness to others is the only way he can lessen it. He knows he'll never heal it.'

'How sad,' Fien says. 'He must be very lonely.'

'I'm not lonely,' Giles calls from behind the wall. 'This is what I was born to do. To serve others, and to serve my god through it.' He reappears with plates heaped with bread and ham, tomatoes, and cheese.

'Who exactly is your god?' Fien says as the others grab at the food. 'And how do you manage to get hold of food this fresh?'

'My god is the one who saved my life, the one who watches over me and my congregation each and every day, who blesses me with kindness, and lets me live the way I do.'

'And the food?' Ben says.

'I have my own little garden at the back here,' Giles says. 'And I have a baker who is part of my congregation who lives in fear of the extremes as much as I do. He prays with me, and brings me bread. Every day.' He sits down in one of the vacant chairs. 'Mistrust is easier than trust, so I can understand your questions.'

'And if war comes?' Fien says. 'Can you find a middle path between the Royalists and the Parliamentarians? Because England will again call on you to make a choice.'

'There's no choice to be made for me,' he says. ' It's simple. God is my only master. Nothing else matters.'

'But Henry the Eighth made himself supreme ruler of state and church,' Fien says. 'I read about it.'

'That's very true,' Giles says. 'But it doesn't apply to me; it doesn't apply to anyone who has faith.'

'Why?' Fien says.

'Because those of true faith don't rely on organised religion.' It's Ishtar's voice that cuts through the warm must of the vestry.

Giles nods an acknowledgement to her. 'Thank you, my child. That is exactly it. That's the thing no-one seems to understand; your god is what you hold in your heart, not what people and traditions and rituals tell you to believe.'

'But no-one will ever follow that path.'

'There are enough of that persuasion to sustain me,' Giles says.

'And when they break down your doors, and force you to give them an answer, what then?' Ben says.

'Then I'll welcome them with open arms and tell them what I believe.'

'They'll tell you you're not a king's subject nor a believer,' Fien says. 'They'll burn you again.'

Giles takes a very small sip of the wine he brought through after the food. 'And I will not burn,' he says and smiles.

'That's easily said.'

'It's easily done, too.'

'How can you say that?'

'Because I'll be protected. I know I will. One way or the other, I will survive.'

'Have you ever heard of the Immortality Clock?' Ben says.

Giles sits up straight. 'Yes, I have.'

'What do you know about it?' Fien says. 'Is it real? Is it true?'

'How long do you have?' Giles says and leans back.

'It won't be light for hours,' Fien says. 'I think we have plenty of time.'

'Who has it now? Do you know?' Giles says. 'I gave it away once upon a time, a long time ago. It was a poisoned chalice.'

'You owned it?' Fien says, her eyes bright, her mind spinning.

'A gift from some god,' he says. 'That's what saved me from the flames. I'm surprised you hadn't guessed if you know of the clock.'

256

'Who did you give it to?'

'I can't remember. It was a very long time ago. There's a residual effect, you see, if you've owned it for a long time.'

'How long's a long time?' Fien says. 'Ten years, twenty?'

Giles laughs. 'Oh no, my child. That's not a long time at all.'

'Then what?'

'I … I think I gave it away about two hundred years ago.'

Chapter 36

'But you're supposed to die if you give it away,' Fien says, breathless.

'That's what I'd understood, but that's not what seems to have happened,' Giles says.

'It's impossible,' Fien says. 'No-one's truly immortal, especially not without the clock.'

'You didn't ask me how long I'd had it for before I gave it away.'

'So how long did you have it for?'

'Too long. That's why I gave it away.'

'That's not an answer.'

He leans forward, the muscles in his neck straining under his abused skin. 'Do you really want to know? Do you really want a precise answer? Are you ready for what I would have to tell you?' His eyes are nothing if not gentle and understanding. 'The human mind can only understand so much.'

'Tell me,' Fien says. 'I can cope with anything you say.'

'I was given it when the one they call Christ was born,' he says. 'There. I've told you.' He watches their faces drain of blood. 'I owned the original clock for one and a half thousand years.'

'It can't be that old. There were no watches then.' Ben says.

'It's older than even that,' Giles says. 'What does it look like now?'

'It's inside a casing carved from one emerald,' Fien says.

'That must be very pretty,' he says. 'When I had it, it was in a plain silver case.'

'How does it work?'

Giles shrugs, and some kind of pain strikes at him. 'I wish I knew.'

'And how long will you live for now that it's not been yours for nearly two hundred years?'

'I don't know. And I don't really care. I expect to die every day. I've had too long a life, too wearisome an existence. If I'd known then what I know now, I'd never have accepted the gift.'

'But ... but.' Fien struggles to catch her breath. 'I thought you could still die a violent death, even if you owned it.'

'That's a myth someone's dreamed up over the years. If you were now the rightful owner of the clock, and I stabbed you, you'd not die.' He puts his hand on his chest. 'The wound would heal, and you'd live.'

Fien jumps up. 'Then my father must still be alive,' she shouts. 'And I've thought for over half a year that he's dead.'

'Maybe he wishes he were dead,' Giles says softly. 'Because the clock doesn't stop the pain.'

'What's the point of it then?' Fien says. 'I've got to get back to Lindsey's ship. Father must be there.'

'The good Lord Lindsey's involved in this, is he?' The sarcasm of Giles's words is undisguised.

'You know him?' Ben says.

'I know of him.'

'He killed my mother,' Ben says. 'With a weapon the clock made for him.'

'The clock can't make weapons.' He shakes his head. 'It did sometimes play me moving pictures of some fragment of the future, things I thought I wanted but decided I didn't need. But it never told me about my own future.' He sighs and leans back. 'Oh, if I'd only understood, right at the beginning. The problem is – imagine you have something that gives you a power no-one else has. You don't want to give that up, do you? And then, when I realised what I had, I didn't want to part with it. Not at any cost. And it turned me into ...

into this.'

'You two stay here,' Fien says to Ben and Ishtar.

'We'll come with you,' Ishtar says.

'You can't go now,' Giles says. 'You need rest, sleep, sustenance.'

'Don't you think it's strange we found you?' Fien says. 'Such a coincidence.'

'Nothing is so strange it can't be believed,' Giles says. 'Nothing is so strange it can't be true. You just have to have faith in the fate you make for yourself.'

'We go as soon as it gets light, then,' Fien says.

'I'll come with you and your friends,' Giles says.

'You don't have to.'

'I want to.'

They all lapse into silence, so much to think about. They eat all the food Giles has brought them, and then some more. And then Giles bids them good night, limps out of the vestry into whatever lies beyond, after he's made up beds for them from consecrated garments, from anything soft he can find. The candles gutter and go out, and even the horses stretch out on the floor of the church and close their eyes.

The vestry faces west, so first light is nothing but a dim haze of gold that reaches across from the east windows in the church. The horses are first to wake. Ishtar and Ben are still shifting in their deep sleep when Giles comes back into the room, to find Fien sitting up under her makeshift covers, staring into the church.

'Did you sleep well?' he whispers.

'Like a baby.'

'Babies don't actually sleep that well.' He chuckles. 'Be prepared.'

'What?'

'You're going to have children with him, aren't you?'

'I … I don't know.'

'You love each other, don't you?' Giles says. 'So, sooner or later, a child will appear, and it won't be by magic.'

Fien opens her mouth and closes it again without saying anything.

'I could marry you both here and now if you wanted me to.'

'Does anyone else know how old you are? The church, the congregation?'

'You have deflected me very well, my child. But this is my church, and no-one asks me any questions.' He shrugs. 'Maybe they're scared of me.' He smiles, an unencumbered smile. 'But you didn't say anything about my offer.'

Fien throws off her cover. 'It's too soon,' she says. 'We could be dead by tonight.'

'Even more reason to think about it. To bind you both together forever even if you do die today.'

'I think we're bound together whether or not we get married.'

'That deep, eh?' he smiles again. 'That's good.' He turns and looks at Ben and Ishtar. 'Time to wake these two. The offer stands, by the way. If you ever change your mind.'

'Thank you.'

'It's my greatest pleasure,' he says.

The four of them get to the Tower soon after the sun had fully risen. The alleys are still only sparsely populated, and they make good time in the light. Lindsey's ship is still there, but there seem to be only two guards where yesterday there were guards everywhere.

'What's going on?' Ben says.

'We could kill them all easily,' Ishtar says.

Fien puts her hand on her sword, then thinks again. 'No,' she says. 'No more lives.'

261

'I'll go,' Giles says. 'They'll not question an old priest who's just looking for something or someone to bless.' He gets off his horse. 'Wait here.'

The watch him limp the short distance down to the quayside, see him nodding at the guards, smiling, bowing, making the sign of the cross, and then disappearing below deck.

'What is he doing?' Ben says. 'He'll get himself killed.'

'He can't,' Ishtar says. 'He can't die, remember.'

'Ah,' Ben says. 'He could get hurt, though.'

'He told us to wait here, so here we'll wait.' She pulls at the reins of her impatient horse.

The sun passes overhead.

'He's been gone for over two hours,' Ben says.

'Be patient,' Fien hisses. Then, as an afterthought, with nothing else in her head and nothing else to say. 'He offered to marry us.'

'Is that what you want?' Ben pulls his horse back an involuntary step.

'I want what you want,' she says.

'You don't think it's too soon?'

'I think it's not essential. I love you. You love me. That's all there is.'

'I can't go down on my knees here. Not now.'

'What's that supposed to mean?'

'It means I want to ask you but properly.'

'There is no properly in our relationship. I wouldn't promise to obey.'

'I wouldn't want you to.'

'Does that mean you want to get married?'

'On equal terms,' Ben says. 'Not on the terms women usually get married.'

'A wedding?' Ishtar says, unbidden.

'Who knows?' Fien says.

'Make a decision,' Ishtar says. 'You both want it.'

'Should I ask him when he comes back?' Fien says.

Ben nods. 'If he comes back.'

'He'll come back,' Ishtar says. 'He has to.'

'One more hour,' Fien says. 'And then I'm riding this horse up across that gang plank and killing anything that moves.'

'Let me go first,' Ishtar says.

'Stop it,' Fien says, but she's laughing.

The hour's almost up when Giles emerges from the ship. He bows to the guards again, makes the sign of the cross again, drifts across from the river's edge into the shadows his new friends hide in, leaps onto his horse as if he were a youth, pulls its reins, starts riding for home.

'What?' Fien says when she catches up with him.

'It's empty,' he says.

'What do you mean it's empty?'

'What I said. There are five guards in all on there. Nothing else. It's a ghost ship, to all intents and purposes.'

'Then where's Lindsey?'

'He marched for Nottingham with the King before dawn.'

'What?'

'They're drawing lines for the war,' Giles says, head low.

'So there'll definitely be a war.'

'Definitely.' Giles sighs deeply. 'Less money for those I care for.'

'And there was no sign of my father.'

'I may not know what he looks like, but I assume he's not invisible,' Giles says, 'There's nothing there. The hold is empty, the commander's cabin is empty, and, down by her keel, the prisoners' cell is empty.'

'Any sign that someone's been held there?' Fien says.

'A few rags with blood on them.'

'That's it?'

'That's it,' Giles says.

'We need to get to Nottingham.'

'And put yourself in more danger?'

'There's no other way. I need to find out if my father's still alive. I need to get the watch back.'

'You're turning into me before you even have it.'

Fien shakes her head. 'Not for me, but to stop it from upsetting the world's balance. I'll break it when I find it.'

Giles laughs. 'You won't. I guarantee it. Anyway, it's still your father's unless he's given it to Lindsey of his own free will.'

'Perhaps Lindsey tortured him into giving it to him.'

'That wouldn't work,' Giles says. 'It has to be an act of kindness, the gift, not an artificial construct occasioned by pain and suffering.'

'Will you marry us before we go?'

'You really are going to ride all the way up there and risk your life?'

'I don't think I have a choice.'

'We always have a choice.'

'Then I choose to go after you have married us.'

Giles inclines his head. 'And what does the boy think?'

'He wanted to find somewhere to get on his knees. I told him not to be so silly, that I knew already what he wanted. And that I wouldn't swear to obey him.'

'That shortens the service,' Giles says, grinning.

'Do we need any witnesses?'

'There are witnesses galore in my congregation.' He pulls his horse to the right, up another narrow unnamed alley. 'And I'll lend you my bed for your wedding night.'

Chapter 37

The church is full when they walk back in. Not just full to the eye, but full to the senses. New candles burn brightly, there is no place for anyone to sit, and even the standing room at the very back of it is almost gone. Fien shrinks back from the sounds of the crowd as she walks out of the vestry, followed by Ben and Ishtar.

'What if someone recognises me?' she whispers.

'Lindsey doesn't even know you exist,' Ben whispers back.

Giles doesn't order her to stand anywhere in particular, nor does he show Ben or Ishtar where to stand. He simply walks to his elevated spot in front of the altar and lifts his arms heavenward. 'Dearly beloved,' he says. 'We are gathered here today to witness that rare thing, a wedding where both parties are willing and able and committed to making lasting vows. We're gathered to see two people honestly in love make a commitment to each other, not as a man ruling over a woman, nor as a woman bowing her head to male violence, but as two people, equal in the sight of the gods, who want to bind themselves to each other for all time. Are you prepared to witness this?'

The crowd sings its approval.

Giles walks, suppressing his limp for once, to the very back of the church, where the ailing and wasted have found their places after all the others. 'Will you be a witness to this marriage?' he says. He only has to ask twice, and walks back towards the altar with one man on crutches, and a young girl with only one arm. 'Your willing witnesses,' he says to Fien. 'Willing with all their heart.'

'Thank you,' Fien says, and strokes the face of the man on crutches, and shakes the one remaining hand of the girl with one arm.

'Are you ready?' Giles says, looking first at Fien, and then at Ben.

They both nod.

'Very well.'

'Will you, Fair Fien of the Sea, daughter of Piet The Trader, take Ben of the Unknown, son of Lil the Red, to be your lawful husband, and will you remain with him for eternity?'

'I will,' Fien says, and hears her words echo around the church.

'And will you, Ben The Valiant and Striving, son of Lil the Brave, take Fien of the Knives, daughter of Piet the Living, to be your lawful wife, and will you remain with her for eternity?'

Ben, looking at Fien, staring into her eyes, says loudly, 'I will.'

Giles, a fire of ages in his eyes, bows his head. 'There are no more words to say. You are man and wife.' He holds out to them a pristine piece of parchment and a quill. 'Sign here,' he says, and they sign where he shows them. And their witnesses make their marks as best they can. He lifts the paper above his head, spread wide and glowing white in the gloom of the church. 'These two are now man and wife. Rejoice.'

And the singing in the church is deafening as the sun swings from east to west and sends a shaft of golden light down the length of the nave, a spotlight on Giles, Fien, and Ben.

Giles turns to Ishtar. 'I'll not leave you out of this.' He turns back to the newly-weds. 'I think you have a ready-made child, don't you?'

They both nod.

Giles raises his right hand. 'My gods, bless this family come together in a time of need for them and for our brethren. Protect them wherever they may go, whatever obstacles they might face, and whatever injuries they may have to endure on their path to justice. Forgive them for the sins they have committed and might commit, in the name of justice. So be it.' He smiles. 'There. You're a family now and will be forever. And now it's the time for feasting and forgetting.'

'Where does it all come from?' Fien says, watching the crowd dig in to loaves and meat and fish and fruit.

'It just arrives,' Giles says. 'That's the one thing that makes me hope I'll live forever now; feeding all the poor and needy and lost and hungry. That's all that matters. Not like the lords in their mansions and castles who care only for themselves and not their people.' He points at the food. 'Tuck in. I need to tend to my flock.' And he wanders off, not with a weary gait anymore, but like a man who has a mission, a man who wants to achieve things, not like a man over a thousand years old waiting for death.

'He's a good man,' Ishtar says. 'And he's asked his gods already to forgive me for killing anyone.'

'I don't think it was quite meant like that,' Ben says. 'It wasn't a licence for you to go and kill as many people as you feel like.'

'I think it was,' Ishtar says.

Fien laughs. 'You're our daughter now, so you have to do as we say.'

Ishtar shakes her head. 'Children are meant to be disobedient, to cause their families grief.'

'I'm not sure that's quite how it's supposed to be,' Fien says. 'Are we ready for this?' she says to Ben.

'I don't think we'll ever be ready for her.'

The rest of the afternoon, they spend in that church, eating, drinking, walking amongst Giles's people, feeding them if they can't do it themselves, holding beakers of water to thirsty mouths, until the sun goes down and the church slowly empties.

'How clean they leave it,' Fien says.

Giles, sitting in the front pew again, sighs. 'They're a grateful flock,' he says. 'They respect the church and each other. ... In here, at least.' He rubs his face and looks tired again. 'So, tomorrow Nottingham?'

Fien nods.

'I can't come with you, of course.'

'I wasn't asking you to.'

'I know, child, I know. Part of me wishes I could. To undo some past injustices. But these people need me.'

'I know,' Fien says.

'Promise me you'll come back and see me now and again, when all this is done,' Giles says.

'I promise.'

'I hope you get what you want. And I don't just mean the clock.'

'Is it wrong to kill someone in revenge?' she says.

'It's always wrong to kill. It's just inevitable sometimes.' He looks very tired now, and sad. 'I've done some of that, too, I'm afraid to say.' He takes a deep breath and gets up. 'I need to do some night wandering, out there where I'm needed often. You were lucky to find me in last night.' He puts his hand on Ishtar's shoulder. 'Do you want to come with me and see London at night? Give your parents a peaceful night?'

Ishtar nods, beaming from ear to ear.

'I'll keep her safe,' Giles says. 'And we'll be back before dawn.'

'You're too kind to us,' Fien says. 'Why?'

'Never ask why, my child,' he says. 'The reasons are always there, and we don't need to understand them. I like you, that's probably the best reason of all.'

Ben and Fien watch the crippled priest and the Persian girl stroll off towards the main door, one gaunt shadow, and one small, taut one, and then they're gone. The door clangs shut, and is locked from the outside.

Fien turns to Ben, her eyes bright, and smiles. 'Are you happy?'

Ben nods. 'Although I can't believe we've just done what I think we've done. It happened so quickly.'

'No regrets?'

'No regrets.'

'Shall we find this bed Giles was talking about?' Fien says.

They wander into the vestry, push open the door to the part of the building they haven't yet explored, past the kitchen, huger than they'd expected, to a narrow staircase.

'Up here?' Ben says.

'It must be.' She feels herself tremble. She's excited and afraid.

Ben holds the candle high, and the light pine of the wall panels reflects its brightness. The stairs end in a small room, already ablaze with candles burned almost halfway down. A simple pair of plain curtains hides the small window. The bed takes up most of the space.

'Clean linen,' Fien says. 'He's changed it specially for us.'

Ben clears his throat, and puts the candle down on the small sideboard. 'What a wondrous man.'

'He may be a saint, for all we know.'

'Like you,' Ben says and pulls her towards him.

Their lips meet. Their tongues meet. They let their hands explore each other's bodies through their clothes. There never is anything like the first time, never again. He pulls his shirt off over his head, and Fien does the same.

She unties her knives and puts them down on the floor, next to the bed, carefully, protectively. 'I need …'

'Shh,' Ben says, and puts one warm hand on her breasts, another on the naked small of her back.

'Mmm.'

And then they're naked, and their hands cannot rest, and their hands have to caress each nook and cranny of each other's bodies, so familiar after all those months together, and yet so unfamiliar without the protection of clothes and adventure and grief. The invisible barrier falls, and they find the bed slowly, gracefully, carefully, together.

Ben looks down at Fien, her hair spread across the pillow. 'Your hair looks like a halo,' he says. 'You must be an angel, not a saint.'

'I'm neither. I'm Fien and I'm your wife.'

He kisses her sweaty chest. 'I'm neither either. I'm Ben, and I'm your husband.' He kisses her forehead. 'Did you like that?'

'I was afraid at first,' she says. 'I thought it would hurt, but it didn't.'

'Do you want to try it again?'

She nods, tears suddenly in her eyes. 'I love you.'

'I love you, too.'

The candles have burned down by the time they next wake, and they hear the echo of comfortable footsteps downstairs.

Chapter 38

'Good-bye then,' Giles says.

They are at the church doors, the sun up for a few hours already. Their horses have copious saddlebags stuffed full of provisions by Giles who doesn't appear to have slept.

'Thank you, Giles,' Fien says into his ear as she hugs him, a hug she doesn't want to end, because she feels safe with this holy man. 'See you again soon.'

'I hope so, I do hope so,' he says.

Ben comes in for a hug now, grateful to the old man for offering them sanctuary and hope. He grunts his thanks, and Giles slaps him on both shoulders.

Come on, boy, you have much to look after now. Think of the responsibility.' Giles laughs.

Ishtar lets him pick her up, give her a sharp hug. 'Thanks, Papa Giles,' she says. 'I'll be back.'

'You're very welcome my child. Now don't go wasting those knives on people who don't deserve them.'

'I won't.'

The three mount their horses, sit back in the creaking saddles.

'Take care, you folk,' Giles says. 'I don't want anything bad to happen to you.'

'It won't,' Fien says. 'You can be sure of that.'

'You'll always be welcome here,' Giles says.

The three nod, turn their horses, take one look back, raise their hands as one, and gallop off into the next alleyway pointing north.

Giles smiles, nods, wipes a tear from his worn eyes, turns, and pushes open the church door. Inside the empty building, he drops to his knees in front of the altar, puts his hands together, and bows his head. He mumbles into the silence, words no-one else would be able to understand, words of his first language, from far

far away.

When they're finally clear of London, a sense of freedom comes over them. Fien, tired of pretending, throws off her disguise and travels as a woman, albeit a woman in trousers who rides like a man. Her back bruised, she makes a big holster for Lindsey's new-fangled rifle, fixes it onto the leather of her saddle, so she can grab it if she needs it.

After two days' riding, they see a column of dust a few miles off. Ben rides ahead, telescope in hand, to get a closer look. He's back within a few hours.

'We've caught up with some sort of army,' he says.

'What did they look like?'

'I think they're the king's men.'

'Did you see Lindsey or the king?'

Ben shakes his head. 'But then they may have been hiding at the heart of the troop.'

'I suppose so,' Fien says. 'Do we want to get to Nottingham before them? Do we need to?'

'If we try to overtake them, we could be spotted. And although they don't know who we are, they might start asking awkward questions.' He jumps off his horse. 'And they might wonder what that contraption on your horse is.'

'And maybe Lindsey would realise who we are.'

'Exactly.'

'Let's stop then,' Fien says. 'If my father's still alive, we've got more chance of getting to him when they're stationary, not when they're moving. They're bound to be more on their guard when they're marching.'

'No killing today then,' Ishtar says, feigns disappointment. 'This is boring.' And then she laughs. When the other two react, she drops her head, pushes out her bottom lip. 'I didn't fool you then.'

'No,' Fien says. 'But you didn't expect to, did you?'

Ishtar shrugs.

'Better luck next time,' Ben says.

'I ought to try this damned rifle before we get anywhere near Nottingham,' Fien says.

'What about the noise?' Ben says.

'Did we hear anything when it killed Lil?'

'No.'

'How far from the shore were we when he hit her?'

'A mile and a half?' Ben says.

'That's a hell of a long way. I need to start closer than that.'

'How many bullets have you got?'

'I haven't counted them.'

'Then do,' he says.

She looks at the gun, mouthes numbers to herself. 'Ten in the compartment fixed to the gun,' she says. She finds the box she stole from Lindsey's cabin, counts the bullets out onto the ground. 'And another twenty in here.'

'I suppose that's enough to practice with,' Ben says.

'If all I want to do is kill Lindsey, yes. But not if I've got to stop a whole army.'

'We're not trying to stop a whole army,' Ben says. 'Are we?'

Fien shrugs. 'I don't honestly know.'

'We're not. And that's final. We're looking for your father and Lindsey. The king and his opponents are nothing to do with us. Let them sort it out amongst themselves. We're not here to get involved in a war.'

'We already are,' Fien says wearily. 'And don't you want revenge?'

'That's different, Ben says. 'That's not taking on a whole army.'

'It is if he's leading it.'

'War's a conflict of principles, artificial or not. Revenge isn't about winning wars. It's about getting back at someone who's done something bad to you.'

'Let's not argue.'

'You're right. It's all abstract and hypothetical anyway. We're not instrumental in this war. We're just in it. Innocent bystanders.'

Fien puts the bullets back in their box, the gun back in its holster. 'I still need to practice.'

'Then we hang back, find somewhere quiet and hidden, and you can practice. You only need one shot.'

'So we stay here?'

'Yes. For the time being.' Ben grins. 'Although I suggest finding a forest for your practice. Good places to hide are forests.'

'I think I know that.'

'Good.' He gets up. 'I'm going for a walk.'

Fien shrugs. 'Fine.'

Ben is back an hour later. He looks at Fien, mimics her sullen face. 'I think I've found the perfect place.'

'What?'

'For you to practice.'

'I thought you'd gone off because you were angry with me.'

'Well, I wasn't, and I didn't.'

'I can't see a forest from here.'

He raises his finger. 'Ah. That's because it's not a forest.'

'I thought …'

'So did I.' He hits his head with a flat palm. 'But a quarry's even better. It's wide and open. Good distances.'

'Take us there then.'

'Can't we have lunch first? I'm starving.'

'Yes, we can have lunch first.' Fien throws the saddlebag with the food across to him. 'But you have to get it ready.'

Two hours later, Ben leads them through trees and undergrowth to a hidden hole in the ground. It must be at least two miles across. Sheer cliffs, bitten into by the primitive teeth of the age, edges showing in every cut, and a hole as deep as the sun can reach.

'Will this do?' he says.

'How do we get down there?' Fien says.

'We climb, of course,' Ishtar says. 'It's easy.'

'It'd be easier to just walk round this crater and set up a target on the other side.'

'But that's a huge distance, and you said you wanted to start with half a mile.'

'So I changed my mind.'

'Women.' Ben huffs and puffs. 'That's not what I intended.'

'One shot,' she says. 'And if that doesn't work, we'll climb down.'

'You afraid?' Ishtar says.

Fien laughs 'No. I just don't want to waste time with this. I just want to spend my time thinking about how I'll kill Lindsey and get my father back. If the first shot hits at two miles, I don't need to worry about anything shorter than that.'

'Fair enough,' Ishtar says. 'I'll be the target.'

'What are you talking about?'

'You can shoot something off my head.'

'Don't be stupid. Just a board with some markings on it will do.'

'I'll take it then,' Ishtar says, sullen again.

'Why do you like danger so much?'

'It makes me feel alive,' the girl says. 'It makes me feel real, not like I'm just someone's dream.'

Fien watches Ben and Ishtar creep around the edge of the quarry's crater. She puts the gun's telescope up to her eyes, and she can see them precisely, can see every movement of every exposed muscle, wonders how someone could have ground the lens to such a perfect magnification. It's better than *The Odyssey's* telescope, better than anything she's ever seen. She finds a boulder to rest the gun on, the copper and gold glittering in the sun, the barrel feeling war, and homely in her hands, as if it were something to be loved rather than a bringer of death.

The target is up. With the naked eye it's almost invisible, but Fien can see it through the eyeglass on the top of the rifle. She loads a bullet into the side of it, pulls the lever that clicks it into place ready for a shot. She slows her breath until even she can't tell if she's still alive, feels for the wind with her other senses, thinks about how a bullet must drop like a bird at the end of its flight, aims two hand widths above the centre of the target they've marked on a broken log, and pulls the trigger.

There's no sound from the rifle, just a silent explosion of smoke from the side of it. She keeps watching through the lens, watching, counting, hoping, biting her lips. And then, the slightest eruption of wood dust from the log. And the centre of it's gone, blown away by some invisible force, blown away by the magical bullet from the future she can't understand. It's almost as if it guided itself. She closes her eyes and collapses against the rocks.

Ben crashes into the ground beside her, out of breath. 'Are you alright?'

She opens her eyes, dazed. 'Yes, yes.' She shakes her head. 'It wasn't the gun that made me faint. It's what it did.'

'What?'

'Did you hear anything?'

'No.'

'Did you see the wood?'

He nods. 'Bull's eye.'

'All that distance. Two miles. I didn't even have to aim properly. I just thought of the piece of wood and the centre mark. And pulled the trigger. And … and then the bullet hit. It would've hit there even if the log had moved.' She sobs. 'Lil didn't stand a chance. And I just used the gun that killed her.'

'You'll use it to avenge her.'

'There's another thing,' she says. 'Look through its telescope.'

Ben picks up the rifle, holds it first at arm's length, afraid of it.

'Go on,' she says. 'Look at the log through it.'

Ben puts the glass to his eye. 'Dear God. It's like it's right here, under my nose. I've never known a telescope to be so powerful.'

'No. That's what I was afraid of.'

'Why?'

'Lindsey. He … He must have seen me, must have seen us, when he shot Lil, when we pulled her up onto the ship. He must know exactly what we look like.' She stands up, unsteadily. 'And he must know exactly who I am.'

Chapter 39

Lindsey's pacing around the King's room in Nottingham, matching the King's own footsteps.

'We're not getting any support,' Lindsey says when the silence becomes too much for him.

'None of you are trying hard enough, obviously,' the King says.

'Have you talked to the others?'

Charles shakes his head. 'There's no need. I can tell you're all losing your faith in me.'

'That's ridiculous. There are just too many in this damn city who oppose you, and who won't be persuaded or bribed.'

'Then beat them into submission.'

'And that would achieve what? Will the beatings last onto the battlefield when we'll be forcing brother to fight brother?'

'What do you suggest?' Charles drops down into a hard chair. There are no cushions, not like he's used to, and he winces.

'We need to fall back to somewhere where we have support,' Lindsey says, tries to ignore the itching on his chest where the wound is finally healing.

'And where would that be?'

'Somewhere southwest from here. Stafford seems like a good place.'

'Is there anything else you want to tell me?' Charles crosses his arms, leans back, still grimacing at the discomfort of the unsuitable chair he had been provided with.

'The Earl of Essex is moving towards Northampton with ten thousand men.'

'How long have you known this?'

'I heard not half an hour ago.'

'Why not march there and intercept him?'

'We've only got two thousand men, your Highness. I'm sure we could get many more in Stafford, and maybe Shrewsbury after that.'

'You're moving us west not south.'

'It's some way south,' Lindsey says. 'I think we can draw Essex across to us, engage him somewhere far away from London. We don't want London to fall, do we?'

'No, we don't,' Charles says, mimicking Lindsey's tone. He gets up, stretches his legs. 'Do they have better chairs in Stafford and Shrewsbury?'

'I'm sure we can find you one, Sire.'

'Make sure you do. And give the signal to move on out. I can't bear this drab place any longer.'

'Yes, your Highness.'

Summer slows and stops. The leaves begin to change their colour, and the nights have an edge to them, not quite autumnal yet. The King's army moves slowly across the English landscape, not yet bedraggled, not yet spent, still full of humour and hope. The army grows, and as it grows, it feasts on the land, leaving behind it poverty and hunger. By the time it reaches Stafford, it numbers well over fifteen thousand men, some on horse, and the most on foot.

Charles reclines in a chair he likes, sips at a glass of wine, smiles and looks across to Lindsey. 'This is much better,' he says.

'We still need more men, your Highness.'

'I meant the chair.'

Lindsey balls his hand into a fist. 'I am pleased, your Highness.'

'I can think better now.'

'Splendid news.'

'Even more splendid news is that Essex is coming across the country to us, not moving towards London.'

'You made a wise decision,' Lindsey says, and forces a smile. *But he's now blocked our way back to London, you fool.*

'Yes, I did, didn't I?' Charles says.

'The not so splendid news is that Essex now has almost twenty-five thousand men.'

'Ah, but they're mainly rabble, aren't they? Not fit to fight the King's own troops.'

'That remains to be seen.'

'You doubt the ability of my army, Lindsey? That's almost treason.'

'I don't doubt the ability of our men, your Highness,' Lindsey says wearily. 'Not at all. I doubt the ability of even the best soldiers to resist a force that outnumbers them by so many. Even the rabble can kill.'

'God will back us. I will uphold the Protestant religion, the laws of England, and the liberty of Parliament. Nothing will stop me.'

Lindsey tries not to shake his head and almost succeeds.

'You want to say something, Lindsey?' Charles says.

'I'm tired, your Highness.'

'Get more sleep. Get a decent bed. get me more men.'

Lindsey gets up. *You pompous bastard* is what he wants to say, but he knows he can't. He thinks of all his wealth, back on the ship, thinks of the clock Piet still has round his immortal neck, still holds out hope for it, that he might be given it after all. 'I am going now, your Highness, to find you more men, and to find a better bed.'

'You might want to find yourself a good woman, too, while you're at it,' Charles says. 'That might give you more energy for the battles to come.'

'I'm sure it will, Sire, I'm sure it will.' Lindsey steps out into the cool night. He can hear the murmur of the army all around him. If he were king he'd move them on much more quickly, move to Shrewsbury the next day, gather more men about him sooner, and then head back across England eastwards and destroy Essex and his roundheads. He snorts. *What does that painted clown understand about warfare anyway? Once I'm commanding the army, things will change, and we will win, and that puppet can keep the throne, and I'll keep the money.*

Head high, he walks to his quarters. Inside, Piet, his hands still bound together, is eating, messily. His bruises have gone, his face less haggard.

'Enjoying your food, Piet?'

Piet nods, doesn't stop eating, manipulates his spoon as best he can with his shackled hands.

'You're a pig,' Lindsey says.

'You're just keeping me alive in the hope I'll give you the clock.'

'I know I'm predictable.' Lindsey sits down opposite him. 'Maybe I'm just keeping you prisoner so you can watch me kill your delectable daughter.'

'She won't fall into that trap.'

'Oh, you're sure about that, are you?'

'As sure as a father can be about what his daughter does when she believes him to be dead.'

'You're a fool.' Lindsey grabs a bowl and spoons some meat and beans into it. 'By the time I've finished with her you'll wish you could die.'

'And that's meant to persuade me to give you the clock?'

'I think I've given up on that, Herr Brants,' Lindsey says, his mouth full, his hands trembling with tiredness. 'It's your daughter I want now. What's her name again?'

'I never told you.'

'That's right, oh yes, never, during all those hours of torture did you give her away. How brave you are.'

'You're fighting a lost cause, Lindsey,' Piet says.

'Which one would that be? The King or your daughter?'

'Both,' Piet says and pushes away his empty bowl.

'Only time will tell,' Lindsey says. 'And you, for one, have plenty of that. I'll make some pretty little pictures for you to keep in your mind, my friend.' He calls the guards. 'Take him away. Stick him back into that luxurious cart of his.'

The next morning, the army moves on to Shrewsbury. Even the King has become impatient.

Prince Rupert stands in front of the King, his clothes muddy and bloody. 'We drew them towards Worcester,' he says.

'And you won,' Charles says.

'Just a cavalry charge, Sire. Most of them ran away.'

'But the road to London's clear now?' The King is sitting at a table, maps strewn everywhere. He is starting to make sense of this war now.

'Yes, your Highness.'

'Do you think we should march towards London now then, or head to Worcester to destroy Essex's army there?'

'It's difficult to say,' Rupert says. 'If we don't head for London, he might try to double back and block the way again, and the battle at Powick Bridge will have been for nothing.'

'You've done well, my boy. Earned your spurs, so to speak.' He gets up and claps Prince Rupert on the shoulder. 'Some wine?'

'I think I should go to my men.'

'One glass of celebration's allowed the victorious commander, isn't it?'

'Very well, Sire.'

Charles motions the servant to fill up their glasses. 'You're making a name for yourself, my boy.'

'It was only a skirmish,' Rupert says, remembering his modesty.

Charles waves the words away with a thin, impatient hand. 'Drawing a line in the sand,' he says. 'That's what it was. We'll beat the rebellion out of the rabble yet. And I want you there, at my side.'

'Your Highness. You do me a great honour.' He bends his knees and bows.

'Oh, away with you, my lad. It's what any magnanimous king would do.'

Prince Rupert drains his glass and walks out into the light.

Lindsey rushes towards him, his hand outstretched. 'Well done, young man. A skirmish well met, I hear.'

'So it would seem,' Rupert says, a broad grin on his face. 'Next time it will be the whole army, I think.'

'Infantry work,' Lindsey says. 'And we'll save your best cavalry to the last.'

'That's not how we did it in the war in Germany,' Rupert says.

'It's a bit different here,' Lindsey says. 'Rules of engagement and all that.'

'There are no rules of engagement in any war.'

'Oh, Prince Rupert, don't take it amiss, what I said. You're still a young man, and I'm an old man of war.'

'Change does come, my Lord.'

'Yes, yes.' Lindsey pats the boy on his shoulder. 'And it will, it will. Just not right now.' He takes a gold coin from his pocket. 'There, go and celebrate your skirmish with your men. That should keep you all happy for the night.'

'I don't need your gold,' Rupert says and starts walking again. 'I need some decent company.'

'Suit yourself,' Lindsey says. 'You'll be under my command when the time comes.' He slips into the king's quarters.

Chapter 40

The weeks drag. Ishtar is bored, bored with following these foolish armies around, bored with having to spend nights alone in her own tent while Fien and Ben sleep in theirs. She's bored of waiting for something to happen, wants something to happen. So she starts to make night forays when she knows the other two won't be paying any attention, when she knows she'll not be missed for five or six hours at the dead of night, and she can see the fires from the ever-growing army of the king in the near distance. She can always be there and back in the time she gives herself. She starts to wage a war of her own on the king's men, on these slovenly, overdressed drunkards who think they'll win battle after battle because some god is on their side.

She recognises their uniforms easily, even in the dark, by touch, by smell, by the way they move, their overweight bodies too slow to get away from her. They move clumsily, as if they'd never been asked to do battle before, as if it was somehow against the rules for a young girl with wild hair to appear out of the dark and slit their throats without first giving them a warning. She likes the look of surprise on their faces. She likes killing. But then they are the enemy. That's what Ben and Fien have told her. That's what she knows. Because Lindsey is one of them, and he killed their leader, and he supports the king.

The army stays in one place for too long, sometimes for weeks on end. She limits her killing to two maybe three men every night. She revels in the cooler nights, something which surprises her, used as she is to the heat of home. She creeps, belly down, through the grass and rushes, until she finds them, laughing and rolling in the grass. Their smells, their sounds, offend her, and she often cuts them open without waiting for them to defend themselves. She does it quietly, secretly, hidden away at the far extremes of this growing camp of men. Why should she care that they're husbands, fathers, brothers? Why should she care that they're men like she's a girl, dragged unwittingly into conflict? There's nothing that makes them good, in her eyes. They are the enemy.

She takes great care to clean her blades a long way away from their camp. She doesn't want Fien and Ben to know what she is doing. She doesn't want them to know where she goes when they're making all sorts of strange sounds in their tent. What she does is what she does. It's her little secret. When they ask her why she's so tired, she blames it on the damp climate, on the worms of cold running up her legs, on the lack of sun. She never tells them she gets hardly any sleep because of the silent crusade she's started.

And then one night, when they've finally started moving south again, when they've reached a tiny village none of them know the name of, she doesn't retreat after she's killed a couple of the outposts. Instead, lured by the smell of burning pork, by the lights, by the ease with which she's managed to pick them off, she slides, on her stomach, further into the centre of the village, where there's louder talking, where the lights are brighter. She hides behind barrels of what she assumes is beer, behind crates of what she knows to be gunpowder, until she reaches a tent that's bigger than the others, more complete than the others, cleaner than the others, with guards around it. She wonders whose tent it might be. It can't be the king's, surely. He must be quartered in one of the houses around the village.

Intrigued, she crawls round the back of the tent, her belly on the ground, her fingertips making sure she avoids anything that might make a sound. Her breathing is slow and deep. She's behind the tent now, and feels for the binding that's sure to be there. Finally, she finds what she's looking for, undoes it slowly, her fingers not yet numbed by the coolness. When she lifts the cloth of the tent slightly, warm air seeps through the gap, and she hears voices.

'There'll be a battle tomorrow, you can be sure of that, Brants,' a sharp, angry voice says. Whoever he's talking to doesn't answer.

She makes the gap a bit wider, squeezes through it.

'And we'll win,' the unseen man says. 'And then I can focus on finding that damn daughter of yours.'

'I told you she wouldn't come.' The other voice is calm, slow, weary to the point of pain.

'She's not very loyal to you then, is she?'

Ishtar pulls herself fully through the gap. She finds herself behind more crates, fortunate to be hidden from view. She moves along them, until she can risk pushing her head around their furthest corner.

All she can see is the back of a tall man, the back of his bald head, and bloody spurs on his boots. Opposite him, sitting at a tiny table, is a man of similar age, unshaven, grey hair falling almost to his shoulders, his hands tied so tightly his fingers are white. His eyes are in hollows, and there's a singular white mark on either side of his nose. He's not looking at the standing man with the bloody spurs.

'I said she's not very loyal to you then, is she?'

'I heard what you said, Lindsey, and I don't care if she's loyal or disloyal as long as she's safe.'

Ishtar pulls herself quickly back behind the crates. Lindsey? That's the man they're after. *I could kill him now*, she thinks. *He'll be dead before he realises I'm here.* And that must be Fien's father.

'Such a good father you are,' Lindsey says. 'Shame you didn't manage to keep your family together.'

Ishtar is trembling with rage now, listening to the

snide earl insulting her friend's father. She pulls out one of her daggers, heavy and round in her hand. *It would be so simple. And then take Fien's father back to her.* She weighs her knife in her hand. What if she misses the precise point, and he manages to shout out, and the guards come rushing in? What then? She'll be lost, the father will be lost, and Lindsey will know Fien's around here somewhere, and he'll go to find her with his army. She puts the dagger back in its sheath on the inside of her left wrist. No chance of just rescuing the old man, either. She sits there until she's stopped trembling, tries to think of another way, of something else she could do.

Footsteps behind her on the frosty grass. She curls up into a ball. The footsteps pass around the front of the tent, and the material parts. A guard. That's all.

'The King wants to see you,' the guard says, rubbing his hands against the new cold.

'Now?' Lindsey says. 'I thought he'd be asleep by now.'

'The King doesn't sleep. … It's a call to war, I believe.'

'Very well.' The sound makes Ishtar think he's turning back to Fien's father. 'I'll be back, and by then I'll have worked out what to do with you, my friend. And there are guards all round the tent, so don't even think of running.'

'I wouldn't ever run from you,' Piet says.

Ishtar hears Lindsey and the King's guard leave the tent, waits for their footsteps to fade, and stands up, behind the crates, one of her fingers on her lips. She skips across to the man still sitting at the table, the man with a strange look on his face, his hands tied together, motionless on the rough table in front of him. She's next to him with a couple of bounds.

'Don't be afraid,' she says, her hair touching his face,

287

her whisper in his ear. 'Are you the father of Fien?'

Piet nods. 'Where is she? She's not here, is she?'

'A few miles away, asleep, I think. With her husband.'

'Her husb …?

'No questions now. She's safe.' She releases one of her daggers, slices through the rope binding his hands together. 'We need to go. Can you crawl?'

'It's the first thing I learned,' he says, a smile slowly lightening his dark face.

Ishtar fumbles in her belt. 'A spare knife. Not a very special one. Take it. So I know you can defend yourself. Now come.' She leads him to behind the crates where she came in.

He's too big to fit through the tiny gap she made.

'Wait,' she says, pulls at the fabric gently, trying not to make a noise. She eases it apart further and further, until the colour of the night spills into the tent. 'Now,' she says.

They both slip out into the coldness. He shivers.

'It'll pass,' he mutters when she looks round at him.

They move as slowly as they dare, as quickly as they dare, in between sleeping men, snoring men, fires extinguishing, footsteps here and there, staying in the shadows, face down, face down, fingers aching with the strain of being unheard and feeling their way at the same time. They stop every ten yards, let their breath catch up with their bodies, ignore the clammy night dew clinging to them, soaking through their clothes, the wetness on their skin uncomfortable, stinging, chilling.

'Almost away,' she whispers, as she recognises the edge of the camp, the edge of the village. 'Gently.' Her hair clings to her face.

A shape appears in front of them, big feet, big legs, big chest, red face. 'What have we here?' he hollers. 'A girlie for us to feast on?' He bends down, and falls on his face, blood spurting from the gash in his neck.

288

'Quicker,' Ishtar hisses as she pulls her knife from the dead man's throat on their way past. 'Run when I tell you.'

There are raised voices to their left.

'Jimmy, Jimmy, where you gone?'

'Come on, lads, we need to find him.'

'He's just fallen over drunk.'

'No, he ain't. There's something there.'

The rush of boots behind them.

Ishtar looks behind her again. She fears the old man will fall behind as she moves her nimble limbs as quickly as she can.

'Go, go,' he says. 'I'm as quick as you, for now.'

And then they're clear of the camp, on the road out of the village, still crawling, until the last of the fires is tiny behind them. They jump up onto their feet, backs aching from the last half an hour's effort. They don't have time to catch their breath; they move on, a quick walk, out through the fields, until the trees swallow them and they're gone.

Chapter 41

Lindsey has to duck as he enters the house the King has occupied. Still furious at Piet's refusal to even seem afraid of him, he tries to calm his breathing. 'You called for me, Sire?' He bows.

'Indeed, Lindsey,' the King says. 'Rupert here has captured a couple of Parliamentarian cavalry men. It appears Essex's army is just a few miles north of us.'

'We've managed to get the London side of them?' Lindsey says, ignoring Prince Rupert.

'Excellent news, isn't it?' Charles starts the small-stepped pacing that so irritates Lindsey, and slaps his right fist into his left palm. 'This is our chance to put an end to this threat to the kingdom before it gets anywhere near our great city.'

'We march now?' Lindsey says.

'Yes.'

'So what are we waiting for?'

'Rupert was wondering if we should avoid battle and head back to London instead.'

'That would be dishonourable,' Lindsey says.

Rupert opens his mouth as if to speak, but says nothing. He stares at Lindsey.

'I thought you would say that,' Charles says. He nods at one of the guards. 'Get the others in here. We need a full council of war.'

'Is that really necessary?' Lindsey says. 'You've just said this is our chance to quell this rebellion once and for all. What's left to be discussed?'

'I want to know what they're thinking,' Charles says. 'If those generals tell me their men aren't ready, we can't go.'

'So we've been wandering around the countryside for nothing these past three months? We can take them by surprise. If we didn't know they were just a few miles away from us, they're not going to know we're just a few miles from them.' Lindsey sinks into the nearest seat without thinking, then remembers he's not supposed to sit down if the King's still standing, and jumps up. He curses himself. 'Where's halfway?' He strides across to the map table, pulls one of the maps towards himself. 'Edge Hill, that's where.' He puts his finger on the place's mark on the map. 'If we move out in the next hour, we'll be there before them, and we can occupy the high ground. They'll have to come down from their side, and once they're in the valley, we can take them with cannon and with the infantry, and leave the cavalry till last to sweep up behind them, and kill every last bugger of those bastards.'

'I think it would be better to send the cavalry in first, after the cannon,' Rupert says, wiping his lips with a white handkerchief perfumed with his favourite woman's scent.

'Oh, for God's sake, put that rag away,' Lindsey says. 'This is a place for men not for boys.' He wipes his nose with his sleeve to make the point. 'Oh, but that's the way we did it in Germany, you're about to say. Well, this isn't Germany, it's England. And, from what I've heard, the damned cavalry has a tendency to break away from the rest of the army and chase the fleeing cavalry. We can't lose shape. We mustn't lose shape. Stay on the field of battle and mow down those wretches who are on foot. This is a real war.'

'With all due respect,' Rupert says. 'Horses are the most powerful weapon on a field of battle.'

'Exactly. On a field of battle. Not off it. Not chasing some minor players on their horses who've turned and run while their infantry wreak havoc on the ground.'

'Sire.' Rupert turns to the King.

'I'll decide tomorrow,' Charles says. 'If there is a tomorrow. The others may decide it's best to make for

London.' He puts down his glass. 'Here they are now.'

'For Goodness' sake,' Lindsey says under his breath. 'Governing by committee never worked.'

'Gentlemen,' Charles says. 'Welcome to my humble abode.' He waits for them to fall into line. 'Here's the thing. There is news. Essex is some hours' march up the road, north of us. Do we attack him, or do we move our army to London?'

'We fight,' a grizzled old voice says.

'To London.' Another voice.

'We stop them here,' the same voice says. 'Or we never stop them.'

'Aye,' a third one says. 'To battle.'

'To battle.' The chorus speaks, shouts, bellows.

'Are you sure?' the king says. 'Absolutely sure?'

'We're sure.' This time there is no dissenting voice.

'Then prepare your men for battle,' the king says. 'We march within the hour. We should be there by noon.'

The generals nod. Charles shakes each of them by the hand. 'We will see each other on the field tomorrow, and may God bless us with a swift victory.'

The room is filled with a pall of sweat and smoke. Only Charles, Rupert and Lindsey remain.

'Another glass before we move?' Charles says.

'No,' Rupert says. 'My bladder.'

'What sort of boy are you?' Lindsey snarls. 'You were just playing at war in Germany. I suppose you all slept late and broke for tea at four in the afternoon.'

'I'll ignore that,' Rupert says.

'If you ignore a single command I give you later, I'll find you and kill you,' Lindsey says. 'As God is my witness.'

'Gents, gents.' Charles raises his hands in what is meant to be a calming gesture. 'We will ... I will decide the order of battle when it's called for. In the meantime, go and get your troops ready. I'll ride now,

292

with my guards and my sons. We'll await your arrival at Edge Hill.'

'Sire.' Rupert bows so deeply, his nose almost touches the ground.

'Your Highness.' Lindsey clicks together the heels of his boots, as he did when he was training in Holland. ' At your command.' He turns and leaves the room, beats his way through the guards, until the foetid air gives way to the frosty morning. 'At last,' he says to himself. 'At fucking last.'

He wanders through the camp, watches the men pack up their gear, longs for the old days, when he and Essex, in Holland, trained side by side, when they were nothing but infantrymen, nothing but Foot, when warfare was precise and not governed by guesswork, when you could almost calculate how many men you would lose until you broke through enemy lines, when it was as simple as moving pieces across a chessboard.

'Bugger Rupert,' he mumbles as he approaches his tent. 'He's mine tomorrow, and he'll do as he's told. Hold your bloody shape, hold your shape.' He nods at the guard outside the tent. 'Any change?'

'Nothing, Sir.'

'Good.'

Lindsey walks into the tent, eyes unseeing. 'We're on the move, Piet. Get ready for your cart. Maybe I'll parade you in front of all as my freak of nature. The man who can't die.'

No response. He looks up. The tent is empty except for the crates of wood and some cut rope on the ground. 'Hell,' he roars. 'The daughter, the bloody fucking daughter.'

Chapter 42

There's movement below the horizon. Ishtar and Piet, sweating, follow the path north, only a few more yards to go until they reach the tents. They support each other, tired as dogs, hair plastered to their skulls. He's twice as tall as she is, but she look stronger. The clearing in the forest they finally reach is silent, peaceful almost. A bird calls. A cluster of birds answers.

'This is where you live?' he says.

'We've been following the armies,' she says. 'For too long. Boring.'

'Is that why you came to rescue me?'

She shrugs. 'It wasn't a plan. I was just out killing King's men. Lucky I found you.'

He nods, his white hair a wave. 'Very lucky indeed.'

'We need to wake Fien and Ben.' She walks towards the larger of the two green tents. 'She'll want to know you're here.'

'Don't scare her,' he says.

'I'll be gentle,' Ishtar says. 'I always am.' She walks up to the tent. 'Fien,' she hisses. 'Fien.' Louder. 'I've got your father.'

A grunt. The tent rustles, shakes. A suppressed scream. Then Fien emerges, wrapped in whatever clothes she can find, her hair down past her shoulders now, eyebrows white gold, eyes wide open. 'Papa.' She cries, the tears rolling down her face and dripping onto the ground. She falls into his arms, a child again, lost somewhere. The ring on her left hand glints red in the light of the sinking harvest moon. 'Papa. I ... I thought I'd never see you again.' She sobs, her head on his shoulder, her hair tangled, mussy, sleep dripping from it. And then she's back to being a woman, stands tall, taller than him now who's bowed by over half a year of captivity and torture. 'You must come in.'

Piet is lost for words, can't find anything to say against her torrent of tears, of growing up, of changing in front of him by what feels like decades not years, takes the hand she offers him, follows her into the tent where his new son-in-law is hurriedly pulling his trousers on.

'Sit, sit,' Fien says, drags her father down next to her.

Ben turns round, shirt still open, hairless chest, stomach flat and featured, tries a shy smile, embarrassed at Fien's father's presence, quickly buttons up the shirt, reaches out a long brown hand. 'How did you find us?' He's not awake, really, doesn't understand the reality of what's happened.

'Your girl,' Piet says. 'The one with the hair. She found me, rescued me.'

'With a bit of luck.' Ishtar has crept into the tent, too, half in, half out, now curls up in the corner. 'Lindsey had to go see the King.'

'What were you doing out there?' Fien says. 'Getting yourself into danger?'

Ishtar looks at the ground, changes her mind, doesn't want to lie. 'I was bored,' she says. 'I've been bored for a long time. So I've been night walking.' And she tells them about her killing trips, although she halves the numbers of throats she's cut.

'No wonder you've been tired,' Fien says.

'Not as tired as you,' Ishtar says.

Fien blushes to the same shade of red as Ben does. Adulthood seems an artifice in the presence of a parent.

'Don't worry about me,' Piet says, and smiles. 'I was a newly-wed once.'

'You're not angry?'

He shrugs. 'Should I be? ... How can I be?'

'I thought you were dead.'

'You'd have fallen in love anyway,' he says. 'Even if I'd been there, right by your side.'

Fien sniffs. 'Yes, I would have.'

'Do you have plans?'

'We have an appointment with revenge.'

'Oh,' he says. 'Not on my account, though, not now.'

'He has to pay for what he did to you, and for what he did to Lil.'

'The pirate,' Piet says.

'The trader,' Ben says. 'She was my mother.'

'I'm very sorry.' Piet crumples. 'I … I …'

'You don't have to say anything.'

'He made me show him the future,' Piet says, not listening. 'I was in so much pain, and I couldn't give him my daughter.'

'How long did it take to build the gun?' Ben says.

'Months. I didn't really understand what he wanted it for.'

'He'd been hunting my mother ever since their paths first crossed and she refused to give him her body.'

Piet puts his head in his hands. 'Sorry.'

Ben puts his hands on the old man's shoulders. 'It can't be changed. And I don't blame you. You didn't pull the trigger.'

'And now I have the gun,' Fien says. 'And I'll kill him with it.'

Piet shakes his head. 'You mustn't take that guilt on your shoulders,' he says. 'I'll do it.'

'No, no,' Fien says. 'You can't. It's my duty.'

'Its no-one's duty,' Piet says. 'We could just walk away from here now.'

'But the clock,' Fien says.

'What about it?'

'We need to get that from him.'

'He hasn't got it.' Piet puts his hand into his shirt, pulls out the tiny green jewel, still hanging from the knotted grubby strap. 'He tried to wear it, and it burned him. He tried to make me gift it to him, but I wouldn't.'

Fien sees the scar on her father's chest, where his heart is. 'He killed you?'

'He tried to.' Piet touches the scar. 'It hurt. I ... I didn't realise, didn't know that it would keep me alive through that. It was like I started to leave my body, like I could feel the blood flooding from my broken heart, and then, just as suddenly, I was back inside myself, and whole again, and the wound closed. It ... it drove him insane, I think, and me, too, probably.' He drops the clock back into his shirt. 'I have to do it. You can't live a life of killing.'

'We've all killed more than a few times now,' Ishtar says.

'But some of us don't enjoy it,' Fien says.

Ishtar pulls a sullen face, then stops. 'The battle,' she says. 'Lindsey says there'll be a battle today.'

'You can't be part of that,' Fien says. 'You'll definitely get killed.'

'I wouldn't get killed. I'm too fast for them.' Ishtar bares her daggers and grins. 'No, that's not what I meant. That's when we can get Lindsey. With the rifle.'

'We don't know where the battle will be, and it's too risky.'

'I should have tried to kill him last night then,' Ishtar says. 'I didn't take the chance.'

'You shouldn't have rescued me,' Piet says.

Ishtar shakes her head. 'Yes, I should. That was more important. And I couldn't be sure of a silent kill. In a fight that doesn't matter.'

'You're a child. You shouldn't even have been there,' Ben says.

'Then let's go and find the battle,' Ishtar says. 'We'll hide somewhere.'

'And just shoot him instead of facing him?' Fien says.

'That's what he did to Lil,' Ben says. 'He didn't fight her fairly.'

'And that makes it right?' Fien says.

'Yes, it does,' Piet says into the strained silence. 'Especially if I do it. And I'm not going to change my mind. We either leave for wherever it is you want to go, or we find the battle and I fire the shot.' His face is grim and set.

'That's decided then,' I suppose,' Fien says. 'Now all we have to do is find him.'

Chapter 43

Five hours. That's how long the Royalist army's been marching for. Lindsey looks back over his shoulder and watches the seemingly endless stream of men snake its way across the fields, down lanes, up and down hills, to the midway point between the two armies. He's on the last rise already, with King Charles and the generals, and that damn fool Rupert. He digs the spurs into his horse's side and rides forwards, halts next to the King.

They face northeast, look down into a gently-sloping valley, still in shade, while their faces are covered in the early morning autumn sun, a cold sun, one that gives no warmth or comfort to anyone.

Charles leans on his saddle, twirls his moustache with one leather-gloved hand, his eyes looking into the distance, across to the hill, on the other side of the valley. 'That's where we think they'll come from, yes?' he says.

'Yes, your Highness,' Lindsey says.

'So we just sit and wait?'

'We put our men into battle formation here at the top, ready for them.'

'Surely, our cannons won't reach that far.'

'We'll roll them down into the field when the battle commences,' Lindsey says, his mouth desperate at the sophisticated words he's having to use, his eyes quickly taking in the shape of what will soon be a bloody battlefield, figuring what regiment to put where, how to force his way into the left side of the enemy, and the outcome, with the Royal Standard held high over the opposite escarpment. His imaginings are cut short by the King's sharp voice.

'We'll make ourselves targets down there in the dip, won't we?'

'They'll come down that hill over there themselves, to

engage.'

'How can you be so sure of that?'

'Essex and I studied together in Holland, Sire. I'm sure that's what he'll do.'

'What if his views have changed?' Prince Rupert says, his voice snide and patronizing.

'I don't think they will have. We both fight the same way – honourably.'

Before Rupert or the king can say anything more, lone figures appear at the summit at the other end of the valley. Something glints in the distance. It must be a telescope. Lindsey pulls his own out of his saddlebag, and focuses on the glittering light. He so wishes he still had the gun he made according to the plans Brants called out of the clock for him. He could pick each and every single one of them off, right now, and he wouldn't care if it was honourable or not. He doesn't think about Piet's daughter. 'It's Essex, sire, on his white horse as usual.'

'Your tone isn't that friendly Lindsey,' the King says. 'I thought you two were old friends.'

'*Were* being the word. He's chosen the wrong side.' Lindsey grits his teeth. *And he's too honest*, he thinks. *He doesn't want fame or riches, more fool him.*

And then more figures appear, not alone anymore. A whole army, a flood of men, on foot, with their pikes cutting into the lightening sky, pikes that look long enough to puncture the clouds, if there were any. The green hill top grows black with the mass of men.

'Get them into battle groups,' Lindsey shouts out. 'Stay here at the top to start with. We wait until they attack.' He turns to the king. 'This will take some hours, to get all the men into their rightful places. And we're still waiting for more men to arrive, just as Essex probably is.'

'Very well,' Charles says. 'See to it. You're the

commander.'

Rupert looks at the King, his eyes burning, but he says nothing.

Behind them there's a clanking, a huffing and puffing, shouting, singing, the stamping of feet on the hard ground. More men marching up the hill, pushing through those already arrived, getting into the right place, trying to find the courage to go into battle, the first for many of them.

Charles takes out his telescope, and takes it away from his eye almost before he's used it. 'There are so many of them, he says. I can see them better without the damned glass. I never saw the rebels in a body before. They're supposed to be my subjects, not my opponents.' His face is filled with sad anger. 'I will give them a real battle, I will. God, and the prayers of good men, assist my cause. We will prevail.'

All the generals, even Lindsey, raise their arms and shout their assent, their vigour, and as news of the king's words spread along the line, the men begin to shout their huzzahs, shaking their spikes towards the other side, up into the sky, all around. And their echo is a chorus of boos and hisses, followed by a cheers and shouts of their own, a chanted *Parliament, Parliament.*

The sun has now past its highest point. The days are short, and still no sign of an attack from the Parliamentarians.

'Will they keep us waiting all day?' Charles says. 'The battle must be won in the daylight.'

'We can provoke them into attacking,' Lindsey says. 'We'll group the men into the Dutch formation, eight ranks deep, and march some way down the hill with the guns. And the cavalry waits until we've drawn most of the poison from their bite.'

'Ridiculous,' Rupert says. 'Deploy your men like the Swedes do, chequerboard fashion, and let my cavalry cut a swathe through the opposing ranks first.'

'That I won't do,' Lindsey says. 'It's foolhardy, difficult to control, and your men won't keep their shape, I know it, and any advantage we may gain will be lost.'

'This is tiring, gentlemen, and a decision must be made,' Charles says.

'The decision is yours, you Highness,' Rupert says.

'Absolutely,' Lindsey agrees.

Charles scratches his face, smoothes down his breeches, searches the sky for an answer. He coughs, and rubs his beard one last time. 'Very well. Let Rupert charge when he wants to, Lindsey. He can report directly to me. And use that damn chequerboard formation, but command your men on my behalf.'

Lindsey shakes his head, all thoughts of richness gone from his mind in the hour of battle. 'I'm very sorry, your Highness, but I cannot and will not do that. I resign the foolish title of General-in-Chief you've given me, and beg your leave to go and fight with my own Lincoln regiment with the rank of colonel, pledging my loyalty to you in perpetuity.' He turns his horse.

'Don't be like that,' Charles says. 'I just think this way is easier.'

'And my way is more honest, to stand with my men, and to fight on your behalf without a petty squabble.'

The king nods. 'Very well. God Speed to you, Robert. I will see you after the glorious battle.'

Lindsey gallops away, off to find his regiment. It's an irony to him that he finds it squarely opposite Essex's banner. *Now we'll see who can fight best*, he thinks. *And who's richest after the bloody war is over.* He watches the guns roll down the hill not half an hour later when Essex's army still has made no move, sees the infantry at the centre arrange themselves into the Swedish pattern. And then he hears the cannons loosing their shots, from both side, without much effect; only a few bodies ripped apart on either side, by flukes of range and terrain.

The King, knowing he's out too far from the guns to die, rides from one regiment to the other, shaking their commanders' hands, wishing them well for the now imminent battle. He's in full sight of the Parliamentarian army who respond first by jeering and booing again, and then finally advancing down the hill along the whole front, firing their muskets at will.

The Royalist centre moves, too, and then, amidst all the shouting and braying, the metallic thrumming of armour and arms, a split-second of silence. Rupert raises his right arm. 'With your swords, charge,' he yells, takes off down the hill without looking back, his sword flashing through the heavy air, towards the left flank of Essex's army. His cavalry follow him, all swords aloft, and drive into their opponents, slashing, driving, harrying.

Essex's cavalry manage only to get one shot off from the saddle, and then, confronted by mad Royalist horsemen, turn and flee. A whole regiment of Parliament horses turns in the middle of the battle, and changes sides, now chasing, with the Royalists, the fleeing cavalry, all the way back up the hill on the other side, and out beyond the battlefield.

'Bloody fool,' Lindsey shouts. 'You've lost our advantage, you idiot. Just what I thought. All shape gone, all advantage lost.' He jumps from his horse at the foot of the valley. 'To me, men, to me. For God and country!' *And for me.* He throws himself into the fight at the head of troops. As he slashes his way across the field, blood running down his sword arm from his enemies' bodies, as he manages to start climbing the hill towards Essex, he glances to his left and thinks he sees a shock of blonde hair. He stops, midway through a killing blow.

Chapter 44

The moon was still up, a huge red sphere grazing the trees, when Fien, Ben, Ishtar and Piet broke camp and rode their patient horses, Piet and Ishtar together on one, eastwards, towards where they thought the armies might meet. Now, the clash of battle reaches them, hidden behind one of the hedges well behind the Parliamentarian lines, and they can see, through the gaps in the undergrowth, the full ferocity of the fighting.

'Like against like,' Fien says. 'This will be no place to enjoy living, no matter who wins.'

'Nowhere is very different,' her father says. 'It's never a question of the people for the people, just a question of the people for themselves, the person for himself. That's the way it's always been, and nothing will ever change.'

Fien takes the telescope from the rifle. 'You could even get the king from here with that thing.'

'Is that what you'd want to do?' Ben says. 'Change history rather than just one greedy man's destiny?'

Fien shakes her head. 'We'll let him live,' she says. 'And let whoever's supposed to win the battle win the battle.' She finds Lindsey with the lens. 'I think Lindsey's lost already, anyway. The way he rode away from the king, his head low. And now he's in the main fight, on foot. Even if we don't kill him, he's bound to die.'

'Give me the rifle,' her father says.

She shakes her head. 'I've changed my mind,' she says. 'I'm going to do it. I have to do it. I want to. If hadn't been for Lil I wouldn't be here.'

'Fien.' Her father's voice is hard and sharp. 'You don't have to take this on your shoulders.' He moves to free his right hand, grabs hold of the fraying strap, pulls it

305

and the clock out from under his shirt. 'Here, have this.' He pulls the loop down round her head before she can stop him, the watch gently falling onto her chest.

'No, Papa, no. What are you doing? You'll die.'

'Not now, not here,' he says. 'That much I know.'

'I'm still not giving you the gun,' she says, fixes the sight back into its place, wriggles forwards to the edge of the hedge. She pulls the guard and hears the bullet engage, steadies herself on her elbows and stomach, closes one eye and looks through the scope. She thinks of Lindsey, and there he is, looking straight at her, as if he knows she's there. His sword halts in mid-blow. She presses the trigger, lightly.

Lindsey's thigh bone shatters. *She missed*, he thinks. *Impossible.*

Fien sees him crumple, blood staining his white breeches. *Not a quick death for you.*

Lindsey. *On purpose. Bitch.* The pain cripples him. Rebels on horseback surround him. 'I surrender,' he says. 'I surrender.'

'You missed,' Ben says.

'Only his heart.'

'He may survive.'

'He won't.' Fien pulls the rifle back from its firing position. 'He'll bleed to death. He deserves it.'

They carry Lindsey into the nearest shed, try, for humanity, to stop his bleeding, but cannot. The pain is insufferable. *Bitch, you fucking bitch*, he thinks. *I should've put one of those wonderful bullets through your head instead of your pirate friend's.* The straw digs into his back. He feels his life seeping away into it. *I should have had that clock,*

that green diamond giving me eternal life. I'd have healed by now.
He tries to stand, but he can't. He tries to talk, and
some hoarse words jump from his mouth and fall onto
the ground.

'Let's go,' Fien says. She looks down onto the
battlefield. Both sides are retreating now, and the sun
has gone down behind her. Everything is shadow,
everything is dark. And the cold comes, sweeps down
from the empty sky, rises from the hardening soil. 'Let's
go back to Aldeburgh.'

They jump onto their horses and ride eastwards, away
from the battle, away from Lindsey, away from civil
war. They ride through another moonlit night, as fast as
they can.

Lindsey's vision blurs. He feels hot and then cold. They
bring a fire to him. There's talk of Essex coming to see
him. He talks at them about disloyalty and rebellion
whilst knowing he's the greatest rebel of all. *Who'll save
my ship and its riches now?* he thinks. He falls asleep,
wakes, falls asleep again. It's fitful at best. Fresh blood
pumps from his wound, the straw beneath him sodden
with what should be nourishing him. He catches a
glimpse of a slice of the moon through the shed door
when the surgeon finally comes to him. The man takes
one look and shakes his head.

'You should have called me sooner.' His breath
becomes solid when it touches the cold air. He places
his hand on Lindsey's forehead. 'Sorry.' He throws a
thoughtless dressing onto the broken leg, into the hole,
the bullet lost somewhere on the battlefield. He gets up
and leaves, not looking back.

*It should've been mine, that clock. They should've been mine,
all those jewels and diamonds. You should've been mine, Lil,
with your red hair and your wildness.*

Lindsey's hot, then cold then hot, and then cold. It invades him from his fingers and toes first, as the moon begins to fade. It creeps along his arms and legs, like the tendrils of poison ivy, making him immobile. It grows into his thighs, his hips, the centre of his being, crawls up his spine, until he can't feel the pain anymore. He can't focus his eyes, his thoughts are flying from this to that, some seeking forgiveness, some cursing the women he thinks have crossed him. And Piet, who should be dead, with a knife to his heart.

The first sun lights the summit opposite from which he came charging down the day before. 'The battle?' he says to anyone who'll listen, although he doesn't know who's there. 'Who won the battle?'

'No-one,' a voice says out of the darkness that is the darkness of his eyes, because the day begins brightly. 'No-one lost, no-one won.'

'Such a waste,' Lindsey says, his lips jelly, the cold right there, in his heart. One last pain, sharper and harder than any. He jerks upright, unable even to soothe it with a hand to his chest. 'Such ...' He falls back, his eyes open and afraid.

Chapter 45

It takes them six days to get from Edge Hill to Aldeburgh. They manage to buy a fourth horse from a coaching inn in Bedford. They're always hiding, dodging troops from either army, troops on the run, or troops hoping to join in some major campaign. When they reach the outskirts of Cambridge, they hear the king has pulled all his troops back to Oxford for the winter. There'll be no more fighting this year.

The further east they travel, the fewer troops they see, and they can finally ride in full gallop, in full sight, and feel the final hours of October on their backs, and, at night, find shelter in the inns, drink by a roaring fire, and be warm, rather than shivering in tents hidden in some forlorn undergrowth on the north side of some hill in a deserted part of middle England.

Their travels don't take them back in a straight line, but rather following the shapes and alignments of the tracks broken by the nature of England's agriculture, ancient hedgerows framing their route. When the skies grow huge, they know they can't be more than two days' travel from the coast.

The light changes on that final day, the sun reflecting from the sea back into the cloud at some obscure angle.

'We're nearly there,' Fien says. 'I can't wait to see Harry and the boys.'

'Me, too,' Ishtar says, and grins. 'Even the killing got a bit boring in the end.'

'Will there ever be peace?' Piet says. 'Here or anywhere?'

'We don't know, do we?' Ben says. 'And we probably shouldn't. Knowing would stop us from doing what we do.'

'And what is it we do?' Fien says.

'Living,' Ben says. 'Just living.'

Fien feels a lightness of spirit as they ride down the slope into Aldeburgh. From up here, she can see *The Odyssey*, masts proud into the sunny, crisp sky, and the still ocean beyond them. She turns to her father. 'You'll like these people,' she says. 'You'll really like them.'

'I owe them my daughter,' he says. 'How could I not like them?'

Harry greets them with a bear hug, all four of them. Piet smiles, embarrassed. 'We're just one big family,' Harry says. 'And now we're all back together.'

They tie up the horses, board the ship, eat and drink and talk late into the night.

'Tomorrow,' Fien says to Harry. 'Tomorrow, we have a look in the hold and see what exactly we have, and exactly what we should do.'

'Don't you want to rest?' Harry says.

'That's exactly what I want,' she says. 'I saw some lovely villages on the way back here, and some houses I wouldn't mind living in.'

'Leave the sea, leave the coast?'

'Why not?'

'You'd miss it.'

'The place I'd like most is only a day's ride from here.'

Harry grunts, folds his arms over his belly, and sighs. 'I hate to say it, but I'm not sure I want to go out there again.' He nods at the sea. 'Too many memories, too many dangers. I'm an old man now.'

'Come and work for me,' Piet says. 'Legal trade. There's lots of it still to be done.'

'What with?' Harry says. 'The ship's Fien's and Ben's.'

'You should have her, Harry,' Ben says. 'That's what Lil really would've wanted, not some children still green behind the ears driving her round the globe without knowing what they're doing.'

'You'd be the flagship of the Brants fleet,' Piet says. 'But you could still do exactly as you wanted. Live here in Aldeburgh if you like.'

'And you?' Fien says to her father. 'What are you going to do?'

'I'd thought of getting myself to London and taking back what's mine from Lindsey's ship.'

'They'll know by now he's dead, and they'll have looted it all themselves.'

Piet shakes his head. 'I don't think so. If the King's in Oxford, so will everyone else be who had anything to do with Lindsey. They won't even think about sending anyone down.'

'So should we sail for London tomorrow?' Harry says. 'One last adventure for us?'

'First we check the hold, like I said,' Fien says. 'And then we go.'

There's enough in the hold for each and every one of the crew to be rich and independent. Fien grabs a handful of loot from each trunk, gold, pearls, ear-rings, precious stones set and unset, without even looking at it, and puts everything into a small wooden box, which she closes and locks.

'What's that for?' Ben says.

'I want to give it to Giles when we get to London,' she says. 'It should help him keep his flock. It's the least he and they deserve.'

Ben nods, and kisses her. 'You're too good to be true,' he says.

'So are you,' she says, and kisses him back. 'I'd have no courage without you.'

Three days later *The Odyssey*, still disguised as *The Eagle*, sails up the Thames into London. There are no soldiers to stop them, no Royal Standard flying over the Tower, no waves on the river to stop their progress. It's night-time when they drop anchor next to Lindsey's ship,

311

when they board her from her starboard side, when Ishtar gives up her habit of killing, and merely threatens the remaining guards with her curved daggers, and watches Harry tie them up and dump them in a corner like forgotten rubbish.

With Piet, they swarm into the hold of the ship, only to find that most of what Lindsey stole from the house in Antwerp almost a year ago is still there. They haul it across to their ship in a few hours and are done before the sun rises again.

Harry lifts the bound men onto chairs in what was Lindsey's cabin. 'You're still alive, boys, and that's lucky.'

Ishtar snarls at them.

'She's mad, you see, and it took a lot of persuading to stop her from slitting your throats, and you should be grateful to me for that.' Harry laughs. 'I've got a proposal for you.' He licks his lips. 'And you've got a day to think about it. You can either have this ship and go your merry way with it, but God help you if you ever cross any one of us. Or we can kill you and take the ship anyway.'

One of the men struggles against his gag. Harry rips it away from his mouth. 'What?'

'We'll take the first option.'

'Fair enough. We'll be out of here tomorrow. In the meantime you can stay here under the watchful eye of my young assistant.' He smiles. 'Good choice, lads, good choice.'

When he gets out on deck, he sees Fien on dry land, with a small cart. Ben's with her.

'Back in a few hours,' Fien shouts up to him.

Harry waves at her.

'I hadn't expected to see you again so soon,' Giles says to Fien and Ben.

'We had some unfinished business,' Fien says. 'It

seemed obvious to come to you.'

The priest's face shrivels when he smiles. 'And I'm still alive, as you can see.'

'We have a gift for you,' Fien says, and hands him the box and the key to it. 'We thought you might want something to help you and your people.'

'That really wasn't necessary,' Giles says. 'My life enriches me.'

'It was necessary,' Ben says. 'Without you, this would have all turned out wrong.'

'I am grateful,' Giles says. 'And I accept your generous gift.'

'Don't open it till we've gone,' Fien says. 'I don't want to give you the chance of not accepting it after all.'

'Very well,' Giles says. 'Bread, cheese and wine?'

They feast for a good few hours.

That night, Fien stands on the deck of *The Odyssey*, stares out at the fires of London, and wipes her eyes.

'Are you alright?' Ben says.

'Yes,' she says. 'I just fear I'll never see Giles again.'

'Then that's the will of the world.'

'I know,' she says. 'I just wish the world were smaller and happier.'

He hugs her, stops, puts his hand on her cheek. 'You're not wearing it.'

'What?' she says.

'The clock.'

'You're right,' she says. 'I don't want to be immortal if you can't be. I want to grow old with you. I want to die with you at my side. And then, if there's another life after that, I want to live it with you.'

'Have you told your father?'

'No,' she says. 'He'll find out soon enough. When he can't do anything about it.'

A dark, cowled figure creeps through Cheapside at about the same time, pulling a simple handcart behind it. The wheels turn silently, well-greased. The figure stops in front of one of the many shops and workshops that abound here. This one's temporarily empty. The figure opens the door with a sleight of hand, pulls a box from the cart, carries it into the building, and closes the door.

Giles lights a small torch, keeps the flame behind his hand. He walks across to behind the counter, and gets on his knees. He sweeps through the dust on the floor with his free hand, until he finds what he's looking for. There, the outline of a trapdoor. He lifts it, and holds the torch down into the void. The floor down there is one of soil. That's good.

Back on the shop floor, he limps to the wooden box he's brought with him, lifts it up onto his shoulder, and carefully carries it down into the cellar with him. Down there, he plants the torch into the ground, and digs a hole in one of the corners of the room, twice at least the depth of the box. He sits down, unlocks the box and opens the lid.

On the top of the pile of jewellery sits the small emerald clock. He picks it up, opens it, and winds it, then very slowly and deliberately closes it again, wraps the grubby strap around it, and pushes it down into the mess of wealth in the box. 'Enough,' he whispers. 'Enough.' He puts the box into the hole and levels the soil over it. He makes the sign of the cross over the closed hole.

Upstairs, he brushes dust and dirt back over the trapdoor once he's ripped the heavy iron ring from it. 'No-one can find you now.'

The sun rises just as he gets back to his church. The first of his flock are waiting for him. He welcomes them with open arms.

Epilogue

London, the present day

The Director of the Museum of London is in her office, preparing the next big exhibition. Her desk is covered in uncountable papers, her computer beeps every few seconds with new emails. Only a few months to go until the exhibition launches. The draft posters are at the top of the pile of papers – *The Cheapside Hoard: London's Lost Jewels*. She frets over them. Maybe not quite right yet

Her mobile phone rings.

'Yes?' Her thoughts are still with those posters.

'Hazel here, Sharon. I think you need to come down here and have a look at something.' The voice is calm, but has a nervous edge to it.

'A problem?'

'Not as such.'

'But important.'

'Well, yes.'

'I'll be there in a minute.' She gets up, walks out of her office, locks the door behind her, and walks quickly through the corridors of the museum and down a couple of flights of stairs.

In Hazel's office, the blinds drawn against the daylight, the table's clear except for one piece of the collection – a watch made from one emerald. Hazel's staring at it, chin on her hands wrapped in blue plastic gloves.

'So,' Sharon says. 'This is what it's all about. The best part of the whole collection. It's not broken, is it?'

'Not beyond what was broken when it was found, no,' Hazel says. 'There's something else. Something very strange. Well, two things, actually.'

Sharon sits down opposite her friend, hands on knees.

'Does it mean we won't be able to exhibit it?'

'I hope not.'

'Spit it out then.'

'You know we x-rayed the corroded movement, and found nothing extraordinarily special about it?'

'Well, except that it's an astounding piece of engineering,' Sharon says.

'Besides that, of course. And we all assumed it was a Ferlite watch because his signature's on it?'

'It's a fake? After we thought it was the design he based all his other watches on?'

'No, no, let me finish.'

'Sorry, sorry. It's just I'm behind with some of the exhibition stuff. The posters don't look right.'

'Don't worry about them. ... It looks like Ferlite was the faker.'

'What?'

'I decided it would be an idea to radiocarbon date the movement. It looks like the movement was made around 2 BC.' She hands a piece of paper to Sharon.

'You're kidding me.' She reads the paper quickly. 'This can't be right.'

'I've had it tested three times by three different firms. And there's another thing.'

'This is getting better.'

'Lawrence and your predecessors never looked at this properly, I think. But we always assumed they did. We've all been admiring the brilliant cut of the diamond so much we never looked beyond that. So I played a bit, sorry. ... Just watch. No pun intended.' She puts the clock on a glass shelf, a light bulb directly below it, and carefully opens the lid. She turns off all the room lights and flicks the switch under the clock.

Letters swirl about the room, indistinct at first, and then crystallising into sharp, defined script, silver to the eye.

'Dear God,' Sharon says. 'That's even more beautiful than the watch. It looks like Aramaic.'

'That's exactly what it is,' Hazel says. 'The language of Christ.'

'And what does it say?'

'I am your immortality.'

'People will think we're mad if we tell them this.'

'We can't tell them. It's simple. ... Oh, and we need to put it behind leaded glass.'

'Why?'

'Because there's some uranium-238 in it. Not that much, admittedly.'

'And?'

'It's got a half-life of nearly four and a half billion years.'

They both stare at the dancing characters, at the silver light, an expanding universe of stars.

THE END

Historical Notes

Like all historical fiction, *The Immortality Clock* has several grains of truth at its centre.

The Cheapside Hoard was indeed discovered by workmen in 1912, with many of the items sold to George Fabian Lawrence, also known as Stoney Jack, who as well as being an antiques dealer and pawnshop owner, had been appointed Inspector of Excavations to the new London Museum in 1911.

One of the biggest treasures of the hoard is a clock made of a single Colombian emerald, with the movement signed by G. Ferlite. The clock, along with the rest of the hoard, were exhibited at the Museum of London in 2013, and there are plans to make the hoard a permanent exhibition in the new Museum of London in West Smithfield, London, from 2024.

Historical commentators have suggested that the hoard was put together by Gerald Polman, a Dutch jeweller, in the East Indies in around 1631, who died on his way back to England.

Robert Bertie, First Earl of Lindsey, was involved in litigation over Polman's jewels as Treasurer of East India Company, but died at the Battle of Edgehill in 1642, of the wounds described in Chapter 44.

The rest of the story is invention, as you would expect. Or is it? The truth is always stranger than fiction.

RP

Printed in Poland
by Amazon Fulfillment
Poland Sp. z o.o., Wrocław